Also by Jane Ashford

The Duke's Sons

Heir to the Duke
What the Duke Doesn't Know
Lord Sebastian's Secret
Nothing Like a Duke
The Duke Knows Best

The Way to a Lord's Heart

Brave New Earl
A Lord Apart

Once Again a Bride
Man of Honour
The Three Graces
The Marriage Wager
The Bride Insists
The Bargain
The Marchington Scandal
The Headstrong Ward
Married to a Perfect Stranger
Charmed and Dangerous
A Radical Arrangement
First Season / Bride to Be
Rivals of Fortune / The Impetuous Heiress
Last Gentleman Standing
Earl to the Rescue

HOW TO CROSS
a
Marquess

JANE
ASHFORD

Published by Sourcebooks Casablanca, an imprint of Sourcebooks
P.O. Box 4410, Naperville, Illinois 60567-4410
(630) 961-3900
sourcebooks.com

Printed and bound in the United States of America.
OPM 10 9 8 7 6 5 4 3 2 1

Prologue

ROGER BERWICK, MARQUESS OF CHATTON, PEERED through the growing dusk at the passing London street. It did not look familiar. In fact, it appeared that his hack was headed east, into neighborhoods he'd never penetrated during any of his visits to the metropolis. He rapped on the ceiling of the cab with his cane. "Where the deuce are you going?" he called. "I told you White's club in St. James's Square."

"You said Whitechapel," the driver replied.

"Are you mad? Why would I want to go to a back slum?"

"I heerd you. Whitechapel, the Cub, you said, clear as clear."

"I did not!"

"You calling me a liar?" asked the driver, leaning so far over the top of the carriage that Roger feared he'd fall into his lap. "'Cause if you ain't suited, you can get out of my cab and walk, yer high and mightiness," he added, suddenly belligerent.

Roger realized the man was drunk. Which fit with the neighborhood they were traversing. Despite the filthy March weather, with its tendrils of icy fog, there were people slumped against the dilapidated buildings on either side, women as well as men, victims of an excess of blue ruin. Some of them wouldn't wake, if what Roger had heard about the ravages of gin was true. There were also other figures, upright and alert, hulking in the shadows. He wondered if it was time to twist off the bottom of his cane to reveal the sword inside.

"I did wonder if you'd like the Cub," the driver added, his voice gone meditative. "Mean, dirty sort of boozing ken. But what I say is, you never know with a toff. Right barmy, some of 'em. I've had gentlemen wanting me to take them to Limehouse or the stews around the docks."

"Well, I do not," said Roger, gritting his teeth. Nothing about this day had gone right. In fact, it was shaping to be one of the most exasperating days of his life.

The man went on without seeming to hear, taking on the tone of an inebriated philosopher. "And bawdy houses. Very popular, they are. I know 'em all. You want to visit the liveliest ladies in the city, young sir? Better than the Cub, I can tell ye. I could take you there in a trice."

"No!" It was difficult enough not to be angry after his recent visit without the addition of a sodden cabdriver. Roger fought the temper that was said to go with his red hair.

"Eh, well, it's not far now."

Roger controlled his voice and spoke carefully. "We appear to have had a misunderstanding. Please turn back." He enunciated the next sentence very clearly. "I want to go to White's club in St. James's Square." When there was no response, he added, "Did you hear me? White's club in St. James's Square."

"Bit late to be changing your mind," the driver grumbled. "That's right the other way around. I was heading home after this. Best you get down at the Cub as agreed."

Which it hadn't been, except in the fellow's addled brain, Roger thought. But he'd never find another cab in this neighborhood. "Naturally I will pay you for your trouble," he said.

Two large figures shifted in the darkness at the side of the road. The mention of payment hadn't been wise, perhaps. But how else was he to convince the driver? Roger unsheathed his sword stick and held it so that the blade could be seen in the light of the carriage lamp.

Muttering about the stupidity of passengers who didn't know where they wanted to go, the driver backed his horse and maneuvered to turn the hack around. Roger kept his eye on the lurking bravos as he pulled his greatcoat closer. He wiggled his toes inside his boots. His feet were chilled. And his gloves seemed inadequate. The grimy streets seemed to intensify the cold somehow. He was relieved when the driver finally got the cab going in the right direction, the melancholy streets of the slums receding behind them. No one had offered to molest them in the end. Roger relaxed a little. If the man kept to his job this time, he wouldn't be late.

Roger rarely made the long, hard journey down to London from his home in Northumberland. He was here now only because his former in-laws had insisted on a face-to-face meeting. So that Arabella's mother could relieve her feelings by berating him, apparently. She'd gone so far beyond the line today that Roger had nearly shouted at her. He was proud of that *nearly*. Though it had been a near thing, he hadn't responded in kind. He had behaved like a gentleman despite the glaring injustice of her remarks. And they had at last finished all the necessary business between them. He wouldn't have to obey one of the Crenshaws' summonses again. The relief was considerable.

He looked out at the fashionable precincts of London now passing outside the cab window. This trip hadn't been a complete waste. He'd been here to receive the Earl of Macklin's mysterious invitation. Roger had no idea why such an illustrious figure had asked him to dine. They weren't friends, though Roger remembered being introduced to the older man at some party or other. He did know that Macklin had been a suitor of his mother's, thirty years ago, because she liked to enumerate the many desirable partis who'd pursued her when she was the reigning belle of the *ton*. Of course the invitation couldn't have anything to do with that. In fact, Roger couldn't imagine why he'd been asked to share a meal with the earl. He was quite interested to find out, though a bit worried about what he would find to say, as usual. He'd never mastered the art of light conversation.

Stepping into the brightness of White's was like entering a different world. The rich wooden paneling and golden candlelight of the gentlemen's retreat replaced the icy fog. There was a buzz of conversation and a clink of glasses from both sides of the entryway. Savory smells rode the air, promising a first-rate meal. His fingers and toes would soon be warm, Roger thought, whatever else this occasion might bring.

Surrendering his coat, hat, stick, and gloves to a servitor, Roger followed a waiter to a private corner of the dining room. There he found Arthur Shelton, Earl of Macklin, awaiting him. Though the man was old enough to be Roger's father, he hardly looked it. His dark hair showed no gray. His tall figure remained muscular and upright. He was talking to a man with a snub-nosed face, dun-brown hair, and dark eyes. Roger offered the two of them a polite bow.

Lord Macklin acknowledged it with a smile. His face showed few lines, and those seemed scored by good humor. He gestured toward the snub-nosed man. "Daniel Frith, Viscount Whitfield, may I present Roger Berwick, Marquess of Chatton," he said.

Puzzled, Roger greeted the other man, whom he had not previously encountered. "And Peter Rathbone, Duke of Compton," added their host, looking over Roger's shoulder.

Roger turned to discover a younger man behind him. This fellow couldn't be much past twenty, he judged. Compton had black hair, hazel eyes, and long fingers that tapped uneasily on his flanks. He looked inexplicably uneasy. What could be the matter with him?

Roger remembered that he'd been told, not long ago, that his face fell into forbidding lines when he wasn't paying any heed to his expression. The source was a young lady who had a unique talent for irritating him, and Roger had wanted to dismiss her comment out of hand. But it had come when he'd caused a small child to cry merely by looking at her, so he was concerned there might be a grain of truth to the observation. His father's features had been a bit craggy, and Roger knew he resembled him. He tried for a smile. Compton shied like a nervous horse.

"And here is the last of us," said Macklin. "Gentlemen, this is my nephew Benjamin Romilly, Earl of Furness."

The new arrival resembled his uncle in coloring and frame. Anyone, seeing them, would have known them for relations. Furness looked glum rather than hospitable, however—more like a man stepping into a boxing ring than one joining a convivial supper party. Once again, Roger wondered about the motive behind this gathering.

"And now that the proprieties are satisfied, I hope we can be much less formal," their host added.

They stood gazing at one another. Could the earl have some sort of business proposition in mind? Roger wondered. A few landowners around the country were investing in canals and opening coal mines. But his property was nowhere near Macklin's estates, so that made no sense.

"Sit down," said their host, gesturing at the waiting table. As they obeyed, he signaled for wine to be poured. "They have a fine roast beef this evening. As when do they not at White's? We'll begin with soup, though, on a raw night like this." The waiter returned his nod and went off to fetch it.

Roger appreciated the hot broth. His stomach had been giving him trouble for months, and this was just the thing to soothe it as well as warm him. "Vile weather," Whitfield said.

The others agreed. Compton praised the claret, and then looked worried, as if he'd been presumptuous, which was rather odd behavior for a duke. The rest merely nodded. Roger leaned forward and then couldn't think how to ask what this gathering was about without being rude. He searched for some alternative remark, and found none. So he downed his wine instead. He was immediately given more. All the glasses were being emptied and refilled rather rapidly.

Steaming plates were put before them. The rich aroma of the beef both tantalized and unsettled Roger. He was hungry, and yet his iron digestion had deserted him lately. Or not so lately. Since the Crenshaw affair began, really. And today's rancorous visit had brought it all back. The horseradish sauce was clearly out of the question.

"No doubt you're wondering why I've invited you—the four of you—this evening," Macklin said. "When we aren't really acquainted."

Roger leaned forward again, eager for an explanation.

"You have something in common," Macklin went on. "*We* do." He looked around the table. "Death."

Had the man actually said *death*? Roger checked his companions, and saw astonishment on their faces. Clearly, they knew no more than he. That was a crumb of comfort. He hated being at sea in a social exchange—a discomfort that was all too familiar. So many of his troubles came through not finding the right thing to say.

The older man nodded across the table. "My

nephew's wife died in childbirth several years ago. He mourns her still."

Furness looked more furious than grief-stricken as the table's attention shifted to him. He obviously had not expected this information to be shared with strangers.

The earl turned to the viscount. "Whitfield's parents were killed in a shipwreck eight months ago on their way back from India," he continued.

Whitfield looked around the table as if he couldn't understand how he'd come to be here. "Quite so. A dreadful accident. Storm drove them onto a reef. All hands lost." He shrugged. "What can one do? These things happen." His expression said he didn't intend to discuss it.

"Chatton lost his wife to a virulent fever a year ago," Lord Macklin said.

Though the remark wasn't a surprise, given the foregoing, Roger felt a surge of anger. The phrasing brought back all his in-laws' unfair denunciations. "I didn't *lose* her," he replied. He could feel his face reddening, as it did with any strong emotion, the curse of his pale skin. "She was dashed well *killed* by an incompetent physician, and my neighbor who insisted they ride out into a downpour." Much as the Crenshaws wanted to blame him for Arabella's death, it had *not* been his fault.

Roger saw the others pull back slightly. He'd spoken too emphatically. The proper tone was such a damned difficult thing to gauge, most of the time. And those words hadn't been right either.

"And Compton's sister died while she was visiting a friend, just six months ago," their host finished.

The youngest man at their table flinched. "She was barely seventeen," he murmured. "My ward as well as my sister." He put his head in his hands. "I ought to have gone with her. I was invited. If only I'd gone. I wouldn't have allowed her to take that cliff path. I would have…done something."

Useless regrets, Roger thought. He'd had his share of those. And more than his share, he sometimes felt.

"I've been widowed for ten years," said Macklin gently. "I know what it's like to lose a beloved person quite suddenly. And I know there must be a period of adjustment afterward. People don't talk about the time it takes—different for everyone, I imagine—and how one copes." He looked around the table. "I was aware of Benjamin's bereavement, naturally, since he is my nephew."

Furness gritted his teeth. Roger thought he was going to jump up and stalk out. Whitfield showed similar signs. But the earl spoke again before either of them could move.

"Then, seemingly at random, I heard of your cases, and it occurred to me that I might be able to help."

"What help is there for death?" Roger said. He might have wished there was, but death was an inalterable fact. There was no making up for it, as his in-laws had repeatedly pointed out to him. His temper flared. Arabella's mother had flat out called him a murderer. A mixture of despair and ire made his stomach roil. He was sorry he'd tasted the beef. "And which of us asked for your aid?" he muttered. "*I* certainly didn't."

Whitfield pushed a little back from the table. "Waste of time to dwell on such stuff. No point, eh?"

Compton sighed like a melancholy bellows.

"Grief is insidious, almost palpable, and as variable as humankind," said their host. "No one can understand who hasn't experienced a sudden loss. A black coat and a few platitudes are nothing."

"Are you accusing us of insincerity, sir?" Roger found that his fists were clenched on either side of his plate. No doubt his face had gone as red as his hair. But he wouldn't have the Crenshaws' insinuations echoed by a stranger. On the left, Compton edged away from him.

"Not at all," answered the earl. "I'm offering you the fruits of experience and years of contemplation."

"Thrusting them on us, whether we will or no. Tantamount to an ambush, this so-called dinner." If he'd had the least inkling that the meal would be a repeat of his earlier appointment, he never would have come.

"Nothing wrong with the food," said Whitfield, sticking his unwanted oar in. "Best claret I've had this year."

"Well, well," said Macklin. He seemed serene, not affected by their responses. "Who knows? If I've made a mistake, I'll gladly apologize. Indeed, I beg your pardon for springing my idea on you with no preparation. Will you, nonetheless, allow me to tell the story of my grieving, as I had hoped to do?"

Despite himself, Roger's attention was caught. He'd never heard anyone call grieving a story.

"And afterward, should you wish to do the same, I'll gladly hear it," added the earl. He smiled. The expression cut through Roger's annoyance. He received the sudden impression of a wise, reliable man—one who took the time to listen rather than dictate, utterly unlike the choleric blusterers he'd grown up around. What if his mother had married Macklin rather than his father? he suddenly thought. Roger would have had a different life, in a softer region than the Scottish borders. Which was a ridiculous notion, because he wouldn't have been himself, but somebody else entirely. And that was sillier still.

The earl said his piece. And then the others spoke, briefly, with varying degrees of enthusiasm and candor. Compton came very near tears, while Furness was tight-lipped and laconic. The talk was surprisingly engrossing. And when they were done, Roger found that the simmering anger the day had brought was eased. Which was a boon he certainly hadn't expected to receive from a dinner at White's, he thought as he headed back to his hotel.

One

ROGER URGED HIS HORSE TO GREATER SPEED ON THE firm sand at the verge of the waves. A good gallop could always relieve his feelings. And late July was surely the best time for it here at the edge of the North Sea. The Northumberland wind still had a bite, but the sun was warm on his back, and there was no sign of rain. The stone pile of Chatton Castle, with all its attendant responsibilities, receded behind him. The shore stretched ahead. For an hour or so he could be solitary and carefree.

And so, of course, a figure on horseback appeared ahead, riding toward him. The mount's glossy gray coat and the rider's neat silhouette told him who it was. Roger muttered a curse. His luck was out today. "You're on my land," he said when their paths intersected.

"Not according to my father," replied a haughty young lady in a fashionable riding habit. "He would say that you're on his."

"The deuce. Is this that stretch?" Roger looked around and realized that he'd come farther than he'd noticed. He was on a piece of land at the edge of his estate that was the subject of a border dispute, started by his father and hers some years ago. The ham-handed way the two men had tried to settle the matter had roused a world of troubles.

"You know it is," she said.

Roger looked at her. In one sense, he'd known Fenella Fairclough all his life. They'd grown up on neighboring estates and met at various children's parties in their youth. In another sense, however, he hardly knew her at all. A female had no right to change so much between the ages of seventeen and twenty-three, Roger thought. She'd been a gangling, tongue-tied girl when she left for the north five years ago, after the fiasco of their rejected betrothal. She'd been fearful and retiring, the sort of female one was surprised to hear had been present at a soiree or assembly. And she'd come back the opposite of all those things—forthright, impatient, alarmingly astute. Not to mention far more curvaceous. The first time he'd seen her again, on her return to the neighborhood, he hadn't recognized Fenella.

She had the same pale-red hair and blue eyes, the same pretty oval face, but the expression was far different, and the words that issued from that full-lipped mouth could sting. How well he knew that! "You're out alone, without even a groom?" he asked. She'd scarcely ridden in their youth, finding horses large and intimidating as he remembered it. The gray she was on now would have terrified her then.

"As are you," she said.

"A completely different case," Roger said.

Her eyes flashed. "I suppose I can ride as I like on *our own* land."

"Hah!" It was a distinct hit. Almost amusing, if circumstances had been different. "You're all too ready to ride anywhere, even through a tempest."

Exasperation tightened her jaw. "Please tell me that you're not going to start with this again. I thought you'd given up that stupid story at last."

He had. And he rather wished he hadn't referred to it now. But the visit to the Crenshaws had kicked up all sorts of inner turmoil. The ranting of Arabella's parents, particularly her mother, in London had brought everything back. Coupled with his tendency to utter the wrong word at the wrong time, it had tripped him up.

"I am very tired of telling you that expedition was Arabella's idea, not mine, Chatton. And that I did my best to stop her."

"Splendid. I'm tired of hearing it."

"You don't hear. That's the problem." Miss Fairclough sighed. "Can we not leave this behind us? You haven't mentioned it in months."

Easy for her to talk of moving forward, Roger thought. She didn't have to face Mrs. Crenshaw. An irritated sound escaped him.

"You are the most intractable man," said Miss Fairclough.

"Intractable, is it? Did you learn such words north of the border?"

"I learned to express my opinion."

"No matter how misguided. Typical from someone whose mother was a Scot."

Her lips twitched. "Have we descended to childish insults? Very well. *Your* mother is a soft southerner."

"You like my mother! And she's always disgustingly kind to you."

Miss Fairclough's face softened. "She is kind. Though hardly disgusting."

"Oh, you can do no wrong in her eyes."

"On the contrary."

Their eyes met. Roger could tell that she was remembering, as was he, that his mother had wanted him to marry her. When she was a biddable girl, not the waspish young lady she'd become. Roger didn't recall his mother's reasons. He knew they hadn't been related to the cold merger of properties that their fathers had proposed. They'd both rejected that scheme, five years ago. And of course they'd been right. Absolutely right.

"I must go," said Miss Fairclough.

Strictly speaking, he ought to offer to escort her. But Roger didn't care. He wanted his solitude back. And he knew she wouldn't welcome his company. He settled for a bow from the saddle and watched her ride away. Really, she'd become a bruising rider in her years away.

❧

Fenella urged her horse toward home, fuming, as she nearly always was after an encounter with Chatton. She was so tired of hearing about the notorious ride into the storm that had brought on his wife's fever and led to her death. His position was quite unjust. The expedition really had been entirely Arabella's idea.

Fenella *had* tried to talk her out of going. But the newly minted Marchioness of Chatton had not been a persuadable person. Indeed, Arabella had been spoiled and stubborn. Add discontent to that, and you had a volatile mixture.

Silently, Fenella acknowledged that she hadn't liked Arabella at first. But she'd begun to feel sorry for a girl of nineteen taken so far from her home and discovering that she didn't like the windswept coast of Northumberland or, indeed, her new husband. Fenella had watched the newcomer realize that a title didn't make up for a lack of common interests or clashing temperaments.

With Fenella's sympathies roused, and Arabella very lonely, they'd become friends of a sort, despite Arabella's chancy nature. Wistful tales of London revealed that Arabella's parents, particularly her mother, had engineered the marriage, intent on social advancement. Fenella suspected that they'd forced Arabella to relinquish a prior attachment, over which she sometimes wept. For the Crenshaws, Chatton's position had been everything, his personality irrelevant. And so two young people had been yoked together with little chance of happiness, as far as Fenella could judge. It was sad. And none of her business, of course. Indeed, her history with Chatton made Arabella's confidences awkward. Yet she couldn't have rejected her, Fenella thought as she rode. It would have been cruel.

Three and a half years with her Scottish grandmother had taught Fenella a good deal about kindness. Which was ironic on the face of it, because many thought her grandmother a terrifying old lady. Grandmamma came from a long line of border lords who had harried the English and feuded with each other for centuries. She was as comfortable holding a pistol as a teacup. And she'd explained to Fenella that kindness could be quite a complicated exercise, requiring thought and care.

The time with her grandmother had made her feel older than her years, Fenella thought. Certainly more than a few years older than Arabella. Fenella often wondered what might have come to Arabella, and indeed Chatton, if she hadn't died so young. But that would never be known.

On this melancholy note, Fenella reached her home and turned to the stables, where she left her mount. Looping up the long skirts of her riding habit, she walked to the side door of the great brick pile where she'd grown up. She'd missed Clough House while she was gone. Yet she wasn't entirely glad to be back.

A housemaid met her on the threshold, as if she'd been waiting there. "The master's asking for you, miss."

"I'll just change out of my habit," said Fenella.

"He's fretting."

Fenella adjusted her grip on her skirts and started for the stairs.

Her father's illness had changed him. He still growled and demanded, but the tone was querulous now. And too often bewildered. It had startled Fenella when she'd been called back home to oversee his care.

She was struck again by the irony of the situation as she walked up the stairs. Her two sisters had always gotten on better with Papa, mainly because he'd made no secret of his bitter disappointment that Fenella wasn't born a son. "Third time's the charm," he'd used to mutter. "Only it wasn't." He'd shadowed the last years of her mother's life over this supposed failing, and he'd seemed to feel that Fenella owed him extra obedience to make up for the lapse. And so he'd thought to marry her off like a medieval magnate disposing of his chattel. Well, he hadn't managed that.

But Greta and Nora had families of their own to occupy them and had happened to settle far away. Everyone had thought it Fenella's duty to come home, and so she had. Part of her had welcomed the chance. She didn't wish to be forever estranged from her father.

How did it feel, Fenella wondered, to have the defiant daughter in charge of his sickroom? What if she'd accepted one of the offers of marriage she'd received in Scotland? Where would he be then? But they never discussed such things. They were not a family who spoke of their feelings, she thought as she entered his room. Before her stay with Grandmamma, she'd hardly recognized what her feelings were. "Hello, Papa," she said.

"Where have you been?"

"Out riding."

"Enjoying yourself, eh? Using my horses. With no thought for me lying neglected here."

In fact, Fenella's mount was her own, a gift from her grandmother, though the mare was eating the estate's fodder, of course. "On the contrary, I made certain Simpson was with you."

"That doddering excuse for a valet! I sent him away."

Simpson had been with her father for as long as Fenella could remember. He was probably hovering behind the dressing room door right now in case he might be needed. Her father really was the most difficult of patients. "Shall I read to you?" she asked.

"Pah!" He shoved at his coverlet. "I want to be up out of this damned bed." He tried to rise, and rediscovered the weakness in his right side, which he forgot from one day to the next. The drag of his arm and leg kept him from the outdoor pursuits he loved. And the vagueness of his mind made other favorite amusements, like cards, vastly frustrating for all involved. The doctor had said that her father would probably never recover from the bout of apoplexy that had felled him. Fenella didn't blame Papa for cursing. But that didn't make tending him any easier.

Her father fell back onto the pillows. "Why does no one come to see me?" he asked. "Chatton might stop by, I would think, knowing I'm ill."

Well aware that he was referring to the current marquess's father, and indeed to a time before they'd fallen out, Fenella didn't know what to say. The first time he'd complained of this, she'd told him his old friend-foe was dead. But he never remembered.

"Or Pierson," her father added. "Many's the good turn I've done him. He might spare me half an hour's visit."

It would be good for him to see familiar faces, Fenella thought. But the Piersons had moved to Kent years ago. Her father had no friends left nearby. She'd send for the vicar again. His conversation could soothe, when it didn't infuriate.

"But I've only *you*," he went on. "If you'd been a son, as you were *supposed* to be, I wouldn't be laid low like this. And no one to come after me on the estate."

Resisting the urge to argue with him, Fenella went to change her dress and then discover where Simpson was lurking so that they could discuss what to do.

୬ଚ

When he reached home, Roger found his mother entertaining a visitor to Chatton Castle. Their neighbor Harold Benson was sitting with her in the small drawing room that overlooked the sea. Benson, short and round and bald, always reminded Roger of the drawings of Humpty Dumpty in children's picture books. Now, he jumped up and offered a bow, proving that he did bend in the middle.

"Roger, just in time!" said his mother. "We are talking about the historical pageant on Lindisfarne at the end of August. I've been telling Mr. Benson that of course we will do all we can to help."

If his mother had had a coat of arms, that might have been the motto engraved upon it, Roger thought. Her impulse was always to help. The problem was that the consequent obligations piled up until she was hard-pressed to fulfill them all, and then she bounced from one to another like a fly trapped by a closed window, buzzing with anxiety. Waving Benson back to his chair, Roger sat down beside her, wondering if he could keep her from going distracted over this pageant. A happy smile lit her face. Fair-haired and slender, her features scarcely lined, she didn't look her fifty years of age.

"It's to be bigger than I realized," she went on. "With Romans and Vikings and Saxons. And monks, of course."

"Isn't that a poor place to hold a festival?" asked Roger. "The road out to Lindisfarne is underwater at high tide."

"There's a well-marked path," said Benson. "People only need to take care and mind the tides. And the holy isle has been the scene of a positive panorama of British history." Benson was an avid scholar, their local expert on just about everything. Particularly in his own opinion. On his small, neat estate just south of Roger's lands, Benson inhabited a house overrun by books.

Roger's mother clasped her hands. "There will be a special presentation of speeches from *Macbeth* by a leading London actress. Only think!"

Their visitor's plump cheeks creased with distaste, making him look like a dyspeptic chipmunk. "Very dramatic, I'm sure. Of course Shakespeare got that story wrong in almost every respect. The chronicles give no hint of such machinations. Macbeth was an unexceptional king of Scotland. And nothing at all is known about his wife!"

"What day is it to be?" asked Roger before Benson could launch into a lecture on medieval politics north of the border.

"The last day of August," answered Roger's mother.

"I'm glad it's all going smoothly," said Roger, hoping to plant the notion in her mind that not too much help was needed.

"Ah," said Benson.

The concern he packed into that brief syllable told Roger that the bad news was coming.

"We do have rather a problem over who is to

portray Saint Cuthbert. Such an important figure in our local religious traditions, you know."

"I'd think some vicar or bishop would be pleased to do so," said Roger.

Benson made a wry face. "Precisely. Too pleased. A rather fierce, ah, competition has developed in the church over the role. I understand that a parish priest and a canon nearly came to blows. Shocking. I've thought of suggesting that it should be a great man of the neighborhood instead."

"You don't mean me?" said Roger, horrified at the thought.

Their visitor looked equally perturbed. "No! That is, no, Lord Chatton. I would never… There's no thought of that."

Roger sat back, relieved and somehow a bit piqued at the vehemence of Benson's rejection.

"I certainly hope you *will* take a part in the pageant," Benson added quickly. "There are all sorts of roles. Viking raiders, marauding Saxons or Scots."

Was he seen as so bellicose? Roger wondered. But since he didn't want a part in the least, it didn't matter.

"I think Roger should be a Roman commander," said his mother. "With a toga and a chariot."

He choked back a horrified laugh. Where had that idea come from?

"Ah, strictly speaking, the Romans were not a force this far north in England," said Benson. "And chariots, you know, would never have been used on——"

She went on without seeming to hear. "You could use one of the swords hanging above the hall fireplace," she said to Roger.

"Those are claymores," said Benson. "The two-handed medieval sword, you know. Nothing to do with the Romans."

"And I'd be hard-pressed to wield one," said Roger. "Lord knows what they weigh."

"The Romans carried a much shorter weapon called a *gladius*," said Benson. "But as I said, we had few Romans hereabouts."

He spoke as if Roger was longing for a role but was worried about taking it. Roger set to work to dispel that wrong-headed notion and managed to avoid promising any sort of participation in the August pageant, amusing his mother even as he annoyed their scholarly neighbor.

Two

THE FOLLOWING DAY BROUGHT A SURPRISE TO
Chatton Castle. As Roger was looking over a list of
rent rolls, he was informed that a traveler had arrived
and was asking for him. The card he was handed
startled him, but when he went to the front hall, he
discovered that Lord Macklin was indeed in his house.

"I'm on my way to Scotland for some fishing," said
the newcomer. "When I found we were passing your
home, I thought I'd stop to see you."

"Splendid," said Roger, and found he truly meant
it. He'd recalled the dinner in London quite often
since the spring. The occasion stood out in his mind
as both unusual and, somehow, comforting. He was
genuinely glad to see the earl. "I hope you'll stay a few
days." He noted Macklin's traveling carriage standing
outside. An older man who was clearly a valet waited
beside it, along with a homely youngster Roger
couldn't immediately categorize.

"I wouldn't want to inconvenience you," said
Macklin.

"Not at all. We'll be glad of the company." Roger

turned to the footman. "Have Lord Macklin's carriage taken to the stables," he said. "And tell my mother and Mrs. Burke that we have a visitor." He handed over the earl's card to be delivered with this news. Only then did he remember his mother's youthful romance with their guest.

Macklin had stepped over to the east windows and was gazing out at the cliffside and the expanse of the North Sea beyond. "This coast has an austere beauty," he said. "I haven't been here before."

Roger went to stand next to him. "Yes," he agreed. He knew some found the landscape bleak, but it was his home country and he loved it. "And some unique vulnerabilities. Denmark is there." He pointed directly east. "A matter of five hundred miles for the invading Danes to sail. And Norway is about the same distance there." He pointed northeast. "Once full of marauding Norsemen. That's why Chatton is a fortification rather than an estate house. But we do have an up-to-date wing. We'll make you comfortable, I promise."

"I have no doubt of it."

"Arthur Shelton!" declared a melodious female voice.

They turned to find Roger's mother framed by the arched stone doorway that led to the more modern part of the castle. One hand was pressed against the bodice of her rose-colored gown. The other held Macklin's visiting card. Her blue eyes were sparkling.

"Of course you will remember my mother," said Roger.

"The dowager marchioness," she said with a throwaway gesture, as if to show how ridiculous she found this designation. "Helena Ravelstoke that was."

Macklin blinked, and Roger was suddenly worried that his mother would be humiliated. He'd always accepted her tales of social success. But what if they'd been inflated in her memory?

"Helena Ravelstoke," repeated the earl. He moved forward, holding out his hand. When he grasped Roger's mother's fingers, he bowed over them in the style of an earlier age. "Mademoiselle Matchless, the toast of the *ton*." Without letting go of her hand, he turned back to Roger. "She had every young sprig in London pining at her feet."

She retrieved her hand, but her answering smile was brilliant.

"There were Falconhurst and Gregg." Macklin began counting off on his fingers. "Summerford and Dawes and Wingate, and others too numerous to mention. The Prince called you delectable." He glanced over his shoulder at Roger. "Now the Regent," he explained.

"My mother didn't leave me alone with *him*," replied Roger's mother. "Papa was livid when he mentioned me in that way, but Mama was quite up to the mark. She was pretty well acquainted with the queen, you know."

"Didn't Lensford compare you to Botticelli's Venus?" Macklin said. "Or shouldn't I mention that?"

She laughed. "Such a shocking thing to say." She didn't seem at all bothered by this fact, however.

Was that the painting with the lady on the half shell clothed only in her long hair? Roger rather thought it was. *Not* a proper image to describe a young lady, especially one's mother. He banished it from his mind.

"Many hopes were dashed when your mother

accepted your father's proposal," Macklin said. "Lensford threatened to shoot himself."

"Of course he didn't mean it," she replied. "He was *such* a dramatic young man. I wonder what's become of him."

"Gone to fat," answered the earl promptly. "Lives in Somerset. Breeds prize sheep."

"Oh no!"

Macklin nodded. "Married Wrenly's daughter."

"I did know that. But sheep! Couldn't it have been hunting dogs, at least? What about his poetry?"

The earl shrugged. "He may still write it. But he never published another volume after the one that critic called 'unmitigated bilge.'"

"He was crushed," said Roger's mother sympathetically.

"More of a sulk, I thought." The earl smiled at her in a way that recalled a far younger man.

She gestured. Roger could almost see a fan in her hand, extended to rap the older man's knuckles.

"I was among those spurned," Macklin said to Roger. He didn't seem particularly regretful, however. More amused and nostalgic.

"Hardly that," Roger's mother replied. "And it seems to me you were courting Celia Garthington well before I married."

He acknowledged it with a nod as the Chatton Castle housekeeper bustled in.

"Is Lord Macklin's room ready, Mrs. Burke?"

"Yes, my lady." The housekeeper turned to Macklin. "Your valet is already above, my lord. Would you care to go up?"

He accepted with a nod and a punctilious farewell.

When Roger and his mother were left alone, she said, "How extraordinary that he came all this way to visit me."

"I don't think... He said he was on the way to Scotland for some fishing."

"Well, he needed an excuse," she replied. "But why else stop at Chatton?"

"To see me, he said. I had dinner with him the last time I was in London."

"You did?"

"I was surprised at the invitation," Roger admitted.

His mother looked thoughtful. "Would he go so far as to make friends with you so that he could visit here? Now that I'm a widow."

"Papa has been dead for more a year."

"Indeed. A proper period of mourning, which shows great sensitivity on Arthur's part."

Roger thought she was wrong. He was pretty sure Macklin had been startled to find her here. This could grow awkward. He began to worry that he'd made a mistake in extending the invitation to stay.

❧

Only a few miles away, Fenella Fairclough was also welcoming a visitor, though this one was officially expected, if not quite invited. Fenella's eldest sister had decreed that her son would spend the summer school holiday at his grandfather's home. Her letter had simply assumed the boy was welcome, and Fenella knew there was no arguing with Greta, not without a monumental fuss.

The ten-year difference in their ages meant that she barely knew her sister. Greta had married at seventeen, in her first season, and produced a son and heir for her husband the following year. Two daughters had followed, and now Greta was expecting again. She'd declared that she couldn't deal with her son under these circumstances, leaving Fenella to wonder what that meant precisely. But her father had approved the plan, and she had no reason to refuse. And so ten-year-old Sherrington Symmes had been packed into a post chaise, from which he was now descending, and sent along like a parcel into the North.

Her nephew was thin, with a narrow face, his dark hair a bit long, falling over his forehead. His long fingers moved nervously, and something in his eyes touched Fenella. Apprehension? It was true they weren't really acquainted. Their interactions on family visits had been fleeting. She smiled. "Hello, Sherrington. I'm your aunt Fenella."

"People call me John. It's my middle name." His voice was defiant, as if he expected objections and was ready to fight them off.

Fenella saw no reason to make any. He'd been named after his father, who might have known better, Fenella thought. She'd found Sherrington a ponderous name when it was announced. "John," she repeated. "Welcome to Northumberland."

He looked around without visible enthusiasm.

The servant supervising the unloading of his trunks seemed old for a boy, Fenella noticed. But perhaps he was more of a tutor.

"How far away is Scotland?" the boy asked.

"We're about ten miles from the border here," Fenella replied.

"It's so cold in Scotland that the snakes don't lay eggs," he said. "They're born alive, like mammals."

"Really."

He flushed as if he wished he could take back these words, then raised his chin as if Fenella had reprimanded him. "There aren't any proper snakes here. Nothing like a cobra or a python. Pythons can be feet and feet long. They can crush a goat."

"How?"

"They wrap their coils around them and squeeze." John closed his hands into fists, demonstrating.

He meant her to shudder, Fenella thought. She disappointed him. "And where do they do this crushing?"

"What?"

"Where do pythons live?"

"In Asia and Africa. When I'm older, I'm going to visit my uncle in India and see the snake charmers."

John spoke like a boy who was often contradicted. Fenella decided then and there that she wouldn't. "Well, we may be short on snakes, but we do have cats and dogs and horses. Do you like to ride?"

The servant had left the carriage and was hovering behind the boy. "This is Wrayle," John said. "He's my minder."

"Now, Master Sherrington." The man glanced at Fenella as if to enlist her in a furtive cause. "I'm afraid Master Sherrington's health is delicate. He will require a south-facing bedchamber, with tight shutters, and a restricted diet, with hot milk at bedtime."

The boy seemed to deflate, like a creature resigned to oppression. He also looked as if he was made of whipcord and steel, and not the least bit delicate.

"I'll introduce you to our housekeeper," said Fenella to Wrayle. "She'll see that you have what you need." *But perhaps not everything you want*, she added silently.

He smiled like a man who had established his dominance. Fenella decided she didn't like him. She vowed to have a talk with the housekeeper before Wrayle reached her with his list of demands.

❧

Wrayle was part of the reason that Fenella took her nephew along that evening to a gathering at the house of a local baronet. Sir Cyril and Lady Prouse loved to entertain, and they didn't let the fact that their children were all married and settled elsewhere stop them from inviting young people to gather for a bit of music and dancing. Lady Prouse said that nothing cheered her like watching youngsters enjoy themselves. In a somewhat isolated neighborhood without local assemblies, the Prouse home was a lively social hub.

Fenella hadn't accepted one of their invitations for a while. Caring for her father and his estate took much of her time, but the truth was she hadn't been as active in neighborhood society since Arabella's death. That event, and its aftermath, had cast a pall. But that was clearing, and anyhow she had John to think of now.

The Prouses lived nearby. Their evening wouldn't run too late, and beyond thwarting Wrayle, Fenella thought John would enjoy the jovial atmosphere.

There would certainly be plenty of young people present. Not as young as he, admittedly. But she wasn't
going to mind that.

At this point in her thought processes, Fenella
realized that she wanted to go for her own sake.
Gaiety had been missing from her life recently.
She was ready for a dose of Lady Prouse's shrewd
good humor. And so she put on one of her favorite
gowns, bundled John into the carriage, and set out
for the baronet's.

They were among the first arrivals, but this was not
an occasion for the fashionably late. Others entered
soon enough, all of them friends or acquaintances.
Fenella found John a comfortable perch and a plate
of cakes and went to talk to her neighbors. Those
who evinced an opinion seemed glad to see her.
More were concentrated on their own enjoyment.
A reminder, Fenella thought, not to exaggerate one's
own importance.

A wry smile still lingered on her lips when Roger
entered the spacious drawing room. She was surprised
to see him. He had been mingling in society even
less over this past year. But the conventional mourning period, for his wife and his father, was over. He
certainly had as much right as she to attend. Fenella
turned away to speak to Mrs. Cheeve, the vicar's wife,
who had also just arrived with her husband.

The musicians in the corner struck up. Permanent
employees of the Prouses, they included, as always, a
piper, even though the bagpipe didn't really fit with
many of the usual dances. As well as the fact that the
baronet and his wife weren't the least bit Scottish.

Fenella had asked them about this once. Sir Cyril's gaze had gone distant as he declared, "It's just such a magnificent sound, is it not?"

Now, accompanied by its eerie strains, Lady Prouse bore down on Fenella, took her arm, and turned her around. "There, you two dance," she said, pushing her toward Roger.

Before either of them could react, she'd moved on, putting other couples together based entirely on proximity, as far as Fenella could judge. She meant nothing in particular by these pairings, except to set the dance moving.

Facing Roger, Fenella wondered what she ought to do. They hadn't danced together since she came back from Scotland. Their past, and then a pile of complicating circumstances, had made it unwise.

The bagpipe shrilled, signaling a Highland reel. Fenella's foot tapped. She wasn't the awkward girl who'd been thrown at him five years ago. And she felt like dancing. She extended her hands.

Roger took them. They laced their fingers together, standing very close, and then they joined the others in moving forward and back, hopping and turning in the steps of the dance.

His hands were sure and powerful. He swung her around with practiced skill. She'd forgotten that he was a fine, athletic dancer, Fenella thought. Or, she'd just avoided thinking about it.

They hadn't touched in ages, certainly not since she'd returned from Scotland, and that had been best. She had no doubt about it. But before that, there had been occasions. She suddenly realized that the first of them had been here in this very room. It must be, yes, eight years ago.

Lady Prouse had organized a dancing class to help prepare her daughter Prudence for a London season, and she'd invited all the local young people, even those like Fenella who were not remotely out. Lady Prouse had wanted enough couples to make up sets, and there weren't a great many to choose from in the neighborhood. And so, although she was only fifteen, Fenella had wangled permission to go. She'd argued that the occasion was very informal and strictly chaperoned. Her mother had been ill at the time and had given in to her arguments. And so she'd come here, to this very spot, a pathetically gawky girl with unrealistic expectations. The draperies and furnishings looked just the same.

And then when Lady Prouse had to leave the room to attend to some household crisis, her daughter had cajoled the musicians into playing a waltz. Many of the boys, coerced into attending by their mothers, had been longing for a way to rebel, and they added their voices to hers. The musicians were persuaded, couples quickly came together, and Roger had been somehow left out, with only Fenella unpartnered.

He hadn't been pleased, Fenella remembered. And he'd made no effort to hide his reluctance. But the others twitted him as a coward, or a bumpkin ignorant of the steps of the waltz. And so he had grabbed her, his arm tight around her waist, and spun her dizzily down the room. Fenella had found the dance intoxicating. She'd yielded to his masterful lead, senses swimming, until Lady Prouse returned and put a stop to their scandalous performance. "I wonder how Prudence is," said Fenella.

Roger looked startled, as well he might. She'd been silent through much of the reel, and now she'd come out with this. He laughed. "No one ever had a more inapt name. She's the least prudent creature I can imagine."

Before he could think of that long-ago waltz, Fenella rushed on. "She married a man from Hertfordshire. The Prouses usually go to visit her down there."

Roger nodded. "Do you remember those tableaus she organized one Christmas? Weren't you in one?"

Fenella fought the blush, but it won out. Prudence had given her the part of winged Victory, to her utter delight. Even though she knew it was because she was the slightest girl and willing to perch on a tall plinth. But the diaphanous toga sort of thing she'd been draped in had turned out to be quite transparent when the banks of candles were lit for the tableaus. She'd been virtually naked, four feet above people's heads. Her father had roared with fury.

"Oh yes," said Roger. A spark lit his blue eyes.

He'd remembered. Of course he had. How could he not? "That incident gave me an enduring hatred of sarsenet," Fenella said dryly. "I've never worn it since."

He burst out laughing, which had been her aim. The music ended. Fenella stepped away, more breathless than a bit of dancing could explain. Roger left her with a smiling bow, shifting to another partner for the next dance.

"You and Chatton move well together," said Lady Prouse at Fenella's shoulder.

Fenella turned to find a speculative gleam in her hostess's eye. She resisted pressing her hands to her flushed cheeks. Or saying anything that might encourage matchmaking. "Have you seen my nephew?"

"He asked about our library," replied Lady Prouse, looking mildly disappointed at this response.

Fenella found John among the books. He was reading one about India, and he looked tired. She gathered him up to take him home to bed—and probably face the wrath of Wrayle, but she cared very little about that.

❧

The local church service on Sunday held a good deal of interest for the Chatton Castle neighborhood, which seldom received strangers. Additions to society were always welcome in this isolated corner of the country.

The castle party itself included a distinguished older gentleman. Whispers soon identified him as an earl, and he was seen to be quite friendly with Lady Chatton, rousing a buzz of curiosity. There was also an unknown youngster at the far end of the castle pew, homely but amiable-looking. His status couldn't be agreed upon within the limited opportunities for gossip inside the church. He did not appear the least cowed by noble company.

The group from Clough House also brought a new member, a slender boy soon identified as the old gentleman's grandson. Parishioners murmured that this visit must be pleasant for the old man in his sickness. He hadn't been seen in church, or anywhere else, since being felled by the apoplexy.

The vicar's sermon that day added to the excitement of the occasion. Rather than his usual homily on responsibility or compassion, he stated that his subject would be Cuthbert, the area's patron saint and, he declared, the savior of England. "For after this holy man's death and the many miracles due to his intercession, Cuthbert came in a dream to Alfred, known as the Great, King of Wessex. Alfred was then engaged in a mighty struggle against the Danes, invaders from over the sea."

The vicar paused and raked the congregation with his gaze. Roger, directly under his eye in the front, was taken aback. Reverend Cheeve was usually the mildest of men, but today his green eyes burned with fervor.

The man shook back the wide sleeves of his surplice, put a hand on either side of the pulpit, leaned forward, and continued. "Calling himself a soldier of Christ in this dream, Cuthbert told the king what he needed to do. Alfred must arise at dawn and sound his horn three times. Cuthbert promised that by the ninth hour, the king would have assembled five hundred men. And within seven days Alfred would have gathered, through God's gift and Cuthbert's aid, an army to fight at his side and vanquish the Danes. And so it happened. The battle was won. And England was *not* conquered."

Roger stifled an impulse to applaud. Cheeve might have been rousing a fighting troop rather than preaching. Far more entertaining than his customary platitudes. The vicar did circle back after this to relate his story to his listeners, urging them to put their trust in the lord. But the jolt of energy he'd provided remained in the air. Roger put a bit extra in the collection plate to show his appreciation. He also congratulated Cheeve on a fine sermon as he passed through the church door after the service.

Outside, Roger came face-to-face with Fenella Fairclough, for the first time since their invigorating reel at the Prouses'. And he couldn't help thinking that she looked particularly pretty this morning, curvaceous and assured in a deep-blue gown that echoed the hue of her eyes, with a shawl falling artistically over her shoulders. Her face, half-shaded by a chip straw bonnet, reminded Roger of an antique cameo. If such a piece of jewelry could shift expressions like wind passing over water, he amended.

The press of people leaving the church urged him on, and they moved away together. "This is my nephew John Symmes," she said, indicating a dark-haired boy at her side. "Greta's son. John, this is Lord Chatton, a neighbor of ours."

"You live in the castle," said the boy.

"I do."

"John is spending his holiday with us," Fenella added.

"Ah." Seeing his mother and houseguest ahead, Roger moved toward them. "We have a visitor as well. Up from London. Lord Macklin, may I present Miss Fairclough and…" But young Symmes had faded into the small crowd between one step and the next. He appeared to be gone.

Roger's mother offered happy greetings, and Macklin acknowledged the introduction with his habitual composure. Roger was about to suggest that they depart when Harold Benson edged around Macklin, plump and furtive to the earl's tall and distinguished. Indeed, the self-appointed historian was half crouching, so that his rotund figure looked even more squat. "I'm avoiding Cheeve," he informed them. "He thinks I can guarantee him the part of St. Cuthbert in the pageant, but I can't. That decision is not up to me. He's wasted his oratory."

Benson moved so that Roger was between him and the church door, where the vicar still lingered. "But I have been asked to speak to you again, Lord Chatton. And also to Miss Fairclough. I'm happy to find you together. There's a scene in the pageant that is part of a Viking raid on the Lindisfarne manor, and the committee wondered, hoped, that you two might enact it. As a gesture of support for the enterprise. To help make the venture a success, you know. And reflect well on the neighborhood."

Despite this blatant hint, Roger started to refuse, but Fenella spoke first. "What sort of scene?"

"A Saxon noblewoman repels the Viking attacker with a broom."

"A broom?" asked Fenella.

"She bashes him on the side of the head," replied Benson. "Naturally we would take care—"

"I could do that," Fenella interrupted.

"I'm sure you could," said Roger. "And enjoy it, too. I don't intend to be bashed, however."

"The Viking prevails in the end, of course," said Benson. "He sweeps her up and carries her off and, well, there is another bit, but we could make adjustments."

"Throws her in the midden?" Roger suggested. "Or the pigsty perhaps?"

"After she kicks him in the face, repeatedly?" said Fenella.

Benson looked taken aback. "Whatever the exact, er, outcome, I'm glad to put you down as settled for the roles." He whipped a small notebook from his coat pocket, pulled out a stub of pencil, and made check marks on a list inside.

"Wait," said Roger. He noticed Macklin and his mother watching this exchange with interest. His mother leaned over to whisper to the earl, who would soon know all the history with Fenella that there was to know—from his mother's point of view, Roger thought.

"Rehearsals begin day after tomorrow," said Benson.

"Rehearsals!" repeated Roger and Fenella in unison.

"Just a moment," said Fenella.

"Cheeve's spotted me," said Benson. "I must go." He ducked sideways, scuttled along the path through the churchyard, and more or less ran away.

"Oh dear, I was going to ask him about taking a role myself," said Roger's mother.

"I suspect you'll have your chance," said Macklin.

Without meaning to, Roger met Fenella's sparkling blue gaze. She was clearly irritated and amused and resigned. And why did he imagine he saw so much in a glance? Roger wondered. He couldn't possibly. He was very bad at such perceptions. And yet he *was* certain. Roger felt an odd inner tug of emotion. He couldn't identify it. And when he had been so sure about *her* feelings, too. That made no sense. And it was dashed uncomfortable. He turned away toward his waiting carriage.

On the other side of the churchyard, shielded by a tall monument, Sherrington Symmes, known at long last as John, was kicking pebbles onto the plinth when an older boy walked around the obelisk and joined him.

"Hullo," he said.

John merely nodded. He wasn't in the mood for conversation.

"My name's Tom," said the newcomer.

John kicked a larger rock. It struck the base of the monument, bounced back, and tumbled off into the grass.

"'Dedicated to the memory of Malcolm Carew,'" Tom read from the stone. "'Beloved husband, respected father.' They all say something like that. Have to, once they're dead, don't they?"

John felt a spark of interest in the newcomer.

"I mean, you never see a gravestone saying 'rotten husband, mean old dad, and all-'round clutch-fisted blackguard.' Ain't done." He consulted the inscription. "Plenty old when he died. I suppose nobody shells out for a great spike like this if they didn't like the fellow."

John laughed. "Who are you?"

"Name's Tom," the other repeated.

"Tom what?"

"Dunno." The older boy shrugged. "Don't got a last name."

"But how can you not?"

"I don't remember my parents. Grew up scrambling, like, on the streets of Bristol."

John's interest increased by leaps and bounds. "My name is John Symmes."

"Grandson of one of the local gentry," Tom
answered. "I heard."

"You live around here?"

"No, come up for a visit. With Lord Macklin."
Leaning out, he indicated a tall, somewhat intimidating-
looking gentleman amid the parishioners.

John tried to figure out their association. Tom didn't
seem like a servant exactly. But he couldn't be a relation of that high-nosed man. Not with the history he'd
mentioned and the way he spoke. Still, better to err on
the side of the complimentary. "Are you his grandson?"

Tom laughed. "Not hardly. I'm... Well, I don't
rightly know what. I heard his secretary call me 'the
earl's current project.'" He grinned.

It was an immensely engaging grin. John felt a tug
of liking for this older, homely boy. Which was a rare
experience in his life. "What does that mean?"

"I reckon Lord Macklin wants to make something
of me." Tom's grin widened. "Not going to work,
howsomever."

"I don't understand."

"You ain't alone in that. Do you like walking?"

"Walking?"

"Tramping about the countryside. I'm partial to it
myself. Like company, too. You could come along."

"I'm not allowed out by myself." Much as it pained
him, John had to admit it. He felt it simply wouldn't
be right to lie to this new, intriguing acquaintance.

"Well, you wouldn't be. You'd be with me. You
could tell that aunt of yours that I never get in trouble.
I'm right careful. And we'd just be looking about, ye
know. 'Reconnoitering,' they call it."

"It isn't Aunt Fenella. It's Wrayle."

"Rail?"

"He's my jailer." John enjoyed saying it. Daring to say it.

"Eh?" said Tom.

"They call him a servant, but he isn't really." Now that he was launched, the words went faster. "My parents assigned him to watch me."

"Why?"

There was something about Tom that made you want to be honest with him, John thought. He hoped they could be friends. He would like that very much. But Tom had to know the truth first. That was the only way it could be. And so, although his heart sank, John proceeded to tell it. "I like snakes," he said. "They're quite interesting. And when we were last in London, I found a shopkeeper who sells exotic animals. He had a boa constrictor!" John's enthusiasm for his subject swelled. "A sailor brought it back from the Americas. Fed it on rats on the ship. It was a quite small specimen, really, and they're not poisonous."

"Boa constrictor," repeated Tom as if interested in the sound of the words. "That's a kind of snake?"

John nodded. "So I bought it and sneaked it home. To observe and learn, you know. But it got loose from its cage somehow, and it…" He stopped, swallowed, and then rushed on. "It ate my little sister's new kitten." Here was the depth of his disgrace. John saw again the horror in his sisters' eyes, heard the heartbroken weeping. He cringed.

"Yer joking."

John looked for signs of disgust in Tom's face, and found none. He shook his head.

"Ate it, you say? I'd think a kitten could outrun a snake."

"Constrictors throw their coils around their prey and crush them before they swallow them." The kitten's tail, still protruding from his snake's mouth, had been the terrible, irrefutable evidence that sealed both their fates.

"Garn!"

"I never meant it to get near the kitten! Indeed, I don't know how it escaped my cage. I promise you the wire mesh was quite sturdy."

Tom nodded. "What happened to him?"

"Who?"

"The snake."

"Oh. One of the gardeners killed it. With a hoe. Chopped it into four pieces." John felt a lingering sadness at this summary execution.

"Huh."

There was no sign of withdrawal on Tom's homely face. John's relief made him brave. He drew in a breath and took the risk. "What's Lord Macklin?" he asked.

"What d'you mean?"

"What's his rank?"

"Ah. He's an earl."

John's mind worked. "If I told Wrayle that you're here with an earl, perhaps his ward, he'd likely give me permission to go for a walk. Wrayle's a dreadful snob."

"I ain't his ward," replied Tom. He seemed to dislike the idea.

"No." Disappointment threatened to engulf John. "But Lord Macklin is feeding and housing you, isn't he?"

"For the present."

"And you're not a servant. He doesn't pay you wages?"

"No. Didn't want 'em."

"So you're practically his ward. Let me tell Wrayle." John didn't wish to beg, but he found this terribly important.

"Well." Tom pursed his lips. "I suppose it's all right."

"I'll speak to him when we get back." John's spirits soared. "Perhaps we could go walking tomorrow?"

Tom nodded. "I'll come 'round and fetch you."

Three

FENELLA HADN'T MEANT TO ATTEND THE REHEARSAL for the Lindisfarne pageant. She'd determined to send her regrets to Harold Benson, pleading a press of duties and the exigencies of her father's illness. However, a note from the man in charge of the performance had put paid to that idea. If she'd known Colonel Patterson was supervising, she would have made her refusal clear to Mr. Benson at the first mention, Fenella thought. Now it was too late. The colonel, a hero of Waterloo and scion of an ancient noble family, was expecting her, and one did not go back on a promise to him. The idea of seeing disappointment in the upright old man's eyes when they next met made Fenella shudder.

She'd told herself that Chatton wouldn't appear, and so this whole scheme would come to nothing. But there he was, walking toward her across the wooden floor of the village hall—rangy, frowning, with his red hair agleam in a ray of sunshine, automatically the center of attention even in this crowded room. She'd seen him more often in the last week than in months before that, and his renewed presence was reviving memories at an increasing pace.

The heir to Chatton Castle had been a wild boy, careening over the countryside with his cronies, brandishing wooden swords and makeshift shields, racing their ponies along the beach. Fenella, burdened by her father's criticisms and hemmed in by her mother's rules, had envied them their loud, heedless freedom. She'd watched them from out-of-the-way corners at children's parties, not knowing what to say. She'd fumbled for conversation when they were older and thrown together at neighborhood assemblies. Not that she'd often been asked to dance. And then came their fathers' disastrous attempt to marry them off, which broke her life in two. Fortunately, Fenella thought. She was grateful for her time in Scotland and her grandmother's insistence that she "grow a spine," as the old lady had put it. She was glad she'd risen to that challenge, happy with the woman she'd become.

"I wasn't going to do this," Chatton said when he reached her, echoing her thoughts. "But then I heard from Patterson."

Fenella nodded.

"And as my mother immediately pointed out, one does not say no to the colonel."

"I feel as if I've enlisted."

Chatton laughed. "Or been taken up by Harold Benson's one-man press-gang."

"If he'd said it was Colonel Patterson…"

"I imagine he's careful not to." Chatton smiled at Fenella as he hadn't in a long time. "I was surprised

Patterson took on this job. At least we know the thing will run efficiently."

This statement was amply confirmed as they watched a bit of the rehearsal. The colonel had lined up a group of local men and informed them that they were a procession of monks moving to the sound of a harp and chanting. They were to walk meditatively, with their hands in the sleeves of their monks' robes and their heads bent in the hoods. Since there were as yet no robes, and no harp or chanting, this proved problematic. Also, the colonel once or twice strayed into a parade-ground roar that caused two of the men to snap to attention and salute.

"I always think of Colonel Patterson as a large man," Fenella murmured. "But he isn't." Indeed, he was shorter than most of his amateur actors, but so upright and energetic that he seemed bigger. A lined face and white hair didn't matter in such a dominating personality, she thought. His plain blue coat, riding breeches, and boots gave the impression of a uniform.

"You feel as if he's carrying a swagger stick," said Chatton. "Even though he isn't."

"I wonder what happens if someone doesn't follow his orders?" Fenella replied.

"I don't think we want to find out."

They exchanged a look that held more sympathy than they'd shared before. She was surprised at how gratifying this felt.

The time came for their scene. The colonel allowed a moment for greetings, shaking Chatton's hand and offering Fenella a nod and a glance from twinkling gray eyes. Then Fenella was given a much-used broom from the back of the hall and told to imagine that she was standing under a stone archway in the ruins of the old abbey on Lindisfarne. "Rush up to her like a marauding Viking," the colonel said to Chatton.

He trotted over.

"A Viking," repeated the colonel. "Bent on looting. Bristling with weapons. More than likely spattered with the blood of murdered monks."

Chatton blinked. He tried it again.

"You aren't at a tea party!" growled Colonel Patterson. "Have you heard the phrase 'ravening horde'? You're part of one."

The marquess bit his lower lip—whether in chagrin or to keep from laughing, Fenella couldn't tell. He backed up, gathered himself, and essayed another rush, baring his teeth and shouting, "Charge!"

"Charge?" echoed the colonel.

"Slipped out." Chatton looked sheepish.

"Well, see that it doesn't do so again. But that was good enough for now. Rather effective snarl. See that you practice." Colonel Patterson turned to Fenella, who had very nearly laughed. "Miss Fairclough, you are furious and determined to defend your home."

Fenella swung the broom and caught Chatton on the shoulder, rocking him back a step.

"Hold on!" cried the colonel. "You mustn't actually hit him."

And then they spent a good deal of time working out how she was to repel the supposed invader with a swipe that looked like a leveler but stopped short of striking him. Chatton had to flinch and fall at just the right moment, so that it appeared he'd been felled by her stroke, when it hadn't actually touched him.

It was quite difficult, Fenella found. To make a wide swing with the broom and stop short was more tiring than simply flailing about. She was relieved when Colonel Patterson finally said, "Yes, all right. That will do for now." She started to lower the broom, thinking they were finished, but he continued. "Now, Chatton, you leap up and return to the fray. Miss Fairclough, you try the same trick. But, Chatton, you knock the broom from her hands this time. Thus and thus." He guided them through the movements. "And then you grasp her arms to keep her from hitting you."

Roger did as he was told. Fenella's arms felt slender and supple under the cloth of her gown. Her face was inches away. He hadn't been so close to her in… Had he ever been so close? She wore a heady flowery scent.

"And now, Miss Fairclough, you spit at him," said Colonel Patterson.

"Spit?" She looked startled.

"This is a barbarian invader, come to steal everything you have. He's killed your defenders. Set your church on fire. Now he's dared to enter your house and laid hands on you."

Fenella's blue eyes flamed. She bared her teeth and spit, though to the side rather than in his face.

It might have been funny, but it wasn't, Roger thought. Had he been an invader, he'd have been taken aback by the fiery spirit she'd revealed. A man might be proud to have such a woman defending his native land. Surprised by an impulse to pull her closer, he went still.

"Good." Patterson nodded. "Now, this next part is a bit tricky."

A boy ran into the room. "The monks is calling for ale, Colonel, sir. Saying they was promised a drink for their trouble."

Patterson scowled. "Stay where you are," he commanded. "I'll be back in a moment." And he followed the boy out the door.

Did Patterson mean he was to keep hold? Roger wondered. Such was the colonel's influence that he hesitated to let go. But she was so near. The slightest move and her breasts would brush his chest.

Once he'd noted this, Roger could think of nothing else. Except the feel of her under his hands and the brilliance of her gaze. How long had the colonel been gone? It seemed like forever, and yet not long enough. He should say something. The silence was becoming awkward.

"It's rather like that time you were forced to dance with me," Fenella said.

"Eh?"

"I've been remembering our neighborhood dances for some reason. This was at the Haskins' ball. Mrs. Haskins pulled you over and made you ask me. You were so angry. You'd wanted to dance with her daughter."

Roger didn't remember the incident, though he did recall Sara Haskins. She'd been a lovely girl, the belle of the neighborhood when he was younger. Fenella, on the other hand, was only a vague presence in his youthful memory. A shadowy figure, slipping into view at the edge of a gathering and then forgotten again, utterly different from the way she was now. Had her lips been so full back then? So enticing? Surely he would have noticed if they had been. And yet a woman's lips didn't change after she was grown. Did they?

"That was right before our fathers hatched their stupid scheme."

A tremor went through him at this forthright remark. They'd never discussed the past. When Arabella was alive, the topic was obviously out of bounds. And after her death he and Fenella hadn't talked at all.

"And I ran for my life," she added.

"I admired that," Roger said, words slipping out as they sometimes did, without any advance notice to his brain.

Fenella looked surprised. "My craven flight?"

"More like rebellion." He'd thought of her more after that dramatic departure than he ever had before. Once she'd shown some defiance, a flare of spirit, he'd even wondered what it would have been like to marry her. Not seriously, of course. He wouldn't be ordered about like a vassal.

Roger experienced an odd dislocation. In this moment, he resented her long-ago rejection of his charms. Even though he'd done the same, more emphatically. It was confusing. He had to let her go. He did so, and stepped back. Fenella gazed up at him as if he'd done something strange.

Fortunately, Colonel Patterson strode back in. He looked irritated. "All right, Chatton," he said. "Now you throw Miss Fairclough over your shoulder and carry her through the archway." He indicated the supposed span of stone with a wide gesture.

"Pick her up?" said Roger. He didn't want to touch Fenella again, mainly because he very much wanted to do so. "That isn't proper."

"You're a Viking," replied the colonel dryly. "I don't think propriety is a consideration." He turned to Fenella. "You have no objection? I assumed Benson explained the whole to you."

She shook her head.

"We must leave that bit out," said Roger.

Patterson looked concerned. "I've given my word that the scenarios will be performed exactly as written. They were put together by a pack of historians, you know. Very stern on the subject of accuracy. As bad as headquarters regulations."

Everyone knew that the colonel's word was inviolate. Roger looked at Fenella. "Let's just do it," she said.

"You don't mind?" asked Patterson. "It's only a moment. Through the archway and finished."

She nodded.

"Good girl." Patterson gestured like a commander ordering his troops forward.

Roger bent, set his shoulder in Fenella's midsection, and lifted. His arm went around her knees for balance. Her hip rested against his cheek.

"You'll have to move faster than that," said the colonel. "You're not lifting a fragile piece of porcelain, Chatton. You keep forgetting you're a ferocious raider. And Miss Fairclough, you should kick and beat your fists. Not too hard, of course. Give the effect, as with the broom."

Light blows fell on Roger's back. Feet pumped. Fenella's frame shook against his shoulder. Was she afraid? No, she was laughing.

The boy ran in again. "The monks found the ale barrel! They're bunging it open." He beckoned urgently. With a muttered curse, Patterson hurried out after him.

Roger was left with a lithe, sweet-smelling young lady over his shoulder.

"I must be heavy," she said. "You can put me down."

She wasn't. Roger felt as if he could hold her forever, even though the feel of her body was making his head spin. He set her down. She took a step and stumbled. He steadied her.

"Hanging head down makes one dizzy," she observed.

"I know."

"What?"

"Nothing." He'd felt this strong pull of attraction before, Roger recalled. When she first returned from Scotland to care for her father, there'd been an evening at Chatton. He'd laughed with Fenella over some jest, and the heat had risen between them, intense, surprising. And then he'd glimpsed the avid speculation in his father's eyes, which made him angry, and he'd gone haring off to London the next day to avoid any revival of the old matchmaking scheme. Yes, and he'd fallen into Mrs. Crenshaw's toils almost at once. So his disastrous marriage had been Fenella's fault. Everything was Fenella's fault—from the very inception to Arabella's last, ill-advised ride.

Except. With her standing before him, pleasant and assured, he had to acknowledge that this was a load of pure rubbish.

Fenella hadn't sent him to town. And of course she hadn't been able to keep Arabella from doing whatever she wished. Arabella had been one of the stubbornest people he'd ever encountered. She'd never listened once she made up her mind. He remembered an evening when his wife had stalked out of a dinner party, declaring that she couldn't bear it a moment longer. In the silence that followed, he'd suspected his neighbors pitied him, which had been humiliating. Roger had told everyone that Arabella was referring to a terrible headache, but he was fairly certain they'd known she meant the dullness of the company. In her opinion. The incident had occurred just a few weeks before her fateful ride in the rain. But it was best not to think of that.

Roger felt the mixture of anger and guilt that had been with him since his wife died. Pain lanced through his stomach. He pressed a hand against it.

"Are you all right?" asked Fenella.

He gave her a curt nod. "We'll have to come back to this later," he said. "I have an appointment." He walked away before anyone could question this lie.

❧

"Those two have hit it off," said Arthur as he and his hostess watched Tom and young John Symmes trot through the stone arch that led from Chatton Castle's courtyard into the countryside. The boys disappeared into the tunnel under the wide wall. Arthur offered his arm, and the two of them moved in the opposite direction, into the walled garden at the back of the castle. A riot of flowers filled this sizable space. The walls met sheer cliffs that fell to the sea.

"I like Tom," said the earl's companion, the former Miss Helena Ravelstoke, Dowager Marchioness of Chatton, and an unexpected element of his northern visit.

"Nearly everyone does," said Arthur.

"Is he an eccentricity?"

"What?"

"I've heard that it's fashionable to have one," she added. "A quirk. To make one stand out in society."

"Tom is not that," replied Arthur. "He is, oddly enough, a friend."

"That is rather odd for the distinguished Lord Macklin."

She smiled up at him, and Arthur was once again reminded of a London season more than thirty years ago, when they'd both been young and she'd been dazzling. Helena, as she'd insisted he call her now, had cocked her head in just that way back then. Arthur and his friends had vied with each other to evoke her silvery laugh. He was happy to see that she'd kept her blithe spirit through three decades.

"Tom is a miraculous triumph over his back-ground," he answered. "Circumstances that might have, should have ground him down or embittered him didn't. I was struck by his intelligence and good humor when I met him. I found him good company. And I would like to give him the chance he deserves."

"Chance to do what?"

"That is the question."

His hostess looked inquiring. She'd raised a rose-colored parasol against the sun, and the tinted shade was kind to her face. Not that it needed a great deal of help, even now. "Send him to school?" she suggested. "Set him to a trade?"

"He would hate those things. He'd be off wandering in a day." Arthur admired a swath of scarlet poppies as they walked past. "I've learned recently that helping is not a simple matter. The impulse is easy. Discovering how to go about it is not." As he'd found with the young men he'd gathered for dinner in town last spring, Arthur thought. How long ago that seemed, though it was just a few months.

"I don't quite understand," she said.

Arthur nodded. He wasn't certain he did either. "I've worked out that help isn't forcing your ideas or plans onto people. That's a kind of oppression. Yet simply asking those you'd like to aid what they want may not be enough. Often they don't really know. Or aren't able to choose between alternatives."

"Goodness, how philosophical you've become."

He laughed. "And a dead bore. I beg your pardon."

"Not at all. I'm quite interested. I can't even count all the times I've been asked to help with some scheme or other that's meant to 'better the lot' of those involved. But I've noticed that charitable projects are often just what you said—forcing a plan on people who resent the interference. Even when they appreciate the material assistance. How do you help?"

"By not rushing in with my own notions," Arthur

replied. "By observing and listening. By applying a longer experience of life than...some others." His efforts had gone well so far, he thought, despite some mistakes.

"I like that." Her lips curved in a small smile. "I believe I shall adopt your approach."

"That's too grand a word for it."

"And you're too modest."

They strolled for a while in silence. Helena pointed out a special rose for him to admire. Then she said, "You didn't come here to see me, did you?"

For once, Arthur was speechless. He'd been aware of her assumption and had sidestepped the issue with considerable finesse until now.

"I thought when you arrived that you were looking for me. But you weren't."

She'd tipped her parasol so he couldn't see her expression. "I was delighted to see you again after so many years," he said.

"But not expecting to."

"I had forgotten you married Chatton," he admitted. They moved on a few steps before the parasol shifted, and he could see that she looked ruefully regretful. "I'm past the age for flirtation," he added.

"Oh, Arthur." She gazed at him like a woman amused by the boy he'd been when they first met. "Why are you here? And don't try to fob me off with some story about fishing in Scotland."

He wasn't sure what to say. The confidences shared at that London dinner were sacrosanct, and it was difficult to explain without revealing them.

"One of your missions to help?"

Helena Ravelstoke hadn't been this sharp, Arthur thought. Or he hadn't noticed if she was, his attention being on other elements of her person.

"Never mind. I'll figure it out. You aren't the only one who can observe." She sighed. "I *did* like the idea that you'd been languishing for me all these years."

Arthur caught the twinkle in her blue eyes. Relief preceded amusement. "Perhaps we can be friends?" He hadn't had any female friends when he first knew Helena. At that age, women had seemed too alien, and enflaming, for friendship. But over the years since, he'd made a few.

She smiled. "Yes. Let's do that."

They walked on, talking of gardens and what had become of people they both remembered. Helena pointed out her beehives at the far end of the space. As they turned onto a new path, Arthur said, "Who was that young lady at church? The one who offered to kick your son in the face."

"Ah. Fenella Fairclough." She sighed.

"You don't like her?" Arthur had been intrigued by the exchange he'd witnessed. There'd been a palpable spark between the two young people.

"Oh, I'm very fond of her. I've often wished *she* was my daughter-in-law. But it wouldn't have worked. Though it couldn't have been worse than—" She bit off the sentence and fell silent.

Arthur's interest increased. "Shall we sit for a while?" He led her to a shaded bench set on a rise of ground, offering a panoramic view of the sea. "In answer to your earlier question, I recently noted a group of young men who had suffered unfortunate losses in their lives. I've set myself the task of helping them, if I can. I have some experience with grief."

"Grief." She seemed to examine the word, and then his face. Whatever she found there appeared to satisfy her. "My husband was ten years older than me, you know."

Arthur didn't see what this had to do with the case. But he'd learned that it was best to let people tell stories in their own way.

"He thought he knew best," she went on. "About everything, really, and particularly when my opinion was involved." She gave Arthur a sharp glance. "He was *not* unkind. And I loved him. But he always saw me as a girl, even when I wasn't one any longer."

Arthur nodded to show that he'd heard and understood.

"He hatched this scheme to marry Roger to Fenella. He and her father did, I should say." She shook her head. "They'd been rather enjoying themselves, arguing over the boundary between their properties. Firing off copies of old deeds and writing scathing letters. Then they came up with the idea of a marital alliance, as if they were kings of rival countries or some such nonsense. I told my husband that Roger wouldn't stand for it. But Raymond didn't listen. He decreed that Roger was to go and offer for Fenella. Wouldn't hear a word Roger said. And I expect Fenella's father was even worse. Well, I know he was." She fell silent again.

"So they disobeyed," Arthur said after a while.

His hostess laughed. "Fenella sneaked off in the middle of the night and ran to her grandmother in Scotland. She knew her father wouldn't dare hunt her there! My husband gave Roger a thundering scold. There was bad feeling on all sides. Raymond wanted to cut off Roger's allowance, but I managed to persuade him that would make things worse."

"A belligerent young sprig with no money is liable to fall into bad hands," said Arthur.

"Exactly. And so, after a time, the tempest in a teapot subsided. I think all would have been well, perhaps even better than well, if it hadn't been for Arabella's mother."

"Arabella?"

"She was Roger's wife."

The one who had died of a lung complaint after an ill-advised ride in the rain, Arthur remembered.

"Arabella was beautiful," Helena said in an oddly flat voice. "Truly a ravishing creature. And her mother was—is—a very determined woman." She glanced at Arthur. "I'm speaking as if you are a friend indeed."

"Shall I give my word not to repeat anything you tell me?"

She waved this aside. "It's nothing so dreadful. Roger was dazzled by the exquisite daughter. No one could blame him. And through the efforts of her mother, he was *brought up to scratch*, as they say. As a canny mother is meant to do. I don't know the details, but I'm fairly certain he didn't intend to marry right then. But he offered, and Arabella accepted." She sighed again. "I was delighted actually. She had birth and breeding and wealth enough to satisfy my husband. I wanted Roger to be happy. We went down to London for the wedding. And as soon as I met her, I knew. Have you ever felt your spirits sink to the depths all in an instant?"

Arthur nodded encouragement. He sensed that she had needed to say this for a long time.

"It was too late of course. And I don't know what I could have done. Well, I do know. Nothing. Raymond's health was failing, and he was beyond pleased to see his son safely married. He thought Arabella a paragon." She made a wry face. "Most men did."

"Beauty can be compelling."

"Oh yes. And so my son contracted an unhappy marriage. I could see that he knew it when they returned here from their wedding journey. But those were Raymond's last days, you know, and I was distracted."

"Of course you were."

She met his eyes. "You know what it's like to lose the person you've lived with, cared for, over many years."

"I do."

They shared a moment of silent communion.

"The first time Fenella and Roger met after she came home from Scotland, I saw what a mistake had been made." She looked distressed.

Arthur waited. When she didn't go on, he said, "Yes?" It seemed they had reached the crux of the matter.

"Never mind." She stood up, tilting her parasol to hide her face again. "It's very warm, isn't it? We should go inside."

Arthur had to be satisfied with this, and he rather thought he was.

❧

"You have no family at all?" John asked Tom. He'd inquired before, but he never tired of hearing about

Tom's fortunate situation. It seemed to John that there could be nothing more liberating than being an orphan with no connections at all.

"Shh," murmured Tom. The boys lay on a stream bank in the cool shadows of a willow. Tom's bared right arm hung down into the water, very still. "Here comes a trout. Now watch."

John leaned very carefully, so as not to alert the fish edging up the shallows, sheltering under the bank and beside rocks. He saw it slide out of sight near Tom's hand, just the moving tail still visible. Tom's hand, with fingers turned up, moved by imperceptible inches to that tail. Then it disappeared as he began tickling with his forefinger, gradually running his hand up the fish's belly. John was nearly lulled himself when Tom suddenly tensed, twisted, and pulled the trout out of the water and onto the grass beside them.

John flinched. He couldn't help it. "How did you do that?"

"Learnt it from a poacher," Tom said. "The fish go into a trance, like, when you tickle them." He threw the flapping, gasping trout back into the stream. "It ain't legal to take fish though, unless it's your own stream. You shouldn't be trying it." He dried his arm on the grass and rolled down his shirtsleeve.

"I could never." John's admiration of his new acquaintance, already vast, swelled further. "Where did you meet a poacher?"

"Just rambling, on the way south from Bristol. Fella nearly took my head off with his club before he saw I weren't the gamekeeper."

John was fascinated by Tom's life history. "That was before you met Lord Macklin."

"Yep." Tom turned onto his back and gazed up at the sky through the willow branches. "'Twas the very next day I came across young Geoffrey thinking he was hid in a hollow log and took him back home."

"To Lord Macklin's son's house."

"His nephew."

"Right." John was consumed with envy for Tom's rootless life. It seemed to him an ideal existence, to have no last name with its weight of expectations, to wander wherever you liked. "Are you still thinking of moving on?" he asked. "Just walking off one day in whatever direction feels interesting?" He'd been transfixed by this idea ever since Tom had mentioned it.

"I expect I will," replied Tom idly. His attention had been caught by a pair of dragonflies darting over the surface of the water. "Look at the way their wings go," he said.

John gathered all his hope and courage. "Will you let me come with you?"

"Eh?" Tom turned his head to look at him.

"When you go. Run away. Or, it isn't really. Running. When you walk off to see the world." He clasped his hands, then quickly unclasped them. "I want to see all the snakes in the world. Particularly the spitting cobras!"

Tom sat up slowly, moving rather as he had when he captured the trout. He crossed his legs in the grass. "I'd just be rambling about in England," he answered. "Mebbe Scotland. That's right close, ain't it? No cobras though."

"But you can go wherever you want!"

Tom shook his head. "I can go where my feet will take me. And where I'm allowed in. That ain't everywhere, by any means."

"No one can stop you though."

"Sure they can. I've been chased off and barely missed beatings. I was nearly taken up and put in the workhouse once." Tom held up a hand before John could protest again. "Also. Seems to me it must cost a deal of money to get over to where these cobras live."

John slumped, his dreams of unfettered freedom dissolving.

"You'd need one of them scientific expeditions," Tom continued. "I heard Lord Macklin talking about one of them."

"You mean like James Cook? I've read the chronicles of his voyages. And there's James Strange and the other fellows in the East India Company."

"Yeah. Them."

"I'd *love* to organize a scientific expedition to catalog snakes in India."

"Well, there's people that do that, eh?"

"Like the Royal Society, you mean?"

"Sure." Tom nodded wisely. "You could ask them."

"They want men with university degrees and fellowships and such."

"Huh. Are there fellows studying snakes in them universities?"

John sat very still. With a smile, Tom let him be.

Four

MACKLIN'S COMPANY WAS SOOTHING, ROGER THOUGHT as they returned from a morning ride the following day. He seemed to sense when one wished to talk and when not. And his conversation was always sensible. Should he ever need advice, Macklin was the man, Roger concluded. Not that he did. He had no pressing problems.

"Isn't that Miss Fairclough?" his guest said, almost as if disputing Roger's thought.

Roger looked. Fenella rode ahead of them toward the castle gate, alone, as was her habit. He was surprised. She hadn't visited Chatton since their falling-out. His fault, he acknowledged for the first time.

Her skirts billowed in the wind off the sea, and her horse took offense, sidling and dancing. Roger worried momentarily, but she controlled her mount with casual ease, caught the cloth, and held it down.

"She's the careless young lady you spoke of at the London dinner?" Macklin asked.

"Careless?"

"The one who urged your wife to venture out in bad weather."

"Ah." He'd spoken with extra rancor that night, Roger thought. His feelings had been rubbed raw by his encounter with his in-laws, and he'd been itching for a target. "I don't think she did, really."

"Indeed?" Macklin looked interested.

"Arabella had...strong opinions. I expect she *did* insist on going, as Fen—Miss Fairclough says."

"I suppose Miss Fairclough might have refused to accompany her, to discourage her from going."

"Wouldn't have done any good," said Roger. Opposing Arabella's wishes was tantamount to a declaration of war, in her mind, and she fought the ensuing campaign without mercy. He'd learned *that* the day after his wedding.

"You think not?"

Roger pulled his thoughts back to the present. It didn't do to remember those battles. If he thought of them, he might feel that brush of gratitude, that absolutely unacceptable tinge of relief at the fact of Arabella's death. Suppressing all such inclinations, he spurred his horse to catch up with Fenella.

But she'd already gone in when they reached the castle. Her horse was being tended in the stables. Roger found himself hurrying. He discovered Fenella sitting with his mother in her parlor, laughing with her over some shared jest. The sight of them, leaning together in a shaft of sunlight, stopped him on the threshold.

They didn't look alike. His mother's willowy frame contrasted with Fenella's compact curves. Her hair was silvered gold to the younger woman's reddish tones. Their faces had different lines. And yet they exuded a kinship. The word *delightful* floated through

Roger's consciousness. Arabella had never sat with his mother, he remembered. She'd made certain that the dowager marchioness moved to the dower house, and their visits had been limited to formal occasions. An unpalatable mixture of emotion washed over him, along with a stab of pain in his midsection.

Macklin came in behind him, and Roger moved forward.

"There you are," said his mother, rising. "How lovely. Come and sit."

She proceeded to execute a maneuver rather like a dance, and before Roger finished wondering why she'd stood up at all, he found himself seated next to Fenella, while the two older members of the party were settled a little distance away. Perhaps his mother was taking advantage of the opportunity to flirt with Macklin, he thought. He was still a bit worried about her views on the earl's visit. But when he looked, he found both of them gazing in his direction in an oddly unsettling way. Come to think of it, they didn't flirt. They talked like old friends, and they were watching him now like kennel masters evaluating a promising puppy. Roger blinked. Where had that ridiculous idea come from?

Fenella held out a small packet wrapped in brown paper and tied with string. "I brought you this," she said.

Roger stared at the gift. He had a sudden sense of the world gone topsy-turvy.

"It's a tonic for dyspepsia," she continued. "You put a few drops in a glass of water and drink it if you're feeling ill."

Under her clear blue gaze, he felt uncomfortably exposed. "Why would you give it to me?"

"You kept clutching your midsection at the rehearsal. And looking pained."

"It could have been distaste for the antics they were putting us through."

She smiled a little. "You've done it at church as well."

Roger was embarrassed. He hadn't wanted anyone to know of his weakness. It was then that he noticed she was holding the packet so that it was shielded from the others. "Where did you get this?"

"My grandmother is renowned for her skill in the stillroom. People come from all around for her remedies."

"You sent to Scotland?"

"No, I made it."

"Yourself?"

"Grandmother taught me."

That and so much else, Roger thought.

"I was with her for years," Fenella added. "I needed something to do."

"Besides changing out of all recognition."

Her smile deepened. There were the dimples he hadn't seen in a while, Roger noted. They added an impish quality to her beauty. "Besides that," she said.

Once again, Roger was ambushed by a memory. They'd gathered the leading families of the neighborhood at Chatton Castle to introduce Arabella to local society. His wife had reveled in the occasion, holding court like the queen. Her enjoyment had been a relief. Roger had hoped the admiration she was receiving might ease her growing dislike of her new home. More vocally expressed with each passing day.

Moving through the crowd, greeting friends and

acquaintances, he'd come face-to-face with a lovely young lady, dressed in sea-green muslin, sporting those very dimples. Before they spoke, he'd felt a pulse run through him, like a thread drawing him closer, rousing more than interest. And then he'd realized that this was Fenella Fairclough, the girl he'd refused to marry. He'd turned away, rudely. And from that moment he'd set Fenella at a distance. He was newly married. Such attractions had no place in his life. Not for anyone, and certainly not for this woman, with their history. After a while, he'd managed to convince himself that the moment hadn't happened. But he didn't talk with her or dance with her or hang about any room she inhabited.

He'd tried to discourage Arabella from making friends with Fenella. Which had caused his discontented wife to do just the opposite, of course. Somehow, amazingly, no one had told Arabella their story. Probably because most everyone hereabouts liked Fenella, and hadn't much cared for his late wife. He'd been foul to Fenella these past months, Roger thought. Yet she'd taken the trouble to prepare this medicine. "Thank you," he said, taking the packet.

"You're welcome. It's no great thing."

"It's an unlooked-for kindness. When I've been unkind, at times."

"You've had difficulties."

Was that sympathy in her gaze? After all his rudeness? He could almost imagine that she understood the mixture of emotions plaguing him. The attraction that Roger had suppressed for so long came leaping out of its cage. Ever since he'd held her over his shoulder, he'd longed to touch her again, he realized. "I'm sorry," he said.

"For?"

"The things I said to you, about you, after... Arabella's death." They'd never spoken of her.

"And about others," she answered evenly. "The doctor, Arabella's maid. You were rather free with your accusations."

Roger leaned back. Had he expected immediate forgiveness? Apparently he had. Was he so complacent? His stomach gave a sharp twinge.

"They were quite affected by it, you know. The doctor felt like a failure. And Grace, the maid, was already overcome by grief for her mistress."

Roger searched for words. Frustratingly, none came.

Fenella stood. "I must go. My father will be wondering where I am."

Roger rose. He had to say something, but his mind was a jumble. She'd be shocked if she knew of his attraction, particularly after the way he'd treated her. This woman had run away to Scotland rather than marry him, he reminded himself. His urges were his problem. He turned away to ring for a footman.

Fenella said her goodbyes, fending off an escort to the front door, conscious of Lady Chatton's interested gaze. Roger's attempt at an apology had shaken her, she acknowledged as she strode through the hall, the long skirts of her riding habit looped over her arm. As had the way he'd looked at her. He'd been forbidden fruit since she returned home. Fenella stopped abruptly. "What?" she said aloud. Forbidden fruit? What sort of nonsense was that?

She walked on. The trouble was, since the pageant rehearsal, it was as if she could still feel Roger's hands on her from time to time. His forearm around her knees, his palm against her back. The strength of his shoulder under her. That had been bad enough when he was carping at her. She could scorn his ridiculous attitude. If he meant to be pleasant now, she didn't know what she would do. But this was no more than politeness, Fenella told herself. She wouldn't refine too much on the change. She would remember that the present Marquess of Chatton had been revolted at the thought of marrying her. The word was not too strong. His expression on that long-ago day! Such disgust. She pushed the image out of her mind.

Outside, as she waited for her horse to be brought around, Fenella was surprised to see her nephew John appear from the direction of the stables, mounted on a horse from her father's stables. Automatically, she noted it was a gentle one. She could trust their head groom to match guests and horses. And to send along the stable boy who trailed behind. "Hello, John," she said as he approached. "Have you been visiting here?"

"I came to see Tom."

Her sister's son looked sulky, as usual. He really was a difficult boy. "The young man employed by Lord Macklin?"

"He isn't employed. He's his friend." John's expression dared her to argue with this assertion.

"Is he?" The connection seemed unusual. But it was none of her affair. "Are you headed home? We can ride together if you wait a moment." A groom brought her horse and held it while she used the mounting block. Fenella arranged her skirts and took the reins.

"You don't care about Tom?" said her nephew as they rode out the gates side by side. His tone was a little less gruff.

"What do you mean?"

"You don't mind that I've been spending time with him?"

"Why should I?"

"He's not gentry."

John said this as if it was a phrase he'd often heard. Thinking of his father, a stiff, prickly man, Fenella understood. Fleetingly, she wondered if she had an obligation to consider Mr. Symmes's prejudices. But Greta had sent her son north. She'd have to accept Fenella's choices. "If Lord Macklin has befriended him, he must have a good character. And I'm sure you enjoy some company younger than me and your grandfather." John had not taken to her father so far. The boy seemed afraid of him.

John looked surprised, but he said nothing. They rode on. Fenella's thoughts drifted back to her conversation with Roger. He'd looked sincere when he said he was sorry. She'd felt some honest contrition. It was the first real connection she'd had with him in... well, years. She tried to recall another such moment.

"You've been kind to me," blurted out her nephew.

She hadn't meant to ignore the boy. "As I should be. I am your aunt." He looked as if he might cry, which would be humiliating at his age. "Is something wrong, John?"

"You don't know why I'm here." He bit his lower

lip to stop its trembling. "I thought Mama would have told you what I've done."

What in the world? Fenella remembered how childish transgressions could be magnified in one's mind. Or, in her case, blown all out of proportion by her father's attitude. He'd spent so much time shouting at her. She would never behave like that!

"If you did know, you wouldn't want to be kind," John added.

"I will always want to be kind," Fenella declared. "And you don't have to tell me anything you don't want to." It came out rather forcefully.

John blinked, a bit startled, but then he shook his head. "If you found out why I was sent…"

"For a visit with your family. That's all I need to know."

This assurance seemed to make him more unhappy rather than less so. "So it's all fake," he added as if to himself. He swallowed.

She knew that expression, Fenella thought. Here was a child bracing for a thundering scold. How to assure him that she would not deliver such a thing?

"I bought a boa constrictor," John blurted out. "That's a kind of large snake. And it ate Sally's kitten."

Fenella took a moment to absorb this startling information. Sally was her youngest niece, just three years old. Unbidden, a scene rose in her mind—scales, fangs, baby cat. She hid a shudder, partly at the fate of the kitten and partly at the shrieking chaos that must have ensued. Justified, really, she thought.

"It was an *accident*," John continued, his face a picture of anguish. "The boa was meant to stay in its cage. I brought it mice. It shouldn't have been at all hungry. I don't know how it got out."

Would she, and John's mother, have been more sympathetic if they'd had brothers? Fenella wondered. She remembered the mud-slathered boys of her childhood. Roger and his friends had seemed to delight in noise and dirt. Not snakes, though, as far as she knew. "You didn't mean it," she managed.

"Of *course* not. I *like* kittens!"

He spoke as if he'd been accused of the opposite. Fenella recalled her father's many unfair indictments. "Well, it sounds like an unfortunate accident. I can tell you're sorry it happened."

John nodded. Tears had run down his cheeks. He sniffed.

"So let us say no more about it."

"Really?" The boy blinked rapidly. He sniffed again. "You aren't revolted?"

Again, it sounded as if he'd heard that word before. Repeatedly. "Not at all," Fenella lied. Then, worried she'd been too cavalier, she added, "Although I would rather you didn't bring snakes into the house."

"I wouldn't! Never again!" John gazed at the ground, shrugged, and sighed. "There's no good ones up here anyway," he said, somewhat diluting his fervent promise.

"Ah." Fenella grappled with the idea of a good snake. What exactly constituted its goodness? She suspected this lay in qualities other than beneficence. And then she was struck by an idea. "There's a place you could use, if you'd like to, ah, collect specimens."

John raised his head to stare at her.

"Your mother and your Aunt Nora had a playhouse in our apple orchard." Her two sisters, years older than Fenella, hadn't allowed her inside their sanctum. In fact, they'd made a great point of excluding her from their games. Their father's disappointment in his third child had spilled over onto his other offspring. Fleetingly, Fenella remembered the day she'd read a story about fairy changelings. She'd decided at once that she must be such a magical substitution, so alien did she feel within her family. Now, she rather enjoyed the idea of Greta's son filling her old playhouse with snakes. "I'll show you when we get back."

"You will?"

"Yes."

"You're an absolute trump, Aunt Fenella!"

And just like that, one could bask in a male's unalloyed admiration, she thought. Simply offer a boy a place to keep his snakes.

But matters were not so simple. When they reached Clough House, they found Wrayle lurking in the front hall. John's dour attendant, pinched and disapproving, looked like a scarecrow dressed as a valet. He surged forward when they came in. "Master Sherrington went out without permission," he said to Fenella.

"I was visiting at Chatton Castle," said her nephew.

Though she could see that this address impressed Wrayle, it didn't change his position. "He did not inform me," the man said to Fenella. "I am to accompany him on any outings." His expression was smug, even a bit contemptuous. Clearly, he expected Fenella to take his side.

Wrayle had not made himself popular with the

household. More than just his air of aggrieved supe-
riority, he took liberties. Fenella had had complaints.
She'd been planning to deal with him, though not
looking forward to it. "A stable boy accompanied
John," she said, slightly emphasizing her nephew's
preferred form of address. "He was perfectly safe."

"That is not the *point*," replied Wrayle. "He
requires my supervision."

Fenella was not accustomed to such an insolent tone,
not from anyone. "I don't think he does, really," she
replied. "In fact, I think you'd best return to my sister's
home." That would solve several problems at once. At
her side, John started as if he'd been poked with a pin.

"I was engaged to attend Master Sherrington."

"We'll take good care of him," Fenella said. It
wasn't as if a ten-year-old boy required a valet.

"I'm to watch him and return him to school at
the end of the summer holidays," said Wrayle. He
spoke as if John was an annoying package that must be
hauled around the country.

"We'll make sure he gets there."

"He cannot go alone."

"Naturally not," said Fenella. "Perhaps I'll take him
myself. John could show me his school." She glanced
at her nephew. His eyes and mouth were wide. His
hands were clasped so tightly, they trembled. She
turned back to Wrayle. "But I'm afraid we can't
accommodate you here any longer."

The gaunt man bridled. "You have no choice."

Fenella's temper was not easily roused, but this man
managed it, and not for the first time. "I think you'll
find that I do," she said.

"I'm not employed by you. You cannot dismiss me!"

"I'm not dismissing you, Wrayle. I am simply sending you back to my sister."

Wrayle bared his teeth in a sort of snarling smile. "We'll see about *that*." He turned and charged up the stairs.

"He'll go to my grandfather," John said. "Wrayle always toadeats the person highest in rank."

"Of course he does." Fenella picked up the skirts of her riding habit. "Go and ask William to come to your grandfather's chamber," she told John as she started up the steps.

Simpson the valet hovered in the doorway of her father's room, a thin, aging figure. "That fellow Wrayle pushed his way in, miss. He shoved me!"

"I'll speak to him."

"I am *not* accustomed to such treatment."

"Of course not. It won't happen again. I'll see to it."

Fenella entered her father's room, and found Wrayle leaning over the bed. He looked like a great crow poised to peck out an eye. She started to take a position opposite him, and then realized that she didn't wish to argue with Wrayle across her father's prostrate form. She stopped beside the door. Wrayle shot her a triumphant glance, as if he imagined he would have vengeance for her treatment of him.

"Mr. Symmes sent me," the man said to her father. "I answer to him, and no one else."

Her father looked peevish. Fenella knew he didn't like dealing with domestic difficulties. He thought such things beneath him. "You can't dismiss Sherrington's valet, Fenella," he said.

"Of course not, Papa." Before Wrayle's obvious glee could be expressed, she added, "I'm merely sending him back to Greta's."

"You have no right—" the valet began.

"I'm sorry you were bothered, Papa," she cut in. "But there have been complaints from the housemaids." This was perfectly true. The younger maids, and particularly the youngest, who was just fourteen, had told the housekeeper that Wrayle looked for opportunities to catch them alone and make lewd remarks. The housekeeper, unsuccessful in her attempts to curb him, had told Fenella just this morning. "You know the sort of thing," she added.

Her father looked pained.

"You won't take the word of silly girls," said Wrayle. He sounded utterly certain.

Fenella decided she would get a letter to her sister *before* the man arrived back at her home. Whatever Wrayle might think, Greta wouldn't tolerate such creeping behavior.

"Have them up here," Wrayle said grandly. "I'll soon put their stories to the lie." He looked as if he enjoyed a good wrangle.

Her father frowned. Wrayle's attitude was annoying him. As how could it not? Surely it wasn't so difficult for him to choose between daughter and servant? He waved a pale hand. "Do as you think best, Fenella."

"Sir!" said Wrayle.

"Go away. All of you."

"Of course, Papa. You must rest." Fenella indicated

the door with a gesture. Wrayle looked rebellious, but William appeared in the opening just then. The burly footman, who helped lift her father when such services were needed, looked daunting, as Fenella had known he would. She gestured again. Wrayle ground his teeth, but he went.

Fenella followed. When she'd shut the bedchamber door behind her, she summoned all the hauteur and steely resolve she'd learned from her Scottish grandmother. Or rather had uncovered from deep inside herself, if Grandmamma was to be believed.

"You have half an hour to pack your things, Wrayle. William will help you, and then he will take you over to the tollgate where you can get the mail coach south." A glance at William showed Fenella that he relished his assignment. She wasn't surprised. He had friends among the housemaids.

"I refuse!"

William took a step toward him. Fenella held up a hand. "You really can't stay if we don't want you here, you know."

The man sputtered and fumed. Finally he turned away. William followed. "I shall tell Mr. Symmes how I have been treated here!" was Wrayle's parting shot.

Fenella supposed he might cause problems between the two households. She definitely needed to tell Greta about his poor behavior before he had a chance to complain. Let Greta explain that to her husband.

"You got rid of Wrayle," said a small, awed voice.

She looked down to find her nephew gazing at her as if she had performed a miracle. "He'll be there when you go home," she pointed out.

"That's not until after next term. Mama won't be thinking so much about my snake by then. She'll have a new baby. And Sally already has a new kitten." He seemed to equate the two additions. "I'll send Sally some ribbons. She likes to tie ribbons around their necks." He pondered the plan. "Do you have any ribbons? Ones you don't need, I mean."

"I might."

"Thank you!" John beamed at her, and Fenella understood that his gratitude extended to much more than ribbons. "Is there anything I can help you with?" he added. "I'd be glad to. Anything at all!"

"Perhaps. We'll see."

"Yes, Aunt Fenella."

He practically bowed, and Fenella realized that she'd assumed mythic proportions in his mind. Inadvertently, she'd become the Aunt, the imposing relative so many families seemed to possess. She remembered her own aunt Moira, her mother's oldest sister. Wife of a Scottish laird, she'd been up to anything. Fenella had wistfully admired her forthright manner and fiery spirit. A smile escaped her. Aunt Moira wasn't a bad source of inspiration. "Shall I show you the playhouse now?" she asked John.

He looked ready to jump for joy. "Yes, Aunt Fenella!"

Five

ROGER REINED IN HIS MOUNT ON A SMALL RISE AND looked down at Clough House. A substantial brick edifice, far newer than Chatton Castle, it had been built to replace an earlier building that had burned down a century ago. Rather than facing the buffeting of the North Sea, the house was nestled in a fold of land bordered by a stream and surrounded by gardens rich with trees. The stream fell into the ravine that had given the place its name and ran off to the south. A softer place than his home, Roger thought. Which led him to thoughts of Fenella, as all too many things seemed to do lately.

For years he'd avoided this house, and her. Today, he was calling on her father but hoping to see her. He didn't know if that was wise, but he had to admit that it was true. Beset by constant thoughts of her, he had to discover what she felt about their jumbled connection.

Admitted to Mr. Fairclough's bedchamber some minutes later, Roger was shocked at the change in the old man. He hadn't realized he was so ill. He ought to have come before, despite their dispute. Fairclough had been a friend of his father's before he became his enemy in that stupid way.

He was greeted with a growl from the bed. "Chatton."

"Mr. Fairclough. I'm sorry you've been poorly. I hope you will soon be better."

"Well, I won't. Only one cure for me, and that's a box and a shovel. Come to get the better of me when I'm down, have you? You'll find you're out there."

Roger shook his head. "Not at all. In fact, if you don't feel up to talking, I can come another day."

"That won't help. Say what you have to say and be done with it."

Now that he'd seen the man's state, Roger found that he did have a good deal to say to him. Though he hadn't been invited to sit, he didn't want to loom over the old man. He fetched a straight chair to the side of the bed and sank onto it. "Shouldn't we resolve the border dispute that has dragged on between us for so long?"

"Don't blame me! That was all your father's doing."

"Was it? I don't even know how it got started."

Fairclough scowled. "Your father…" he began. Then he looked puzzled. "I can't seem to recall."

Roger opened his hands in a there-you-are-then gesture. He didn't say that the matter must be trivial, knowing this wouldn't be well received.

"Wait, wait." Fairclough plucked at the coverlet. "No, I've got it. My great-grandfather wanted to buy that parcel of land on our borders, and your

potion that Fenella had brewed for him, which had been helping dramatically.

"I'm ill, not long for this world," said Fairclough. He attempted a pathetic look, but achieved only devious and exhausted. "I'd like to see my last daughter settled before I go."

"I believe we both expressed our opinions on that when the idea was first brought up," Roger replied dryly.

Fairclough waved this aside. "That was years ago, and Fenella's much improved since then. Her grandmother managed to instill some spirit in her. She's in better looks, too."

Though this was true, Roger still felt offended for her. Old Fairclough talked of his daughter as if she was livestock.

"I'd sign over all my right and interest in that land to her, once she was a marchioness. She'll have a third of my estate as well, you know."

As though this would tempt him. If he needed temptation, Fenella supplied all that in herself, Roger thought. And then marveled at his errant brain.

Fenella entered the room on the heels of his confusion. "I just heard you were here," she said.

Roger gazed at her. How could he ever have thought this glorious creature bland or forgettable?

Fenella stopped just inside the door, conscious that both her father and his visitor were staring at her, their expressions quite odd.

"We were talking of your marriage," said her father.

Chatton winced visibly.

"I wasn't aware that I had a wedding planned,"

Fenella said. She managed to keep her voice cool despite the annoyance and embarrassment welling up within.

"You and Chatton. It's still the best way to resolve this land dispute."

The first time her father had spoken such words, years ago, he'd been trying to act the patriarch. Now, he sounded like a petulant old man. Fenella would have felt sorry for him, if his revival of the plan hadn't been so irritating. "The *best* way would be to forget all about it," she said. "All this fuss over a strip of land that's good for nothing but scrubby pasture for sheep. It's ridiculous."

"It's a matter of principle," her father began.

"No, Papa, it's pure stubbornness."

"Don't speak that way to me, girl. You'll do as you're told."

Whatever made him think so? Fenella hadn't, even when she was younger and cowed by his disapproval. Didn't he understand that he had no power over her? Of course Papa didn't know that her grandmother had given her certain guarantees. She had somewhere to go, should she wish to leave. Her father could rant and rail all he liked; it came down to "sound and fury, signifying nothing." Looking at his ravaged face, his remaining wisps of white hair, the gnarled hands that would no longer do his bidding, Fenella was silenced by compassion.

"She won't be forced into marriage with me," said Chatton. "I won't have that."

Did Roger think she needed defending? He was standing very straight, his chin up, gaze resolute,

playing the hero. He looked quite handsome doing it. Laughter bubbled up in Fenella's throat. What a pair of *men* they were. She choked back the laugh.

"Turning on the waterworks won't do you any good," growled her father. "You know I'm not deterred by tears."

Which was a bare-faced lie, as his expression showed. Chatton looked apprehensive, too. She had to go, before she offended them both with a fit of giggles. Fenella turned away.

As she passed through the door, she heard her father say, "Go and turn her up sweet, Chatton. You must have acquired some address by this time." Her back to them, Fenella grinned.

Roger caught up with Fenella as she was sending Simpson back into her father's room. "He's worn himself out again," she said. "Try to settle him down."

The valet departed with a nod, leaving them in the empty hallway.

Roger examined Fenella's face. He saw no evidence of the tears he'd feared to find. She looked calmly lovely. Indeed, her blue eyes were sparkling with… humor? Had she found that scene amusing? That would be encouraging.

"I could have told you he wouldn't let go of the border dispute," she said. "Papa clings even harder to his prejudices now that he can't leave his bed. He has so little left."

"I didn't know he was so ill. He seems to think it's the end."

"The doctor agrees," said Fenella. It was a somber truth that roused an uncomfortable mixture of feelings.

"I'm sorry. I'll come to visit him again. Unless you think that seeing me would make him worse?"

"No, he enjoys visitors. You could talk about things he did with your father. Before their dispute." She hesitated, then added, "Some days he may think you *are* your father."

Roger nodded, accepting the warning. "I'd gladly take his place to cheer an old friend. They used to fish together, I remember. And sample different varieties of snuff."

"Whiskey, too."

"Ah, yes. Rather too much of that, on occasion. My father rode halfway to the border one night on his way home from here. He said his horse finally lost patience and turned back toward Chatton."

Fenella smiled. "Papa would enjoy hearing that. Thank you for calling on him."

"I wanted to see you as well." Roger marshaled his faculties. "To apologize more…effectively." He had written out and memorized several versions of his apology. He'd taken to doing that in the wake of certain unfortunate incidents where words failed him and disaster ensued.

She looked quizzical.

"I wrote to Doctor Fenchurch and told him I was sorry for my intemperate remarks after…after. And that he always did a fine job. Said he was welcome to share the letter, and I'd be happy to vouch for his skills." He'd started talking too fast. Needed to slow down.

"Good for you," said Fenella.

"And I asked Mrs. Burke about Grace. She said Arabella's maid got a very good position in London and is happier now than she ever was in Northumberland. Do you think I should write her as well?"

"This is not my decision to make."

"My mother said it might just remind the girl of an unhappy period of her life," Roger continued. "And it was better to let it lie."

Fenella nodded. "She would know what's best."

"So I hope you see that I truly am sorry." Roger examined her face, but he couldn't interpret her expression.

"You don't have to report to me," she said.

"You rightly pointed out my failings."

"How smug you make me sound."

"You weren't. More admonitory."

She made a rejecting gesture. And yet there was a glint in her eyes. Could she be finding a hint of the ridiculous in this conversation, as Roger was? "So there's just you left," he said.

"Left?"

"To receive my apologies for maligning you."

"Maligning? How grand."

That was the word, Roger thought. He'd written it down. Hadn't he? He couldn't look at his notes just now. But that was it. Yes. He hadn't mistaken it. "Perhaps you know what I mean?" he said stiffly.

Fenella nodded. "I accept your apology. Consider the matter closed. We needn't mention it again." She smiled. "And I hope you don't mean to become utterly humble."

"What?"

"You were always a wild, free spirit as a boy."

"I was an insufferable puppy."

"That too."

Roger laughed. She joined him. He felt as if a great weight had lifted off him. "About the other thing," he dared to say then.

"Thing?"

"Our fathers' misguided plan to marry us."

"Oh, that thing."

She looked rueful and amused and completely lovely. "Why did I refuse, back then?" Roger pressed his lips together. After all his preparation, a string of words had popped out of his mouth ahead of conscious thought. Did this happen to other people?

"You were horrified," said Fenella.

"What?"

"Horrified," she repeated.

"That seems too strong a word."

She shook her head. "No. It's quite apt. You made your opinion very clear when we met at the Duddo Stones, the day after they'd commanded us to marry." Fenella paused as her mind conjured up that dreadful afternoon, as it could still do in crystalline detail. She'd ridden away from home, even though she was afraid of riding back then. She'd had to get away from her father's shouting. The ride had been aimless and sometimes frightening, and when the circle of ancient stones had risen before her, she'd practically fallen off her mount to sit among them. She'd been trying to get up the nerve to remount and head home when Roger had come thundering along on one of his terrifying horses. He'd looked half-demented, with blood trickling down the side of his head.

"We met at Duddo? That can't be right. What were you doing there?"

Clearly, he didn't remember the scene that was engraved on her memory. Fenella was glad, actually.

"I'd been out riding like a lunatic that day," Roger continued. "I know that. Blaze finally turned and tried to bite me when I whipped him on. He tossed me off. I fell and hit my head. I don't even know how I got back into the saddle."

Fenella nodded. That fit with his state when he'd galloped up. He'd slid off his horse and fallen bonelessly to the ground.

"Someone helped me. Was that you? My recollection of that afternoon isn't clear."

"Yes," said Fenella. She'd been frightened and clumsy, but she'd bound the cut on his head with a bit of cloth torn from her petticoat.

"I could never recall who it was afterward. I thought of it like a visitation from the fair folk in their ancient ring."

He gazed at her. Such a different look from that long-ago afternoon, Fenella thought. Then, his eyes had burned with outrage as he raved about the fate planned for him, about the ignorance and tyranny of parents. She'd hated the shouting, cringed under it. Fenella felt a pang of sympathy for the girl she'd been.

"I do recall seeing you at church though. Back then."

That had been two miserable days later. Her father had filled them with discord.

"I was rude to you."

He'd been beastly, scowling at her in front of

everyone. And the neighborhood was well aware of the painful situation, thanks to her father's intemperance.

"I think I said I'd rather marry—"

"A sheep." It had hurt, then. "A 'sodding' sheep." Fenella snorted. "I'd never heard that word before. Your intent was clear, however."

"I was an abominable sprig. Shall I remind you that I'm sorry?"

"That was a different apology."

"True. I wonder how many I owe you?"

A laugh escaped Fenella, clearly surprising him. "I did tell you I'd rather become a nun than marry you," she said. A weak riposte, she thought; she'd do much better today. But his sodding-sheep comment, with all those friends and acquaintances looking on, had been the last straw. It had sent her home to pack her things and sneak off to her grandmother. Which had turned out to be a splendid thing to do.

"You did?"

She nodded.

"Good for you. I don't suppose I heard you. I rarely thought of anyone but myself in those days. I imagined that I knew everything, when in fact I knew nothing. Will you accept my belated apologies for that slur as well?"

And she'd run from marrying this man, Fenella marveled. But, no. He hadn't been this man, at the time. *This* man was dangerously alluring. He inspired an impulse to lean closer, to run a fingertip along his cheek, perhaps. What would he do? She could hardly resist the impulse to find out.

A housemaid appeared at the end of the corridor.

"There you are, miss. This just arrived for you." She held out a folded note.

Fenella stepped back.

"I should go," said Roger.

He sounded breathless. Yes, he should go. The situation was getting out of hand. Fenella nodded.

"I'll come again."

Unsettled by how much she wanted him to do so, Fenella sent him off with the housemaid to retrieve his hat and leave her home. Could anything be more foolish than mooning over a man she'd run away from a few years ago? How her father would laugh if he found out. Laugh and then argue for his marital plan until he drove them all mad. Fenella shook her head. They'd been through that fiasco. She'd refused to be pushed even then, when she was timid enough to jump at shadows. She certainly wouldn't be now. And Roger *had* compared her to a sodding sheep.

Pulled by irresistible currents, she walked to the end of the corridor and looked out the window. Roger was mounting his horse on the sweep of gravel before the front steps. In the saddle, he paused and looked back. Fenella couldn't judge his expression from this distance, but he sat there for a full minute before he turned his horse and rode away. She would have given a good deal to know what he was thinking.

"Sodding sheep," she muttered, a warning reminder. The note crackled as her fingers closed into fists.

Shoving the past aside, Fenella opened the missive and read it. Harold Benson wondered if she might know of a boy who could take a part in their Lindisfarne pageant. A lad of ten years old or so would be perfect. The message was disingenuous. Mr. Benson knew she had a nephew staying for the summer holidays. Clearly, he intended John for the role. Wondering why, when he must have a number of boys to choose from, she read over the description of the scene. Ah, that was it. Laughing, she went in search of John.

Ten minutes later, Fenella knocked on the closed door of her sisters' old playhouse. The little building, built for Greta and Nora when they were small, nestled among flowering bushes at the back of the Clough House garden. Fenella couldn't count the times she'd been denied admittance, and then lurked in the undergrowth trying to overhear her sisters' secrets, before she stopped trying.

"Come in," called Greta's son.

With a tiny, ridiculous thrill, Fenella bent under the low doorway and entered.

John sat on a stool before a wooden table holding some botanical specimens. He'd removed the frilly curtains that used to hang at the windows, Fenella saw. Most of the scaled-down furniture was gone as well. She wondered where he'd put it. What had been a girlhood bower was now neat and functional. Fenella checked for snakes. She didn't see any. But she asked to make certain.

"No," replied John. "I haven't found any worth keeping so far. And I've nothing to keep them in. You can't just shut them in a dark box."

Fenella was reassured by this sign of compassion. John worried about the well-being of reptiles, at least. "I came to ask if you would take a role in the historical pageant on Lindisfarne Island at the end of the month." It would be just before he needed to return to school.

"Pageant? Like a church pageant?"

"A bit like that, yes."

"I don't think I can act." John looked uneasy.

"It's hardly that. More like posing, really."

"Are you in it?"

"Yes." A vivid memory of being hefted over Roger's shoulder intruded. Warmth washed over Fenella.

"What would I have to do?"

"You would be a boy receiving a homily from St. Cuthbert."

"Homily. That's a kind of sermon?"

John was really quite intelligent. Fenella wished he was just a bit more sweet-tempered. "Shorter than that."

"That sounds pretty limp. I don't think I want to."

"You did offer to help me should I need it," Fenella said.

"Does this help you?"

Really very intelligent, Fenella thought, because strictly speaking, it did not. But Mr. Benson would nag, and she thought it might be good for John to join a group effort. Still, she wouldn't lie to him. "I've been asked to help," she said. "And so I'm trying to do so." There was also deceit by omission, Fenella thought. That wouldn't do. "You would have to be covered in mud, apparently," she added. "And a bucket of water would be thrown over you at the end."

Oddly, John's expression brightened. "Right over my head?"

"I suppose so."

"Ha." He smiled at the thought. "All right. I'll do it."

Boys were just odd, Fenella thought as she turned to go. "There's a rehearsal tomorrow afternoon."

"Rehearsal? Do I have to memorize? I'm no good at memorizing." John looked anxious again.

"Your role is silent," replied Fenella. It seemed that way from the description, and she would see that it was.

John nodded, relieved.

A knock came as Fenella was about to open the playhouse door. It signaled the arrival of Tom, the guest without a surname from Chatton Castle, and the little structure was very full all at once. John appeared delighted to see the older boy, however. "We're going to search the garden for adders," he said.

"Adders?" Fenella didn't like the sound of that.

"They're the only poisonous snake in Britain," said John.

"What?"

"They're not *very* poisonous," the boy went on. "Not like a cobra or a black mamba. Their bites don't kill you. And they're fairly rare. I don't suppose we'll find any." He sighed.

Fenella noticed that Tom was looking at her. There was something very reassuring in his homely gaze. "Just looking," he said. "We ain't going to touch 'em."

"Well—" John began.

"No touching of the poisonous snakes," Tom interrupted. "That was the agreement."

"Right," said John.

"Right indeed," said Fenella. She fixed John with a stern gaze. Then she took Tom's nod as a promise.

Six

IF SOMEONE HAD SUGGESTED, EVEN A MONTH AGO, that a rehearsal for a historical pageant would feature as one of the high points of his week, he would have scoffed, Roger thought. But that was how he felt as he arrived at the village hall and watched Colonel Patterson marshaling his motley monks. The bark of his commands was still more suited to a parade ground, but Roger supposed that monks might have stood at attention now and then. Some of them. Hadn't there been warrior monks? Perhaps not monks. Anyhow, it didn't matter. The pageant needed a leader who could whip a group into shape, and Patterson was certainly that person.

Fenella Fairclough entered, followed by her nephew. On this warm day, she wore a simple gown of primrose cambric. She set aside a straw bonnet and a silk parasol, a ray of sun catching her pale-red hair and making it gleam. A pulse of anticipation went through Roger at the idea that he'd soon be lifting her to his shoulder again. She hadn't lodged any objections to the scene they'd been given. Did that mean she enjoyed it as well? Too much to assume, and yet he found he hoped so.

Since their conversation outside her father's room, Roger had strained to remember the encounter she'd described at the Duddo Stones. But try as he might, he got nothing but fragmentary images of the person who'd helped him. He couldn't make the hazy, fairy-tale figure into Fenella. The fall from his horse must have been a bone-cracker.

He didn't remember the sodding-sheep comment at church either. He winced now at the thought of it. What an ass he'd been five years ago! He could remember that, unfortunately. He had an all-too-vivid recollection of his younger self's sulky arrogance. Which had lasted far longer than it should have. That attitude had brought him down when he'd strutted off to London, thinking he was up to every rig and row in town, and been trapped into marriage like the greenest boy. *That* had taught him a whole university of painful lessons.

Colonel Patterson beckoned. Roger moved forward. Fenella came armed with the old broom. "All right," said the colonel. "Marauding Viking. With the snarl."

Roger lunged.

"And Miss Fairclough, your broom," commanded Patterson. She swung. Roger flinched and fell. "Better than before," said the colonel. "Though still lacking ferocity. Inevitable, I suppose." He sighed like a man who has been given inferior materials to work with. "Now up. Another swipe with the broom, Miss Fairclough. Yes. And you grasp her arms, Chatton."

Roger took hold. The cloth of her dress was smooth

under his fingers. Her eyes met his from inches away. A lovely color flushed her cheeks.

"And now you spit at him, Miss Fairclough," said Colonel Patterson.

"I forgot." She managed a half-hearted spit.

"Weak," said the colonel. "You did it much better last time."

"I could say something to incite you," murmured Roger, too quietly to be overheard. "Sodding sheep, perhaps."

"Beast."

"There. Now you can do it."

And indeed her second attempt was more convincing. Roger thought he heard a cheer from her young nephew.

"Right," the colonel said. "Now over the shoulder and off through the archway." He sketched the imaginary span of stone with a wide gesture.

Roger picked her up.

"Quicker," said Patterson. "You keep forgetting you're a desperate raider, Chatton."

Light blows fell on Roger's back from Fenella's fists. Her feet pumped. The movement of her body under his hands was dizzying.

Colonel Patterson made a shooing motion. "Go on. Off through the archway. Run if you can. Carefully though. We don't want accidents."

Roger carried his enticing burden a few yards.

"That's it." The colonel waited an instant, then said, "You can put her down now." Roger did so, sorry their duet hadn't taken nearly as long this time. "You know the movements," Patterson added.

"Which is more than I can say for some. Just have to put a bit more punch in it, eh? Savage era in our local history. Give it a bit more stick."

"Or broom, as the case may be," said Fenella with a smile.

"Precisely, Miss Fairclough."

Young John Symmes came rushing over to them. "That was tremendous, Aunt Fenella!" he said. "You were as good as a play."

Roger thought the boy couldn't have seen many. He lingered beside Fenella, looking for an excuse to prolong their encounter.

"Is this the boy for the homily?" asked the colonel.

Fenella nodded and introduced them.

"You'll be listening to the bishop," Patterson said.

From this Roger understood that the part of their local saint had been given to the highest-ranking member of the church in the area.

"Your job is to be silent and humble," the colonel continued. "You reckon you can do that?"

John shrugged and nodded.

"You'll be wearing a smock slathered with mud. Your hair, too. And no shoes. Have they told you that?"

Oddly, the boy looked cheered by the idea. He nodded.

"And about the bucket of water?"

"Right over my head," replied John with enthusiasm. "Yes, sir."

"That's it." Colonel Patterson looked approving. "At the end, you kneel for a blessing. So not very complicated, eh?"

"No, sir."

"No. I don't think we need to practice that. No one to give a homily anyway. Just be ready on the day, eh?" He turned away to supervise the next bit.

"There's Tom," said Fenella's nephew. He waved, and the lad ambled over to join them. "Are you taking a part in the play?" John asked him.

The homely youngster nodded. "One of the Vikings running in the background. I get to wave an ax."

"Aren't you rather young for that?" asked Fenella.

Tom shrugged. "I wanted a chance to be in a play, and Mr. Benson said some as young as twelve came along in the raiding ships."

John looked interested, and Fenella concerned. Roger stepped in to create a diversion. "You're fond of plays?" he asked Tom. Roger still didn't know quite what to make of this particular houseguest. But then, he hadn't given Tom a great deal of thought, his mind being on other things.

"I am. I been to one in Bristol and then a few in London just lately."

"Really?"

"A…friend of Lord Macklin's got me in backstage and all. I saw everything." Tom's grin was infectious. It was almost enough to distract Roger from his pause before the word *friend*. Roger wondered if the dignified Lord Macklin had a connection with one of the opera dancers. He couldn't quite see that, but the arrangement wasn't uncommon. And you never knew.

"The painting on the scenery is champion," Tom continued. "And they have a way of making waves. Looks remarkable like the sea. Men on either side push these rows of carved boards back and forth. It looked real as real from out front."

"I don't think our pageant will measure up to a London theater production," Fenella said. She was very conscious of Roger at her side. It was as if she could still feel his hands on her. A current of heat seemed to flow from him, as if he was more alive than others in the room. Or as if she was, in his presence.

"This Lindisfarne place," said Tom. "You been there?" He looked back and forth from Fenella to Roger. When they both nodded, he said, "I heard the road to it is underwater at high tide."

"It is," said Roger. "You have to take care not to be on it then. And to check the tide times carefully. As well as the weather. There's a marked path on the causeway."

Tom looked intrigued. "Somebody said there's a walking route over the sand. I'd like to see that."

"We should try it!" said John. "We could run ahead of the tide."

The excitement in his voice made Fenella uneasy. Perhaps she shouldn't have involved him in the pageant on Lindisfarne after all. "No," she said.

"You have to do it during daylight with someone who has local knowledge," said Roger, most unhelpfully. "And never during a rising tide, remember."

"Don't encourage him," said Fenella.

"I wasn't. I just said…"

"Have you walked it?" asked John eagerly.

Fenella tried to control Roger's response with a warning look, but of course it didn't work. He nodded, falsely humble but actually proud, as men so often were over their more reckless exploits.

"Would you take me across?" John gazed at Roger as if he held the keys to the kingdom of heaven.

"No," said Fenella. "Your mother would never permit it."

"She wouldn't know," John wheedled.

"She'd find out," Fenella replied, certain this was true. Greta was like a magpie with information, and she still had friends on the Clough House staff. "Even if she didn't, I'm aware of her wishes. I forbid it."

Her nephew's face fell into sullen lines. "It's not fair."

Part of Fenella wanted to argue that fairness had nothing to do with it. This was good sense, not injustice. But she knew better than to begin such a dispute.

"Let's go and watch the sword fight," said Tom.

John perked up at once.

"It's from the War of the Roses," added Tom. "That's the Lancasters and the Yorks, eh? All killing each other."

As he led John away, Fenella wondered where a lad his age had developed the tact of a diplomat, and where one of his purported background had learned English history. She turned to Roger. "You are not to let John persuade you to take him over the causeway," she said.

He nodded. "Although I wasn't much older when I first tried it."

"*You* are not a good example. You were nearly buried alive digging for treasure in the side of a hill."

Roger blinked in surprise. "How did you know about that?"

"Your…gang was the focus of much admiring gossip among the neighborhood children."

"We were?"

"I think you know you were." She eyed him. "I think you enjoyed it."

This won her a sheepish smile. "We brushed through our adventures pretty well."

"James Farley broke his arm."

"Oh well, yes. He misjudged the strength of a tree branch."

"And Alistair Byrne was trampled by one of the heath ponies."

"He wasn't trampled! It was just a kick, and he nearly got onto the pony's back."

"He had a great bruise on the side of his face. I remember it."

"You should have seen his ribs!"

"His mother was furious."

"But he almost rode a wild pony. Do you know how difficult that is? We all envied him."

Fenella could see it now, but at the time she'd been daunted by some of their exploits, even as she envied them. Wild ponies were not the issue, however. "If John was hurt while under my care, my sister would never forgive me."

Roger looked thoughtful. "I suppose not. Greta has no sense of humor. None at all." He grimaced. "Once, I was setting up a prank in the churchyard. A flapping sheet to simulate a ghost, with a rope I could pull to make it fly away. The vicar—you remember that prig Lynch?—he would have run screaming. But Greta caught me at it and tried to blackmail me."

Fenella stared at him. "Blackmail?"

"She wanted me to dance with some friend of hers twice at an assembly. I forget which, or why actually. Was it to make her beau jealous? At any rate, of course I refused."

"You didn't want to dance with her?" Fenella had never heard this story of her oldest sister.

He shrugged. "I knew that wouldn't be the end of it. Greta would have me under her thumb if I gave in. So I said no, and she went to my father and told him the whole. And the prank wasn't even aimed at her." He sounded as if this still rankled. "Not a forgiving person, your sister Greta."

He didn't know the half of it. And Fenella didn't intend to tell him. The torments of her youth were past. "And so you will not lose her son in a quagmire."

"The sands around Lindisfarne aren't a quagmire. Well, except for one or two spots where the currents have hollowed them out."

"Spots which John would inevitably fall into."

"Do you think so?"

"He has a genius for mishaps. He's in exile here because—" Fenella bit off the rest of this sentence. Her nephew had confided the story of the unfortunate kitten. He probably wouldn't want it shared.

After a moment, Roger said, "I promise not to aid and abet him."

The phrase made Fenella smile. "Thank you." She met his eyes. Their gaze caught and held, as if some urgent communication needed to get through. This had happened at Chatton Castle after her return from

Scotland, she remembered. They'd avoided looking at each other ever since. She turned away.

"I wish I'd met your Scottish grandmother," he said. "Did she ever come to visit? I don't remember it if she did."

"She and Papa annoy each other," Fenella replied, surprised at this change of direction. "My mother always went to see her. Why would you want to meet her?"

"She must be quite exceptional. You became a different person under her tutelage."

Fenella appreciated the admiration in his voice. Perhaps too much. But she also felt a spark of resentment. "She wouldn't agree. She says you can't change anyone. You can only encourage their true natures to emerge if they've been…muffled."

"So she saw your passions simmering under the surface?"

Fenella flushed. Partly with embarrassment, and partly with a sort of forbidden excitement at this perfectly true assessment. She knew the color was visible on her pale skin. If she'd had any doubt, she could judge by the red tingeing Roger's cheeks.

"That didn't come out right," he said. "That is, I meant no offense."

"I'm not offended." There was no reason not to look at him, she thought. Except the shadow of Arabella, which still wavered between them. What did they owe her memory?

A shout from behind made her turn. John was hefting a broadsword that was clearly too heavy for him. He tried to swipe the air. The weapon slashed down and nearly took off the tips of his toes. How did boys survive their youth? Fenella wondered as she hurried over to intervene.

Roger watched her walk across the village hall and take possession of a sword nearly as long as she was. She returned it to its owner with amused confidence and herded her nephew out. Tom trailed after them.

He wanted to go with them, Roger thought. He wanted to follow Fenella around, talk to her, listen to her. And more than that. His interest in his lovely neighbor, freed from the internal chains he'd put on it, was growing by leaps and bounds. Did she feel the same? He was going to have to ask her before he let things go much further. He could at least be certain that the current version of Fenella would tell him the truth.

Roger made his way out of the village hall. The Fairclough party, with Tom, was riding away. Fenella managed her spirited horse with easy grace. Years ago, Roger had overheard her father complaining to his own about the burden of three daughters, and the lack of a son. Fairclough had been ridiculously venomous, he thought now. It was no wonder Fenella had been a timorous girl under that weight of disapproval. At the time, Roger hadn't paid much attention. It was borne in upon him, yet again, what a heedless, self-centered youth he'd been. Was there any way to make up for that now? He found he was determined to try.

❧

Arthur slipped his arms into the evening coat his valet was holding for him. Clayton smoothed it over his shoulders and brushed a speck of lint from the lapel.

"I'd be a sartorial shambles without you, Clayton," said the earl.

The valet permitted himself a small smile, which warmed a round face that was pleasant rather than handsome and softened his brown eyes.

Arthur was grateful for the sharp mind and deep well of common sense behind those eyes. The man had been with the earl for more than twenty years, and Arthur valued his canny insights as much as his personal services. Clayton was a valuable sounding board when the earl was working out a course of action. Arthur reasoned better by talking aloud than through introspection. "What do you hear about Miss Fairclough?" he asked now.

"She seems to be an interesting young lady, my lord. She took over management of the Fairclough estate when she returned from Scotland, as her father is quite ill. Some are happy about that, and others are complaining."

Arthur cocked an eyebrow for more information.

"I've heard it suggested that the latter are a 'gaumless, shiftless lot.'"

The phrase made the earl smile. "Lady Chatton thinks well of her." She'd more or less implied that Roger and Miss Fairclough would do well together, and his host's manner when Miss Fairclough was present seemed to support that opinion. "I think it's time for us to hatch a plot, Clayton."

Clayton didn't sigh. He would never lower himself to do so. But he gave the impression of a sigh nonetheless.

Arthur wondered if his valet was missing the round

of house parties that usually occupied their summers. He knew Clayton had cronies among his noble friends' servitors. "Next year we will be back to our customary routines," he said. But as soon as he spoke, he wondered if he could make such a promise. He was finding this summer so much more satisfying than the last few. "I think," Arthur added in all honesty.

Clayton's answering nod was noncommittal. It was often difficult to decipher what he really thought, Arthur acknowledged. He'd offered more than once to help Clayton into another, more prestigious profession. The man always said he was happy where he was. "More matchmaking, my lord?" the valet said now.

"Who would have thought it, eh? But in this case, there may be a complication. Their fathers tried to force them to marry a few years ago."

"So I have heard," replied Clayton. "Mrs. Burke, the housekeeper here, is of the opinion that the previous Lord Chatton ought to have known better."

"Because?"

"The present marquess was not a particularly... obedient child."

"And what wild young sprig wants to be told who to marry?"

"Indeed, my lord."

A knock at the door heralded the entry of Tom. They'd formed the habit of chatting in the half hour before dinner, which Tom insisted on taking with the servants. Which was undoubtedly wise, Arthur thought, as Tom tended to be. Could such sensitivity simply be innate? He enjoyed hearing about the lad's adventures, and in this case his description of the pageant rehearsal seemed promising. Arthur didn't see just how at present, but it had certainly brought his targets together in an interesting way.

"When is Mrs. Thorpe coming?" asked Tom.

"A few days before the performance, I believe," answered the earl. "It's not as if she needs much rehearsal to recite a speech of Lady Macbeth's." Mrs. Thorpe had played the part on the London stage, to great renown.

"That Mr. Benson says the play ain't true," said Tom. "Claims Shakespeare got it all wrong. Can you do that?"

"What?"

"Call Shakespeare a liar. Ain't he kind of sacred, like?"

"Drama critics have never thought so," answered Arthur with some amusement.

"He's trying to get the pageant to call off that scene," Tom added. "Do you reckon we should tell Mrs. Thorpe?"

Arthur considered the matter. "I don't think it's our place to do so. I suspect the organizers won't want to offend one of the foremost actresses in London. After she has agreed to come all the way up here."

Tom accepted this with his customary good humor and proceeded to tell them more about his part in the pageant.

"It sounds like an interesting spectacle," said Arthur when he finished. "Perhaps I'll go by and watch a rehearsal one day."

"Colonel Patterson's liable to pull you into helping if you do," responded Tom with a grin.

"Colonel Selwyn Patterson?"

"I don't know his first name, my lord."

"Not a large man, but a commanding manner and a fierce gaze. White hair, wiry. I suppose he's about sixty years of age."

"That fits," said Tom.

"I'm acquainted with him." Arthur wondered if this connection would be any help to his plans. He couldn't see how at present, but one never knew.

Seven

ROGER WENT OUT RIDING THE NEXT DAY AT THE SAME time he'd encountered Fenella before, and along the same path. There were clouds today, but the firm sand at the edge of the waves still beckoned, offering an invigorating wind and a sense of boundless freedom. As he'd hoped, after a while a figure on a glossy gray horse appeared, riding toward him. Fenella handled her spirited mount expertly, he thought as she came closer. Of all the ways she'd changed, this one was the most observable. "Shall we ride together?" he suggested.

She smiled at him, and for an instant Roger felt as if his heart had stopped. Had she ever offered him such an easy, open smile before? He couldn't recall one. It lit her face and fired his spirits. "Let's," she replied, turning her horse.

They took a broad, smooth path that led inland from the North Sea, with no large stones or rabbit holes to endanger a horse's legs. After a bit, Fenella drew ahead. Roger caught up and overtook her, just by a head. Fenella urged her horse to more speed and moved a little to the front. He did the same. She followed suit. And then they were galloping full tilt, side by side, bent over their saddlebows, grinning into the wind.

Roger's mount was larger, but he was a heavier burden. She managed her reins with enviable skill. They were remarkably evenly matched, he thought as they hurtled across the countryside, clods of earth flying in their wake. The impromptu race was the most exhilarating thing he could remember in recent months.

When they at last pulled up, Fenella was laughing. Strands of ruddy hair had pulled loose and curled about her face under her small cocked hat. Her face was flushed, her blue eyes sparkling. She looked absolutely enchanting. Then a frown creased her brow. "How funny," she said. "We've come to the Duddo Stones."

Roger turned and saw the circle on a low rise a little way off. The gray stones stood out against a sky of racing clouds. "I didn't mean to head here," he said.

He would have turned away, but Fenella signaled her horse and rode up the incline. Roger dismounted when she did and followed her inside the circle.

The four standing stones were only about his own height, and yet they had a presence that made them seem larger. "You can see the Cheviot Hills from here," said Fenella, pointing south. She turned. "And the Lammermuirs up north. It's no wonder they built their monument here."

"They?"

"The old people. That's what my nurse used to call them. Whoever set up these kinds of places. There are others not far away, you know."

"Yes."

"People still leave offerings at some of them." Fenella ran her hand along one of the lichened stones.

"What sort of offerings?"

"Flowers. Ribbons. Prayers and requests? I don't know."

"You've never done so?" She smiled at him again, and Roger felt that novel soaring sensation in his chest.

"No," she said. "Why didn't I think of that, when my father was being difficult? Do you think some old spirit would have helped me? What did they call them? Genius loci?"

Roger couldn't be bothered with Latin. He couldn't be silent, and yet he didn't know just what to say. "Have you ever... Do you think we... When you came back from Scotland...and then this last year." He paused to gather his wits. Why were words so dashed difficult? "I said and did some things—"

"You kept saying I killed Arabella," she interrupted. She looked out over the panorama, her expression unreadable. "But you've apologized. Remember?"

It wasn't as if his lost wife was here. She was gone. But the constraint that had bound them during her life lingered. Roger made a rejecting gesture. "I was an idiot. Full of anger and guilt."

She blinked at the last word, but didn't ask what he meant.

"I've done more than apologize," Roger added. "I've told people I was wrong. My mother. Macklin. I'll tell everyone."

Still she didn't look at him. "It might be better just not to speak of it," she replied. "People have forgotten."

Conscious that he had repeated the accusation a few months ago, Roger cringed. But that had been far away, in London. He would never say it again. Should anyone mention the idiocy, he would contradict them.

"There's something unusual about this place," said Fenella, pointedly changing the subject. "It's almost as if we're in a room, cut off from the countryside." She walked around the circle, trailing her fingers over the whole rank of standing stones. When she'd made the entire circuit, she glanced at him. "Do you feel that? Or do you think I'm being fanciful?"

He didn't think so. The air felt thicker and warmer here inside the stone circle. His ears buzzed. There were bees in the clover at the foot of the stones, but the sound seemed louder than that. A sweet scent fogged his senses.

Roger gazed through the space between two menhirs. The rolling hills looked too far away, as if viewed through the wrong end of a telescope. He suddenly understood the stories of fairy rings, where one stepped out of the familiar and entered another realm.

"We must hope that years won't have passed when we leave," said Fenella, echoing his thoughts.

He turned to look at her, and his memory finally gave him scattered images from their previous visit here. She'd bent over him when he fell from his horse those years ago. He'd seen her haloed by the sun like a descending angel. She'd put gentle fingers to the cut on his head. Despite his rudeness and really bumptious behavior, despite her fears, she'd tended him. Just as she'd brought him the tonic for his stomach when she noticed his pain. Which she'd had no reason to heed. She was kind through and through.

"Is something wrong?" she asked.

Abruptly, Roger's life spread out in his mind, a panorama of fits and starts, achievements and mistakes. At the same time, he was aware of Fenella in incredible detail. He admired the delicate curl of her eyelashes, the beautiful line of her lips, the intelligence in her eyes, and the grace of her carriage. His mind held a history of her image, beginning in childhood and running up to this moment. And it added up to the fact that this was the woman for him. Immaturity and interference had prevented him from knowing this for far too long. "May I court you?" he blurted out.

"Court?" She looked startled.

He felt his cheeks flush. How did a man gain the kind of finesse that his houseguest Macklin, for example, so amply possessed? *Courting* was a silly word. Yet it expressed his desire to deserve her, to win her, after the way he'd behaved.

"No," Fenella said.

Roger felt as if his heart had dropped to his feet. She didn't want him. He'd wrecked his life.

"My father would be too smug," she added. "I can hear him going on and on, and on, about what a waste it was. Years of upheaval for nothing, and now we're right where he wanted us in the first place. If we'd only listened, only done as he commanded. It would be so vastly irritating."

Roger dared to feel some relief. Those weren't heartfelt reasons. She hadn't said she disliked him. He bent to catch her gaze and searched for an answer in her eyes. They softened under his anxious scrutiny, and she smiled. "What about a clandestine courtship?" he asked. Fenella laughed, and he felt as if he had indeed been reprieved.

"What?" she asked. "Hidden trysts and secret meetings?"

"What else is this?"

"A chance encounter of two neighbors?"

"No."

"What?"

"It wasn't chance. I was looking for you."

"Were you?"

She didn't seem angry, Roger thought. More… speculative? Was that it? He watched as a series of expressions passed over her beautiful features. He thought he saw doubt, interest, even yearning. But who could be sure?

Then she stepped closer, very close, stood on tiptoe, and kissed him.

It was a soft, sweet, simple kiss. And yet desire shot through him like a lightning bolt. He would have crushed her to him, but she drew back. One step, and then another. "Well," she said. "That was…umm."

"Tremendous," said Roger. He reached out, longing to kiss her again.

But Fenella moved farther away. "Unexpected," she said.

"How so? You kissed me."

She acknowledged it with a nod. "Why did I do that?" She looked around at the stone circle. "There's something about this place."

"As if the rules don't apply here."

She looked surprised. "Yes, something like that." She shook her head as if to clear it. "They do, however."

Roger accepted his fate and moved a step back. "Still, I'm glad you did it." He hoped she would say the same.

But Fenella appeared lost in thought. "I didn't know it would be so—"

"Wonderful?"

She gave him a sidelong look.

"Mustn't get ahead of myself," Roger said, then bit his lip in chagrin. He hadn't meant to say that aloud. He quickly suppressed a desire to leap and laugh in triumph. "Perhaps we could try it again some time?"

"Possibly," said Fenella. "Clandestinely."

The small smile that played about her lips made Roger's pulse pound. "Absolutely. Have you a trusted maid who can carry my forbidden letters to you?"

"What?" She burst out laughing. "No, of course I don't. Do you want all the servants gossiping about us?"

"Then how shall we arrange our trysts?"

"We see each other often."

A few glances at church or a dinner party, Roger thought. It wasn't nearly enough. He said so. Then he remembered. "The old oak."

"The hollow tree where your gang left messages for each other?"

"You knew about that?" Roger asked.

"All the neighborhood children did. We read them, too."

Roger felt ridiculously chagrined. His troop of friends had thought the hidey-hole in the old tree's trunk was a deep secret. Now he found his boyish schemes had been common knowledge. But that was years ago. He had no reason to feel betrayed. "We could meet there," he said. "At the oak."

The idea seemed to amuse her. "All right." She turned away. "I must go back. My father gets restive if I'm away too long." She stepped out of the stone circle. "No roll of thunder," she commented. "I haven't suddenly aged a hundred years or my clothes fallen into dust."

"Pity," said Roger.

For an instant he hoped that the word hadn't actually left his lips. That he'd only, fleetingly, seen that dizzying picture in his mind. But then they both flushed, the bane of redheads. He'd spoken.

Fenella walked away. But she gave him a speaking glance over her shoulder. "And by the way, I was never anything like a sheep," she declared.

"No. You were some far more elusive animal, always slipping out of sight at the edge of perception. Not there if one turned to look."

She stared at him. Roger was as surprised as she by the phrases that had come from his mouth. Very nearly eloquent, he thought. How had that happened?

They returned to the horses, cropping grass outside the circle. Roger reached out to help her into the saddle. "I could stand on that rock," she said, pointing to a low boulder.

"So near a fairy circle? Never."

She laughed and let him lift her. Roger kept his hands on her waist for one warm moment, and then went to mount up.

They rode back the way they'd come, much more slowly. Shafts of sun broke through the clouds, illuminating swaths of heath before closing up again.

"Why are you taking care of your father?" Roger asked after a while. "I seem to remember that he always treated your sisters better."

"I'm the spinster daughter," Fenella answered as if this was obvious. "We're meant to nurse aging parents, aren't we?" She made a wry face. "And mind our errant nephews."

"Spinster," he snorted. He couldn't imagine any woman less suited to the word.

"Greta and Nora have families and households to manage," she said. "I don't mind helping out. And should the situation grow impossible—if Papa decided he wished me away, for instance—I can go back to Grandmamma. She'd welcome me."

Recognizing how much he *didn't* want that, Roger dropped the subject.

They rode on, sometimes silent, sometimes talking, until the tower of Chatton Castle appeared on the horizon. Soon they would have to separate if they really meant to keep their ride private. Fenella was about to say as much when two figures popped out of the long grass at the side of the path. It was John and Tom. So much for clandestine, she thought as they rode closer.

"I've got a smooth snake," shouted her nephew. He held up the creature in question, gripping it behind the head.

"Aren't all snakes smooth?" asked Roger.

"I have never had the least desire to find out," she replied.

The boys trotted toward them. "You hardly ever find them so far north," John said. "This one must be an adventurer!" He held it out.

Fenella suppressed a flinch and examined the brown snake. A double row of small, rather indistinct dark spots ran down its back toward the tail. Four parallel, shadowy stripes ornamented its back and flanks. The snake was winding around John's arm as if to squeeze it. "Not a viper?" she asked.

"No," John scoffed. "This isn't poisonous. But you know what, Aunt Fenella? Smooth snakes are one of the ones that don't lay eggs. They have live young."

"Like a dog or cat?" asked Roger.

John winced, but nodded. "They're very rare here. And secretive. I was dashed lucky to find it."

Tom was watching them, not the snake, Fenella noticed. His homely face was full of friendly curiosity. No, clandestine was right off for this particular outing, she concluded. Tom didn't seem like a gossip, but she suspected he told Lord Macklin everything he got up to. Their expedition would undoubtedly be mentioned to the earl. Probably that didn't matter. Macklin was unlikely to care about the affairs of a stranger.

∾⃝∾

At that moment, the earl in question and Roger's mother were sitting in the Chatton Castle garden once again. Having established their status as simply friends, they found they enjoyed a daily chat. Arthur suspected that Helena was lonely, now that she was a widow, and he understood that feeling very well. "Another splendid afternoon," he commented. The sea rolled away to the horizon beyond the castle walls. There were wisps of streaming clouds but no threat of rain. Bees were busy in the flowers and at the hives down the garden. Sweet scents wafted through the air.

"We often have a stretch of fine weather in August," Lady Chatton replied. Her face, shaded by a parasol, was serene.

"I suppose it's quite a different prospect in the winter."

She nodded. "Oh yes. We get some tremendous storms. The spray can reach all the way up the walls. And the days are very short then. The sun is down by four o'clock."

It seemed to Arthur that Chatton must be a desolate place at that season. But he didn't like to say so.

"The thing to do is make it cozy inside," she added, as if answering his thought. "And find pleasant occupations. We often play…played chess." Arthur tried to hide his surprise, but she noticed and laughed. "You don't think me capable. Raymond didn't either. He taught me the moves as if I was an amusing child and would soon grow bored with the game. How I cherish the memory of the first time I beat him in a match. He was dumbfounded."

"Did he mind?" Arthur asked. Many men would.

"He was proud of me." Helena looked rueful. "In his way. Like a man who possesses a rare curiosity due to his own cleverness. And I didn't win often. He was very good." Her expression grew mischievous. "Roger won't play with me. I always beat him."

"Perhaps we can try a match."

"Whenever you like," she said.

Arthur nodded. He'd noticed—in his middle age, certainly not sooner—that it wasn't always easy to be a pretty woman, even in the luxurious ranks of the nobility. He wondered what it was really like, to be constantly underestimated even as one was deferred to. He was aware that his appearance and position often had the opposite effect, leading people to overestimate his abilities. That could be irritating, but not nearly as much as the opposite, he imagined.

"I'll give you the first move," said Helena.

She thought he was worried about losing, Arthur realized. "On no account. I like a fair fight." When she laughed, he moved on to the topic he'd meant to bring up today. "I wanted to speak to you about something." He felt it only right to tell her that he was making plans concerning her son.

She cocked her head, ready to listen.

"I've been doing something rather odd lately. For the last few months, that is."

"Oh good."

Arthur looked down at her, startled.

"I'm always glad to hear that my friends are adventurous. Are you going to become eccentric?"

He'd lost more than he'd understood when Helena Ravelstoke chose another husband, Arthur thought. Yet he'd been very happy with Celia. He had no regrets. "Perhaps I already have."

His companion shook her head. "Still too proper."

He acknowledged her teasing with a smile and returned to his subject. "I told you about the group of young men I'd noticed, who'd suffered unfortunate losses in their lives, and my wish to help them."

She nodded.

"Well, in doing so I've become a bit of a matchmaker."

"You have?" Her blue eyes opened very wide.

"That isn't quite the right word," Arthur said. "I didn't make the matches." He thought of his nephew's case. He had rather pushed that along with some remarks he'd made to a spirited young lady in London. "Or not exactly."

"What then?"

"It's been more a matter of promoting connections that...revealed themselves over time." Arthur found himself searching for the right way to put the matter, a rare experience. "I wouldn't presume to—"

"For whom?" Helena interrupted.

"First my nephew Benjamin and a delightful young lady with very decided views on the care of children."

"Children?"

"Benjamin is...was a widower with a young son."

"And now he is married again?"

"Yes."

"And happy?"

"He certainly seems so. He says he is blissful."

"Who else?" asked Helena.

"Another of the young men I mentioned before and the sister of a ruined baronet."

"Ruined! How romantic that sounds," she said. "So your schemes have gone well." Her sharp gaze suggested that she was aware of where this conversation was heading.

Arthur didn't like the word *schemes*. Yet he couldn't deny it. He nodded.

"And now you've turned your attention to Roger."

"Yes," Arthur acknowledged. "That is, I came to see if there was any help I might offer him. I don't set out to make matches, you understand. Marriage might not be the answer. I'm simply on the lookout for ways to promote these young men's happiness."

"And yet it's always love," she said.

He looked down at her.

"Happiness is always about love."

Arthur considered this statement.

"The happy people I know *love*," Helena added. "Their husbands or wives, their children or other family, their occupations or pastimes, perhaps just their dogs." The skin at the corners of her eyes crinkled in amusement. "Very often their dogs, actually. But someone, something. Those who don't are forever discontented."

"A good point," said Arthur. She'd surprised him once again with hidden depths. "You don't have any dogs here at the moment?"

He'd meant it as a joke, but Helena's smile faded. "Arabella didn't like them." She made a balancing gesture as if trying to be fair. "Raymond's two dogs were old when he died. A bit deaf and feeble, and they *did* slobber over one. She didn't care to be near them. So she didn't want them replaced when they died."

"A puppy?" Arthur suggested.

"Roger got her one. She thought it messy and loud. It chewed up some lace. Roger gave him to a neighbor's child."

The way she said *him* in the final sentence told Arthur a good deal. Best to abandon the subject of dogs for now, he decided. "So Chatton and Miss

Fairclough," he tried instead. "I couldn't help but notice something between them."

"I'd be glad," she admitted. "But that would be a complicated piece of matchmaking. I told you their history." She tapped the handle of her parasol. "What shall I do?"

"You wish to be involved?"

"In helping Roger find happiness? How not?" She held up a finger. "Whatever that may mean. There's to be no forcing."

"Out of the question," replied Arthur. "I wouldn't consider it."

Helena nodded. "So what is your plan?"

"Ah."

"You don't have one, do you?"

"I tend to respond to circumstance." She laughed at him. Arthur joined in. "I try to, uh, provide opportunities for matters to develop," he added.

"Opportunities." She looked doubtful. "I've been doing something similar for months, and nothing has come of it."

Just then the subject of their conversation appeared at the castle door. The marquess surveyed the garden and then began walking toward them.

"Roger looks very satisfied with himself," said Helena.

"He does?"

"Yes. He's walking with a spring in his step. And he's trying not to smile. He's been up to something."

"I accept a mother's keen perceptions," Arthur replied. Chatton did have a lively air about him.

"Hello, Mama, Macklin," said the younger man

when he reached their bench. He stood before them, hands behind his back. He looked up at the clouds racing across the sky. "Not really a day for the outdoors," he commented.

"I thought you went riding," said his mother.

"Well, yes," he said, as if this was a different matter.

"I would have accompanied you if I'd known," said Arthur.

"Oh, ah, I set off early, you know."

Helena was right, Arthur thought. Chatton had definitely been up to something, and he'd avoided having a companion in order to do it. *And* he was very glad that he'd done so. All this was evident in his manner and expression.

"I believe Mrs. Burke is looking for you, Mama," the marquess added.

"Is she?" Helena's tone acknowledged what they all knew. If the housekeeper wanted her, she could easily find her. Nonetheless, Helena rose. Arthur stood with her as she said, "I had better see what she wants then." She strolled away toward the castle. The two men watched her go.

Chatton shifted from one foot to the other. "Are you flirting with my mother?" he asked abruptly. His tone held the awkwardness of posing such a question to a distinguished elder.

"We're old friends," Arthur replied.

"She thinks you came up here to see her."

"She did have an idea about that, but we cleared it up. Quite amiably, I promise you. We've agreed that friendship is the right thing for us."

"Agreed?" Chatton looked skeptical.

Arthur nodded.

"I won't have her hurt."

"Your sentiments do you credit. But you need have no fear."

"Mere friendship?" the marquess asked, again as if he doubted.

"You'll find as you grow older that there's nothing *mere* about friends, Chatton." Arthur tried to sound reassuring, and it seemed he succeeded. The younger man relaxed, as if he'd done his duty and could now return to his own concerns. The question was: what were they? "Shall we walk a little?" Arthur asked.

They moved along the path that led to the far end of the garden.

Arthur tried a question, rather like tossing a baited hook into the water, he thought. "I understand you're acting in the historical pageant with Miss Fairclough?"

Roger suppressed a start. Macklin could *not* read his mind, no matter how close to the subject of his thoughts he'd come. That lad Tom had told the earl about the rehearsal, Roger concluded. He'd tell him about the ride today as well, though he couldn't have spoken to Macklin yet. But today's expedition certainly wouldn't be *clandestine*. Was that idea ridiculous? Roger found he didn't care. He was ready to do whatever was necessary, whatever she asked, to spend time with Fenella.

"So you've reconciled?" asked Macklin.

"What do you mean?"

"After the…misunderstanding over that ride in the rain."

"Miss Fairclough had nothing to do with my wife's death!"

"You said that." Macklin looked him over like a man considering buying a horse. No, he didn't. That was ridiculous. "You seem quite certain, now. As you did on the other side of the question in London."

"Fen—Miss Fairclough is far too levelheaded a person. She tried to keep Arabella from going."

"Ah."

Did Macklin sound skeptical? He mustn't be. He had to convince him. Meeting the earl's level gaze, Roger saw not doubt but genuine interest. He remembered that dinner in London and the clear impression he'd received of a judicious, generous person—a rare man who listened rather than commanding. He'd felt so much better after that conversation, and he'd thought, afterward, that Macklin would be a good source of advice. But what would such a man think of his behavior? He valued the earl's opinion more than he could say and, equally, feared his judgment. But he couldn't offer Macklin anything but honesty. Roger flailed through his chaotic thoughts. The earl didn't break in as he groped for the right words. "I wanted to blame someone for Arabella's unhappy end," he said finally. "I accused others as well. Unjustly." He looked down, ashamed.

"Understandable," said Macklin.

Roger's head jerked up. He saw no condemnation in the older man's face. The relief was immense. But there was worse to confess. "I didn't want to admit that I had any part in it. But I did. I made her unhappy, which made her reckless."

They walked a few steps in silence. Roger braced for disappointment. "I've often wondered about my responsibility for others' feelings and actions," said Macklin.

This wasn't the reply Roger had expected.

"Particularly, these days, with my children and grandchildren," the earl continued. "Those who care the most for my opinion. Or so I think. Occasionally I say or do something that worries them. Even though I try to act with kindness always."

"I didn't." Roger bit off the words. "I got angry. I shouted at Arabella."

"Were you unhappy as well?"

"Miserable." He had never been more so.

"And was that her fault?"

A flare of anger shook him. He recognized it. He'd used it before, as a mask and a bulwark against the very worst. "When she was gone, I was glad the marriage was over." There, he'd said it aloud, as he never had before.

"But you would not have killed her."

"Of course not!"

"And perhaps you tried, now and then, to make things better between you."

"It was impossible. She hated Northumberland, and life at Chatton, and me, I think." His efforts had been a failure from start to finish. The familiar weight of it descended on him.

"I'm sorry for you," said Macklin. "You might have found a way, if you'd had more time."

Roger couldn't suppress a snort of disbelief.

"Or perhaps not. One can't know in such a case. For me, the only answer is to try to do better as time goes by and I learn."

"You?" Macklin seemed a paragon.

"Of course. Do you think I've made no mistakes?"

It felt like a kind of absolution. Roger drew in a breath, slowly let it out. He meant to improve. He intended to take every care. If Fenella would give him the chance, he would show her that he could be a better man. "How do you avoid them now?" he asked. Because it seemed to him that Macklin never made a misstep.

"I don't, of course."

That wasn't good news.

"But I find that I make fewer when I take care to discover others' opinions."

"You make that sound simple."

"Did I?" Macklin shook his head. "Then I have created a misimpression. Asking properly can be quite difficult. And then one must work very hard to hear the answer."

"To hear?" This wasn't the type of advice Roger had expected.

"People aren't always eloquent. And then, we often hear what we wish for rather than truth, do we not?"

Roger hadn't thought so. All he could think now was: here was another social pitfall waiting to trip him up.

Eight

WHEN FENELLA NEXT RODE OUT, AS THE NEIGHBOR-
hood was accustomed to her doing, she turned her
mount to the ancient oak that had been a fixture of
her childhood. The great tree stood alone on the side
of a low hill, where a spring arose and marked the
beginning of a stream, hardly more than a trickle in
this spot, though it gathered force nearer to the sea.
The oak leaned toward the slope, and its branches
dipped down to create a secret space in this spot the
tree had guarded for hundreds of years. Had it been a
sapling when the Vikings harried this coast, as Roger
was supposed to be doing in the pageant? Perhaps that
was stretching the tree's age, but it was fun to think so.

She stopped beside the spring and gazed up through
the arching branches. During her childhood, the
youthful ringleaders of the neighborhood had gathered
here, lords of the juvenile set. Finally, after all these
years, she felt like one of them. Fenella laughed aloud.
Ridiculous to care, but she couldn't help it. Though
she was twenty-three, she'd had no social triumphs to
overshadow old memories. Her grandmother didn't

entertain a great deal, and she'd never thought it right to take Fenella to London for the season and presentation at court without her father's approval. Grandmamma hadn't really wanted to go in any case, Fenella thought. She had no love for cities, or the English.

She'd assured Fenella that a person didn't need the approval of society to be strong and self-assured. Which was true, Fenella supposed, but it required a marked degree of resolution. And there was this. Grandmamma had attended the balls and routs and soirees she now rejected when she was a girl. By all accounts, she'd been lavished with society's approval. So her arguments weren't *quite* definitive.

These thoughts went out of Fenella's head as Roger appeared, riding up the slope toward her, straight and strong on his spirited horse. She couldn't see his eyes from here, but she remembered their fierce blue, the glint of his red hair in candlelight. Fenella felt a tremor in the region of her heart. Was it wise to be meeting him this way? She found she didn't care.

He pulled up and gazed at her as if they hadn't seen each other recently. "A fine day."

It was a balmy northern morning. Clouds lazed across the blue sky. The hum of insects and birdsong wove a pleasant counterpoint. "It is," Fenella agreed.

"We can count on August to give us sun."

"Yes." Their conversation had gone stilted. They had been talking so freely on their last ride. These were the sorts of bland remarks strangers exchanged in a drawing room. Disappointment loomed over her.

"How I hate society chatter," Roger blurted out, echoing her thoughts. "It's the next thing to meaningless, and yet it can be so difficult to produce. Why is that?"

"Because one doesn't really care?"

He looked a question.

"It's not worth much attention," Fenella added. "You know the other person isn't really listening. And most likely doesn't care about your opinion. Probably they're simply marking time until they can walk away."

"Not the case here!" Roger said.

"And so we needn't talk about the weather."

"No."

He looked at her. Fenella stared back and realized that she hadn't improved matters with her disquisition on idle chatter. In fact, she'd sounded fatuous, or pompous. She ought to have said... She didn't know what she ought to have said. It was difficult to think of anything except their visit to the stone circle and the fact that she'd kissed him. Just stood up on tiptoe and kissed him, as if that wasn't a terribly improper thing to do. She ought to be mortified, to be putting distance between them. In fact, she was remembering how much she'd enjoyed the experience.

Of the three kisses in her life so far—kisses from gentlemen, that is—one she had endured in a spirit of inquiry; one she had repulsed, revolted; and the third had made her body tingle and her head spin. It was marvelous how a simple pressure of lips could vary so radically. What did her childhood acquaintance have that other men didn't, to make her feel so dazzlingly alive?

Roger looked self-conscious. She'd been staring...

hungrily? Not that, surely. The word was completely inappropriate.

He turned away, rode closer to the tree, and reached down into a hollow in the trunk. "No messages in here. The neighborhood children don't use it, apparently."

"There aren't many about these days. We all grew up."

He nodded. "We lost Donald in the war. James lives in London. Your sisters married and moved away."

"Alistair is still here, and married. His children may use the oak when they're a bit older."

"He's gone stiff and prosy, though."

Fenella wouldn't have said it herself, but this was undoubtedly true of Roger's old crony Alistair Byrne. "I remember when he walked across that gully on a fallen tree trunk. It bent in the middle, and I was terrified he'd drop onto the rocks."

"By Jove, yes. He did it on a dare. Were you there?" Roger realized at once that the question was tactless. He ought to remember her better from their youth.

But Fenella only nodded. "Among the rank and file, at the back of the audience. How we cheered when he finished."

"He was vastly proud of himself. Never stopped talking about it. And I do mean never. If I called on him tomorrow, I daresay he'd bring it up."

"Despite the prosiness?"

She smiled, and Roger was flooded with relief. The ride was going to be all right. He'd feared, at the beginning, that the proprieties would stifle them, a bitter disappointment after that memorable kiss. But she'd come to the oak, he reminded himself. So she didn't regret it.

They rode up a narrow lane between fields of stubble from the first harvest. The wind rose, bringing a touch of chill. "The days are shorter already," Fenella said. "Sometimes I think of winter hovering in the north like a Viking fleet, waiting to sweep down on us."

"And throw you over its shoulder and carry you off?" Roger frowned at this ill-thought-out remark. But then their eyes met, and he wasn't sorry after all. He was nearly certain that their local historical pageant had set a spark alight in her as well. How to be certain? Macklin had said to ask, but how was he to put the question, precisely?

"It can feel a bit like that when a storm roars in from the sea," she said. "I know some people find that lowering. But I always loved the wildness. I suppose it comes of growing up here. Long, dark winter nights are as much part of home as a day like this." She gestured at the August landscape.

That was exactly it, Roger thought. The rhythm of the seasons and the sea became engrained in the spirit. He'd taken his love of his home country for granted until he was faced with Arabella's hatred of the Northumberland winter. Over and over, she'd urged him to take the revenues his lands generated and move them to a permanent place in London. When he refused, that hatred had been transferred to him, he thought. And her mother had taken it up after Arabella died, as if she owed it to her daughter's memory to despise him.

Roger didn't want to think about Arabella here

and now, and yet in a way she stood between him and
Fenella. His marriage, and its aftermath, had stopped
them from speaking to each other for months. It had
prevented them from becoming reacquainted on her
return. And Fenella had witnessed some of their difficulties. Probably more than he knew, because Arabella
had most likely confided in her. She must have a poor
opinion of his judgment. "You probably wonder why
I married Arabella."

Fenella blinked at this sudden change of subject.
She looked uncomfortable. "It was, and is, not my
place to wonder."

She might feel that, but Roger was determined that
there should be honesty and openness between them.
He'd learned that the lack of those things brought
disaster. "I was herded by her mother like a—"

"Sodding sheep?" she interrupted.

Was she angry or amused or embarrassed? Roger
couldn't tell. He hated that he couldn't tell. He hadn't
realized until this moment how much he wanted
Fenella's approval. He longed to show her that the
wreck of his marriage hadn't been his fault.

She glanced at him, her blue eyes cool and inquiring. They seemed to look right through him.

He'd seen that expression before, Roger noted.
When he'd railed at her about that ill-fated ride in the
rain. Skeptical, he thought, and…weary? In a moment
of rare insight, he realized that she was waiting for him
to bluster and blame someone else for his problems.
She'd heard him do that before, to her. And he'd been
wrong. Dead wrong.

A flock of excuses rose up to distract him—reasonable,

tempting. But under her even scrutiny, Roger had to admit that the core of the matter lay with him. Yes, Arabella's mother had taken advantage, but his own shortcomings had given her the opportunity. "An exceedingly stupid sheep," he said finally. "Stubborn as well."

Fenella cocked her head, surprised.

Roger forged ahead. "I'd been hanging about Arabella at the *ton* parties, along with a bunch of other fellows. She was—" He hesitated.

"Very beautiful," said Fenella.

Roger nodded. There was no denying that. Everyone had agreed that Arabella Crenshaw was an absolute dazzler. "There was a sort of competition among us, to get her alone. We didn't mean anything by it. She was so strictly chaperoned. It was just a lark."

"Like climbing onto the roof of the castle tower?" asked Fenella.

Her tone was very dry. Roger winced under it. "We were a pack of young fools, me most of all, I suppose. Well, obviously."

"Why obviously?"

"Because of the result," he answered. "One day, when I called at her house, I managed it. I saw her alone. I was so pleased with myself, I never wondered how that came about. Imagined it was my own cleverness, I suppose. I tried to steal a kiss. Just one kiss, no more, as Arabella seemed willing. But her mother came in at just that moment. She'd been lying in wait. Like a hunter watching a snare." Roger couldn't help that last bit. Mrs. Crenshaw *had* laid a trap for him. He'd worked out later that he was the one with the highest rank and largest fortune among Arabella's beaus.

"She congratulated us on our engagement," he continued. "When I stammered something about not meaning that, tongue practically tied in knots, she called me a libertine. Arabella cried." Roger still winced when he remembered that scene. "I said of course I wasn't. And then there was a great deal more scolding." It had been a veritable flood of words, engulfing him whenever he tried to speak, and Roger had lost his way in the spate. The feelings of chagrin and shame were vivid, however. He'd been made to feel like a deceiver who had trifled with an innocent girl's affections. The idea that he'd wounded Arabella, so sweet and fragile as she seemed then, had racked him. Of course he'd had to make amends. "Mrs. Crenshaw sent a notice to the papers within the hour, and the thing was done."

Fenella nodded.

Roger couldn't tell what she thought of him. He felt his spirits sink as the details brought it all back. Perhaps he shouldn't have started this story. "My father was so glad," he added. "We'd been at odds since…" He gestured at Fenella and himself.

"Yes."

"Mama was happy, too. Which I was glad of."

"Of course."

Still no sign of her opinion that he could decipher. "I owed it to the title to marry."

"And Arabella was so beautiful," she said again.

Roger acknowledged this with a nod. That had been a point; he admitted it. Seeing her across a crowded drawing room could take a man's breath away. The announcement of their engagement made him the object of envy in his whole set of young bucks. And he'd reveled in it, popinjay that he was. "I was never alone with her again until after the wedding." And then, of course, he'd discovered the extent of his folly.

Roger risked a glance at Fenella. He thought he saw sympathy in her eyes. On their last ride together, he'd begun to feel that he could talk to her about anything. But he couldn't complain about Arabella. That would be ungentlemanly, loutish. He would never do that.

But he yearned to understand, Roger realized. He'd wanted that for months and found no way to achieve it. Macklin had advised asking, and Fenella was the only friend Arabella had made in the neighborhood, ironically. As they were speaking to each other again, could she enlighten him? Still, it took him a moment to dare to say, "Afterward, I found I couldn't put a foot right." He stared into the distance rather than at his companion. "I'm not such a coxcomb as to expect everyone to like me. But I'd never before encountered someone who objected to every single thing I said or did." Nor had he ever felt such an utter failure, he added silently. He couldn't bring himself to say that aloud.

In the short silence that followed, Roger had ample time to regret his impulsive confidences. An urge to spur his horse and gallop off washed over him. They could resume their policy of not talking. It was so much easier than worrying that he'd said the wrong thing and ruined all.

"She cared for someone else," Fenella said.

Roger turned in the saddle to stare at her.

Fenella absorbed his incredulous stare stoically. She'd made up her mind as he spoke, hesitant at first but then increasingly moved by the pain in his voice. Arabella had never sworn her to secrecy, after all. Indeed, she'd been defiantly indiscreet, her need to speak seeming to outweigh all else. Perhaps she'd assumed that Fenella would take her side. She'd certainly vented her spite and resentment of Roger unstintingly, at every opportunity. It never seemed to occur to Arabella that she was burdening Fenella with one of most uncomfortable secrets she'd ever possessed, and straining her affectionate bond with Roger's mother.

"She told me about him," Fenella went on. "Not his name, but…other things. They'd met during the season and fallen in love. They wanted to marry, but her parents objected. Particularly her mother, I believe. The match wasn't grand enough for her."

Roger scowled like a man who could not believe what he was hearing. "Why did she accept me if that was so?" He put a hand to his midsection as if to ease an ache.

"That was her mother's doing. She wove a…fantasy of a bright future on one side and doom on the other, with this less wealthy suitor." Fenella frowned, recalling Arabella's bitterness toward her parent. She hadn't really understood why the other girl gave in to this argument. "I gathered that Mrs. Crenshaw is a… strong personality."

A crack of laughter shook Roger. There was no humor in his face. "A bit like Medusa, actually. One look, and you turn to stone." He grimaced. "Not fair. And I swear she loved her daughter. If you could see her since Arabella's death." He struck his thigh with a fist. "Why the deuce didn't Arabella stand up to her if that was the way of it?"

"She was young." Fenella would make no judgments. "And perhaps not well taught."

"Poor Arabella." Roger's expression grew pained. "So there was this other fellow the whole time. The whole time I knew her."

"Yes." Fenella hated to hurt him, but there was no other answer.

He was silent for a while. "And she never—" He shook his head. "Still, I needn't have walked into Mrs. Crenshaw's scheme."

Fenella was surprised. She'd rather expected that he would go off on a rant about the Crenshaws ruining his life.

"What a prodigious waste. On every front." He met her eyes. "Ask," he murmured.

"What?" This was a different Roger. There was a curious diffidence in his face.

"When you first came back from Scotland and I saw you again, I felt this pull. Like waking up to a... trumpet blast." He examined her face. "I thought you might have, too. Not sure about that." He paused, waiting.

After a moment, Fenella nodded. She could admit it now that there were no secrets lying between them. She felt the attraction more today than she'd done then.

Roger's heart soared. In the face of this confirmation, none of the rest mattered. Old news. Water under the bridge. "Yes." His exultant tone brought a slight smile to her lips. "If only I hadn't been a fool back then," he continued. "But that was rather my forte, wasn't it?"

She gave him a questioning look.

"I made such a point of refusing to marry you. I railed at my father. Told him he had no idea what he was doing. Was a perfect young ass, in short. I didn't want him to think I'd been wrong." Even though he had been, manifestly.

"How to bear the smugness," she said, nodding. "And the I-told-you-so's."

"Precisely. And when I began to suspect that I might have been wrong, I ran off to London rather than consider that fact." If only he hadn't, Roger thought. How different his life might be right now.

"Because of me."

Fenella looked down and away, a shadow passing over her expression. Her jaw tightened. What had he said to make her angry?

"I didn't send you to London," she said.

She used the tone that had charged their jousting in recent months. She thought he was still blaming her, Roger saw; just shifting from one cause to another. Not the ride in the rain, but the trip to town. But he hadn't meant that. Why would she think so? In an unusual flash of insight, he realized that she was accustomed to being blamed for all manner of things. Her father was continually doing it. "No. That was *not* what I meant." It came out forceful, but he didn't care. "I chose to go."

She looked at him, eyebrows raised.

"I decided to leave. For my own reasons." It actually felt rather good to say this. And to believe it. He hated feeling that he was at the mercy of other people's actions. He wasn't! "However wrongheaded my conclusions might have been," he added with a wry smile.

The warmth in his expression left Fenella shaken. She'd been braced for blame. She knew how to dismiss unjust accusations, taught by those her father had been tossing at her for as long as she could remember. But not to have to. That was another matter entirely. Relief was a pale word. Her throat thickened with tears.

She looked away to hide them, blinked them back. Their horses had ambled along at their own direction while their riders talked, and she saw that they'd veered closer to Clough House. Before them lay a dip in the land that was filled with bushes. "The raspberry thicket," said Fenella. "I used to come here and pick berries whenever I could sneak away. How Mama scolded me for spoiling my dresses! But I couldn't resist. I love raspberries."

"I'll pick some for you."

"The thorns will tear your clothes."

"No, they won't. You can sit in the shade over there." He turned his horse toward a cluster of saplings at the side of the thicket, grinning over his shoulder. An antic mood seemed to have overtaken him.

The breeze carried the scent of sun-warmed raspberries. Fenella's mouth watered. "I could pick my own," she said.

"Please allow me."

He spoke like a knight offering some perilous feat of chivalry. She decided to let him.

They dismounted, leaving their mounts to the rich grass on the side of the hill. Fenella settled in the shade and watched Roger plunge into the raspberry bushes. He pulled out his handkerchief and began to fill it with ripe berries. Stains spread over the linen as he added to his haul. She saw the thorns catch at his coat sleeves and riding breeches. They scratched his glossy boots as well. His valet wouldn't appreciate that. But Roger didn't appear to care. He moved deeper into the thicket, until only his hat was visible above the arching canes. And then that too vanished. "Are you all right?" called Fenella.

"Dashed briars snatched my hat," he replied. "Just a… Got it." The crown of his hat reappeared above the branches. He was near the center of the thicket, at the bottom of the dip. It was much harder to get out of that little valley than to go in, Fenella remembered. The slant of the bushes seemed to push one back down.

Roger's face showed above the vegetation. He must be standing on tiptoe. "There you are," he said. "I got turned around."

He moved slowly toward her, obviously having to fight his way out. His head, and then his broad shoulders, came into view. He held one arm in front of his face to stave off the thorns.

"Hotter in there," he said when he finally emerged. Sweat gleamed on his face. He came over to her, bowed, and set his bundle of berries beside her as if they were indeed the result of a knight's quest. Fenella noted an angry scratch across the back of his right hand. At least it wasn't bleeding. She took a raspberry and ate it. The fruit was warm from the sun, sweet and tart at the same time. It melted on her tongue, utterly delicious. "Berries picked here are always better than any others," she said.

Roger sat down in the grass beside her.

"You must have some, too. You did all the work."

He ate one. "Very good."

"Better than that," Fenella said. "Luscious." She held out a berry. He bent a little forward and took it, his lips brushing her fingertips, light as a butterfly's wing, and still it stirred her.

"Luscious," he agreed.

The word vibrated between them, expanding out to encompass far more than berries. The air was heavy with the hum of bees and the scent of fruit under the heat of the August sun.

They were hidden from the world here, Fenella noted. Even the horses would not be easily visible, due to the dip in the land and the height of bushes. They might have stepped outside of time. Her everyday life seemed far away.

Roger took a raspberry and held it out to her. Fenella leaned forward and opened her lips. He put the berry on her tongue. She bit into it, the intense flavor filling her mouth—piquant, delicious, another dart of pleasure. She held out a berry. He followed her example, bending toward her. She set the crimson fruit in his mouth without touching him. He held her gaze as he bit down.

The sultry atmosphere went to her head—the languorous warmth, the rustle of leaves overhead, the soft grass beneath her, Roger's lips red with berry juice.

Hers must be as well, Fenella thought. The same hue, the same taste. The idea seemed to pull her forward, and the next time he held out a berry, she leaned past it and kissed him.

He did taste of raspberries. But the kiss was so much more than that. The sweet taste of the fruit slid slowly into a melting of her whole body.

Strong arms came around her and pulled her close. She put hers around his neck and let herself sink with him onto the grass. The world contracted into a kernel of dizzying sensation.

What kisses, she thought. She'd known she was drawn to Roger, but she hadn't realized it would be like this. His touch set her vibrating with desire. She wanted to give him all he could ask, to take everything he could offer. She pressed up against him. Their kisses wove a tapestry of longing, begging to be unraveled. He murmured her name.

"It went this way," shouted a boy's voice from other side of the thicket.

"Into the brambles?" replied another.

"Right under, the cunning little devil."

"I ain't desperate keen to crawl in there."

"It's John and Tom," whispered Fenella.

"Deuce take them," replied Roger.

"Perhaps it will come out the other side," said John. "We can go around." Footsteps pounded along the edge of the thicket.

Roger pulled her closer as if to protect her from this intrusion. But his instinct was wrong in this case. They couldn't be found embracing. Fenella pulled away and sat up. Her hat had fallen off. She retrieved it and set it on her head, plucking and pinning stray strands of hair into place.

"Must speak to you," Roger whispered.

"Shh. Not now."

"Must." He couldn't stay silent. He had to tell her. This was the tricky bit, where he could win her, or lose everything. If only he could make his damnable tongue form the right phrases, and in a hurried whisper, no less. "These last few weeks, I've...I've seen the truth. What I felt when I saw you again after... everything." This was bilge. "Of course I couldn't say anything. Or even think it. So I didn't. I buried every feeling, every reaction. Got angry. It's always so easy to get angry." He wasn't proud of *that*. "If only I'd just married you five years ago!"

"Shh." She held up a warning finger. "That wouldn't have worked," she murmured, as if saying something he ought to realize.

"It might have. Who can say? We have a great deal in common. And those kisses." He met her blue eyes. Fenella flushed. With pleasure at the memory, he hoped. "I admire and respect you. I think of you constantly." More bilge. How did other men do this?

Roger's horse stamped and shook its head, repelling flies. Its harness jingled sharply in the silence. Fenella froze, wondering if the sound had carried across the dip. Briefly, she thought it had not. But then Tom's voice rang out, louder than before, as if directed across the thicket. "I reckon that snake's gone to ground," he said. "We ain't going to find it again. Let's go down to the stream and look about there where it's cooler."

"But these bushes must be full of specimens,"

replied John. His voice came from the far end of the bushes, moving closer.

Roger closed his eyes and shook his head. Clearly he wasn't pleased at the interruption. Fenella wasn't either, but perhaps it was fortunate. What might she have done otherwise?

"And thorns," said Tom. "They'll rip your coat to pieces. Your aunt won't care for that." Something in his tone made Fenella certain he'd heard the horse and guessed at their presence. Was Tom warning her? Fenella wondered.

"The berries look awfully good," said John.

She had a wild urge to call out that they were delicious. With a wry smile, she suppressed it.

"They'll have some at Clough House," said Tom. "With cream as well. Come along."

"We can't just give up." And with that John rounded the end of the thicket and came into sight on the slope above them. "Oh." He stopped short. "Hullo, Aunt Fenella, Lord Chatton."

"Hello, John." Fenella gathered her full skirts and rose from the grass. "Have you found another snake?" For a place where reptiles were said to be sparse, there seemed to be a great many of them about.

John moved closer. "A little one," he replied with his usual enthusiasm. "I'd have caught it if not for the brambles. I was that close."

Roger stood, making a sound rather like a hiss himself. Tom rounded the bushes and joined them, nodding a greeting. "If the creature has any sense, it will stay in there," said Roger. His irritation was clear, at least to Fenella. And to Tom, she thought.

"We were just going," she said.

"Were we?" said Roger. "I didn't think we were."

"It's time I was getting back."

"Or that *other people* went on their way." Roger threw the boys a discouraging glance. Tom clearly understood it.

"I'll go with you," said John, oblivious. "I want to fetch the small cage that William made for me."

"Not likely to need that," said Tom. "This snake's gone to ground. Better we go to the stream."

"Far better," snapped Roger. He looked at her. "I must speak to you."

Torn between chagrin and laughter, Fenella retreated toward her horse. A gentleman would propose after the interlude they'd just shared, and she was not averse to the idea. But Roger had been pushed into an offer before, following a stolen kiss. It might be silly, but she didn't want their agreement to go like that. Not as it had been with Arabella. And they couldn't speak freely in front of the boys. Tom's amiable curiosity was all too evident.

Roger had followed her. "Not now," she said.

"When, then?"

"When you've had time to think it over. And to be certain."

"I am certain. Are you saying that you—"

John popped up behind him. "Can I ride with you, Aunt Fenella? I have to be quick if I'm to—"

Roger rounded on the boy. "Will you go away?"

John stepped back, startled. Then the cowed expression with which he'd arrived in Northumberland descended over his face.

"Chatton," said Fenella.

"Aren't children meant to be seen and not heard?" said Roger angrily. "And haven't we heard more than anyone wishes to know about snakes?"

Tom moved to stand beside John, a silent protector.

"Enough," said Fenella, the steel of her grandmother's training in her voice.

Roger had the grace to look ashamed.

"You may ride with me if you like," she said to John.

The boy came to her as if to sanctuary. Tom followed along and helped Fenella mount. Roger stood alone, like a man wrestling with a thorny problem. Fenella set her heels into her mare's flanks and turned her toward home.

Nine

"I'm going to ride over and take a look at the place," said John the following morning. He and Tom sat under a tree in the Clough House garden, and John was feeling both resentful and bored. He didn't see that Lord Chatton had any right to speak to him as he had. He wasn't his father, or even his uncle. Aunt Fenella never treated him so. Also, he'd had to release the smooth snake, much as he would have liked to keep it for observation. The creature hadn't been doing well in a dark cage in the old playhouse. Snakes could be tricky to feed, too, and John didn't want to be responsible for another one's death. But he regretted the loss. All in all, life seemed vastly annoying just now. He'd had more than his fill of being a child. "It's only a few miles," he added.

Tom tossed a pebble onto the path. He'd marked out a grid in the gravel and was aiming at the squares in order. He looked tempted.

"I can go and be back before anyone knows," John said. He wanted to say *we*, but Tom hadn't agreed yet. Still, ever since they'd heard of the path across the sands of Lindisfarne, they'd both wanted to see the place.

"You'd have to ask permission," said Tom.

"They'd say no." It seemed to John that a vast web of authority surrounded him. So many people seemed to have the right to tell him what to do. He was more than impatient with it. Tom was not one of them, however. "I can go by myself. You can't stop me."

"I could tell yer aunt."

"If you are a snitch!"

Tom eyed him. John didn't care for that expression. At times, Tom made him feel quite transparent. "Reckon I'd like to see the pathway," Tom said finally.

John jumped up. "Splendid!"

"We'll take care," said the older boy as he stood. "Give me your word you'll heed me?"

"Of course," said John, ready to promise anything in order to escape.

They took the horses in the Clough House stable that they were permitted to use. "I got to stop at Chatton on the way," Tom said as they rode.

"Why?"

"I told the head gardener I'd help him out today. Collecting seed."

"You have to do jobs like that?"

"Don't have to. I like to. You'd be surprised what you can learn." Tom turned his mount toward the castle. "It ain't out of the way," the older boy pointed out.

John could see there was no use arguing, and in fact he didn't want to go to Lindisfarne alone. Tom's company made roaming the neighborhood an easygoing pleasure instead of a challenge. So he gave in.

At Chatton Castle, John waited outside the gates, on his horse, nervous that someone would come along and forbid his adventure. But Tom was inside only a few minutes. Soon enough they were on their way again. "Do you suppose people have really been swept away from the Lindisfarne path?" John asked.

"They say so," replied Tom.

"Can you swim?"

This earned John a sharp glance. Tom nodded. "Can you?"

"Not very well." There was a pond at John's school. But there was also a boisterous group who enjoyed holding smaller boys underwater until they choked. He avoided the activity.

"Well, it's fortunate we ain't going into any water then," said Tom.

He used the dry tone that John had noticed before but didn't always understand. Tom was an odd person. John's father would certainly say that he wasn't a gentleman and disapprove of the friendship. Yet Tom was quite intelligent. He knew all sorts of things. And he could talk to people—anybody, really—with an easy facility that filled John with awe.

An hour after this, Macklin and Roger returned to Chatton Castle from a visit to a new type of cottage Roger was having built on his estate. The appointment, long scheduled, had tasked Roger's patience to the limit. He'd wanted only to ride to Clough House and speak to Fenella.

Why had she refused to let him propose? She'd

known he meant to. He was certain of that. But she'd hurried away as if she didn't want to hear.

A stab of fear went through him. Surely she couldn't have kissed him in that way if she meant to reject him? But why not settle the matter then? Roger could think of nothing but his lovely neighbor. He ached with wanting her. Was she punishing him for past slights? Roger shook his head. That wasn't like her. She'd never done so in the past, even when he'd been at his most annoying. He admitted it; he'd behaved badly. Perhaps another apology was in order? He would gladly offer one, but that didn't feel like the crux of the matter.

Only Fenella could tell him. In fact, why had he come upstairs to change out of his riding clothes? He would go to Clough House right now, insist on speaking to her, and discover what was in her mind. Then he would do whatever was required to win her. *Anything*, Roger thought. *Anything*.

He turned to his bedchamber door, and was caught by a knock on the panels. Roger opened it to find Macklin on his threshold. "I have a note from Tom," the earl said. "He and Miss Fairclough's nephew have ridden up to Lindisfarne to look at the sands."

"Why would Tom do that?" Roger asked. "He knew John was forbidden to go there."

"I suspect that John refused to do as he was told."

All too likely, Roger thought. Fenella's nephew was an irrepressible sprig. Even so, he shouldn't have snapped at the boy as he did yesterday. He was aware of having gone beyond the line there.

"And when Tom couldn't dissuade him, he went along," Macklin added. "Taking care to leave word."

Roger nodded. Young Tom had shown himself to be remarkably levelheaded. "We'd better let the Faircloughs know. I'll go after them."

"I'll accompany you," Macklin said.

They returned to the stable. Roger sent a stable boy off with a note to Clough House and procured a length of rope before they mounted up and started off.

They'd hardly gone a mile when they overtook a gig on the road. Fenella held the reins.

Roger's pulse accelerated at the sight of her. If he'd had any doubts, which he had not, the perfection of her face and form, the spirit in her blue eyes, would have extinguished them.

"I was headed out to see old Mrs. Dorne when your message came," she said. "She's ill." A basket sat beside her on the seat. "I should have known that John wouldn't be able to resist going to Lindisfarne."

"Tom went along," said Macklin. "He'll look after him."

"I'm sure he'll try," said Fenella. "But John does not make that easy."

"We'll bring them back," said Roger.

"Naturally I'm going with you." She urged her horse to greater speed.

Naturally, Roger thought. She didn't hang back and wait for a problem to be solved for her. She didn't moan and lament. She was splendid in every way.

They traveled together toward the coast. When they reached the stretch opposite Lindisfarne Island, they found the boys' horses tied at the inland end of the path.

"The tide has turned," Roger said. "It's coming in."

"Surely they haven't gone over?" asked Fenella. She sounded angry and concerned in equal measure.

Waves were sheeting over the stretch of flat sand in front of the island. The water wasn't deep yet, but the strength of the flow was obvious. "I'll ride out along the path," said Roger. "Wait here."

"I want to come," said Fenella.

"You can't take a gig out there. The horse wouldn't be able to hold it against the waves."

She struggled with the truth of this before giving him a curt nod.

"There they are," said Macklin.

The two boys were pushing through the rising waves, knee high on Tom so far. They leaned against the pressure of the water rushing across the path. Roger could see that the sea was pulling at them. He knew the frightening force of the tide. He'd felt it. Tom was helping John along.

"Is John limping?" asked Fenella.

Roger urged his horse forward. Macklin came just behind him. They coaxed the animals into the flood, keeping to the marked path. Each wave was a warning of worse to come. At high tide, this stretch could be under nearly ten feet of water.

Tom raised an arm in what looked like welcome. The gesture was ill-judged, however, as John was pulled away from him by the slap of a larger wave and flattened on the sand.

Tom bent to help him up. John shook himself, coughing.

Water rushed around the horses' legs. Macklin's mount stumbled, and Roger's objected strongly to the path he was being asked to take. They soothed the animals and pressed on. Not too far now.

A surge of water struck Tom's back. He held on to John and endured the shove and pull. Briefly, he teetered, seeming about to go to one knee. For the first time since Roger had met the lad, he looked apprehensive. "Hang on," Roger shouted over the sound of the waves.

A few minutes later, the riders at last reached the two boys. With a mighty heave, Roger lifted John away from Tom and set the boy in front of him. John dripped on the horse's neck and Roger's riding breeches, soaked through. Tom took hold of the saddleback and leapt up behind Macklin. Carefully, they turned and moved toward dry land.

Water hissed across the sand and pushed at them. The horses hated the fact that they couldn't see their footing. They tossed their heads and threatened to sidle. Progress was growing extremely difficult when at last they reached the shore.

They stepped out of the sea and dismounted. Roger helped his passenger down. The boy was hunched and shivering. Fenella rushed forward.

"It was all my fault," John said before anyone could speak. "Tom didn't want to come at all. And he said we shouldn't go out on the path. He only followed me when I ran out. And then I fell in the water and hurt my ankle so that I couldn't hurry back. I'm a stupid fool. A heedless, stupid fool."

He spoke the final phrases as if he'd heard them before, Fenella thought. He sounded thoroughly miserable.

"Take off your coat," Roger said to him. "You're drenched."

John flinched as if this was an accusation. He clawed at his clothes.

Fenella eased his soaking coat off, and his sodden shirt, wishing she had something to wrap around him. She turned to find Roger holding out his own coat. The fact that it would soon be stained with seawater didn't seem to bother him.

"Tom didn't want to come," John repeated as she swathed him in the larger garment and wiped his face with a handkerchief from the pocket. "He tried to talk me out of it."

"I coulda argued harder," said Tom. He was only wet to the thigh, and he seemed to be recovering rapidly.

"No, I'm to blame." John stood straighter. He looked small and forlorn in the folds of Roger's coat. "You mustn't punish Tom."

Fenella could see that all the older males were impressed by his determination to take responsibility. "Come into the gig," she said. "We must get you home and into dry clothes." She beckoned Tom as well.

"I can ride," said Tom. "I'm not so wet. Only my shoes and stockings."

The fact that John didn't insist on riding as well showed how shaken he was. The others mounted up. Tom caught the reins of John's horse to lead him.

They started back, John hunched on the seat beside Fenella as if awaiting a blow. As the minutes passed without a word, he slowly straightened. "Aren't you going to scold me?" he asked finally.

"You seem to have a good sense of what you did wrong," Fenella replied.

"Yes, but it was idiotic, to go out onto the sand. Tom said I shouldn't."

"He was right."

"And I did it anyway. Like a fool."

"You seem to be sorry," Fenella said, while she thought that being a parent was a more complicated task than she'd previously realized.

"I am! Dreadfully sorry."

"Would you be sorrier if I scolded you?"

John considered this novel idea. "I don't *think* I would be," he said finally. "Perhaps I would feel worse."

"If I talked to you about how I had given you a good deal of freedom, and you had let me down? And about how you might have gotten Tom killed?"

John hunched lower again. "Yes. Then."

She couldn't bring herself to rail at a child who seemed so full of regret. "Well, we will take those points as understood then. Be sure you remember them."

He gaped at her. "You aren't going to punish me?"

"Oh, I'm certainly going to do *that*. You are now confined to the house and garden. The stables will be instructed not to give you a horse, should you ask."

His face showed chagrin, then acceptance. "But, for how long?"

"We will see," said Fenella.

"Criminals get a set sentence in court," said John, some of his rebellious spirit surfacing.

"Would you like me to say for the remainder of your visit to Clough House?"

"No! Never mind."

Fenella nodded. At the moment she was inclined to keep him under her eye until she sent him back to school. Hideous visions of telling her sister that her son had drowned at Lindisfarne were only now receding from her brain. She glanced over to see that John had lifted a corner of the napkin covering the basket she'd brought. "There's cakes in here," he said.

"Yes, for Mrs. Dorne. Who's ill. And old."

"Oh." He let the napkin drop. They moved on along the road. John pulled Roger's coat closer around him. "It's just that I'm so hungry," he added. "The water was dashed cold. And I've had nothing to eat since breakfast."

Having seen the prodigious amounts of food this one small boy could consume, Fenella relented. "Go on then."

She expected him to dive in; instead, he signaled to Tom. When the older boy rode closer, John offered him the napkin filled with cakes. Tom took some with thanks and a grin. Only then did John devour one of the small pastries, in two enormous bites. "Good," he mumbled around the large mouthful. In a remarkably short time, the basket was empty.

They reached the turn where they would separate to go to their different houses.

Fenella noticed that John was shivering harder. The wind had come up, cooling the August day, and clouds threatened rain. She slapped the reins to hurry the gig along.

"I'll come along with you to retrieve my coat," Roger said to Fenella.

"I can bring it, my lord," said Tom. "I'll be return-ing the horses."

Roger looked thwarted. He was an attractive sight in his shirtsleeves, Fenella thought. It would be pleas-ant to have him riding along at her side. But John was her first priority right now.

"The bishop is calling on your mother today," said Lord Macklin. His face as he looked from Roger to Fenella showed remarkably acute curiosity. "We promised not to leave her to entertain him alone."

Roger didn't curse, but he looked as if he would have liked to. He spurred his horse up to John's side of the gig. "There's no harm in searching for adven-tures," he said to Fenella's nephew. "You've a bold spirit. You'll learn to manage them better."

John perked up. That had been kind, Fenella thought, particularly after their last prickly encounter.

Roger gave her a look that warmed her down to her toes before he dropped back and turned with Macklin toward Chatton Castle.

Their smaller party hastened to Clough House, where John was bundled up to his room to change clothes. Fenella went to her own room to shed her riding habit. When she left it, and passed her father's bedchamber, she was surprised to hear John's voice within. Her nephew wasn't usually eager to visit his grandfather. Yet he was in there. The door was ajar; his tones were plain. Fenella paused to listen.

"And then the tide came pouring over the sand," John said. "It felt like a huge hand pushing against my legs. I could hardly stand up. But I knew if I fell, the water would sweep me out to sea. So I leaned against the current and stepped very carefully, even though I'd twisted my ankle."

"That was brave of you," said her father.

"Well, Tom helped me. I couldn't have done it without him."

"Did he?" The old man's voice had taken on the vagueness that meant he didn't recognize the name. "Who are you?" he added.

"I'm your grandson," John replied with a touch of indignation.

"Oh. Are you?" he replied. Fenella could imagine the frown of bewilderment on her father's face. She saw it more and more these days. But this time he retrieved some information. "Greta's son? Or Nora's?"

"My cousin Frederick is only four years old!"

"Who?"

"Greta is my mama."

"So you're a Symmes?"

"John Symmes."

"Eh. I thought Greta's son had some silly grand name. Sanford or the like."

"Sherrington," answered the boy with loathing.

"That's it. A ridiculous mouthful. Thought so when I first heard."

"I hate it!" said John.

"Good for you."

"They refuse to call me John at school," the boy added.

"Tell 'em your father won't pay their fees unless they do," replied Fenella's father. Outside the door, she smiled.

"But that isn't true."

"Are they likely to ask him?"

There was a short silence. Fenella could almost hear John thinking this over. "Probably not," the boy said finally. "They wouldn't want to risk annoying him. Papa can be quite cutting when he's angry."

"I remember that about him," said the old man dryly. "Wondered a bit when Greta... Well, never mind. At least Greta's not a sour spinster like Fenella."

"What do you mean? Aunt Fenella's a great gun. She's been very kind to me. And fair as fair. She doesn't even mind snakes."

Not precisely true, Fenella thought. But she was touched.

"Snakes?" said her father. "Well, it's true she's not afraid of much. Not afraid of *me*. She's stubborn though. Willful as a wildcat."

"I think she's splendid."

"Do you? Ha." There was another pause before her father said, "You might be right."

Blinking back tears, Fenella continued on her way.

Ten

Sitting on what had become their habitual bench in the garden, Arthur and his hostess watched the master of Chatton Castle pace up one path and down another. He walked quickly, head bent, hands clasped behind his back. Though he'd greeted them when he first appeared, he seemed to have forgotten them almost at once. "I've rarely known Roger to be so preoccupied," said Lady Chatton.

"When I bid him good day at breakfast, he said, 'That remains to be seen,'" replied Arthur. "Then he refused my company on a ride and rushed out."

"Oh dear. How rude."

They eyed the subject of their speculations.

"His solitary expedition doesn't seem to have pleased him," Arthur observed.

"No, I would say he's…brooding. Yes, that's it." She nodded.

"A problem, do you think?"

"He seems to think he has one," Lady Chatton answered.

"I have a notion it's to do with Miss Fairclough."

"Perhaps we should ask him about it."

"I don't think he'd like that very much."

"I'm sure you're right." Arthur rose and offered his arm. Roger's mother looked up at him. Then, blue eyes twinkling, she stood and joined him.

Roger kicked at a pebble that lay in the middle of the garden path. It flew off the toe of his boot, struck the trunk of an elm, and bounced back. Fenella hadn't appeared for her ride today. Granted, she hadn't promised to come. And she'd told him from the beginning that the demands of her father's illness might keep her in sometimes. Understandable. But he longed to see her. Alone, as they'd been at the raspberry thicket, not surrounded by servants and lads with snakes and her gloating father at Clough House. Mr. Fairclough would gloat. There was no doubt about that.

He turned, and started in surprise. His mother and his noble houseguest were standing in his path, looking brightly inquisitive. Like foxhounds testing a scent, he thought. And then nearly said *nonsense* out loud.

"Did you have a pleasant ride?" asked Macklin.

"No," said Roger.

"That's too bad," replied his mother. "Why not?"

He should have said yes, Roger realized. Now he had to think of a reason to fob them off. He flailed about mentally, until it occurred to him that excuses weren't really necessary. His intentions were clear. He had no nefarious plan. And he could trust the discretion of these two absolutely. Perhaps he should simply ask their advice. He met his mother's interested gaze, then Macklin's. A man couldn't ask for more sympathetic listeners, or wiser ones. "You like Fenella Fairclough, Mama."

"I do indeed," she replied.

"You wanted me to marry her five years ago, when Papa was urging it."

"I did at first, but it would have been a mistake." She shook her head. "The people you were then wouldn't have gotten on well together."

That was true. Mainly because of him, Roger thought. But Fenella, too. "We're different now," he said. "Both of us."

His mother nodded, watching his face.

"So the case is altered."

"Are you saying you want to marry her now?"

"Yes. You'll say I made a great fuss about nothing in that case," Roger replied. "And wasted a deal of time and…emotion." Mr. Fairclough certainly would. He knew Fenella dreaded that.

"I won't." Her eyes were sympathetic. "We can only do our best at any given time. Hindsight is deceptive."

He hadn't known much five years ago, Roger acknowledged silently. A load of difficulties had educated him since then.

"She seems a very appealing young lady," said Macklin.

"I'd be delighted to welcome her into our family," said Roger's mother.

They spoke as if the match was settled just because he desired it. "I'm not sure what she wants though."

"But you have some reason to think she feels the same?" asked his mother.

He couldn't tell them about the kisses. He wouldn't

expose Fenella that way. "I believe so, but...circum-stances intervened before I could ask her."

"What sort of circumstances?" asked Macklin.

"Her nephew. Snakes."

"Snakes!" his mother exclaimed.

"The pursuit of snakes." Roger strove to recall the conversation that came after their embraces. He'd been muddled by desire. And anger at the interruption. "She said I should take time to think. And be certain." She'd mentioned Arabella. Roger winced.

"And have you?" asked his mother.

"Have I what?"

"Thought? Now that the situation has...cooled."

Could she read his mind? Of course not. But Roger flushed at the memory of lying with Fenella in the grass. "I'm certain she's the bride for me."

"Well then, you must ask her, and find out if she feels the same."

"She might appreciate a formal offer," suggested Macklin. "On your knee, you know. Ladies like that."

"Do we?" said Roger's mother with a smile. "You seem to know a good deal about it."

"Pure hearsay," answered Macklin. They smiled at each other like firm friends.

This was a good idea. He could do that. "I'll go to Clough House now."

"No time like the present," said Macklin.

Scarcely seeming to hear, Roger rushed off.

"There seems to be no need for a push," Macklin added when the younger man had disappeared into the castle.

"Not at the moment." Lady Chatton shrugged. "We must see how he does."

"You think there will be problems?"

"Roger isn't eloquent. His tongue can get in the way of what he wishes to say."

"Sincerity counts for a good deal in these matters," said Macklin.

"When did you become an expert on matrimony?" She laughed at his wry expression. "I shall love having Fenella for my daughter-in-law. How odd that it should come out this way. Raymond would—"

"Laugh?" Macklin suggested.

"No. He'd be odiously smug. As will Mr. Fairclough. I hope he can restrain his gloating until the match is secure."

"Surely he couldn't spoil it?"

"You might be surprised."

◈

Simpson came hurrying down the upper corridor of Clough House toward Fenella. "Your father's asking for you again, miss."

He'd had a bad night. He'd tried to get up and go outside three times. And when he couldn't manage to move from the bed, he'd filled the air with shouted profanity, convinced that an enemy had imprisoned him with invisible bonds. Fenella had helped the valet and William grapple with him, and been excoriated for her trouble. It was lowering to be so roundly cursed by one's own father.

The struggle had left her tired and made her feel that tears were hovering at the back of her throat. It was so difficult to watch Papa's vitality and under-standing draining away with each passing day. She often felt alone with the melancholy and helplessness, despite the staff in the house. They counted on her to be in command, to react with calm good sense. There was no one to confide in, no place to take her worries and doubts.

Roger would listen, she thought suddenly. If she told him, he'd concentrate all his attention on her concerns. He would tell her she was doing splendidly, that the estate was in prime shape under her manage-ment, that her father was fortunate to have her at his side. And then he would urge her to rely on him. She could almost hear him becoming tangled in words, trying to convey these two different sentiments at once. The idea made her smile. He was a man of action rather than speech.

Which took her back to the raspberry thicket and the brief time she'd spent in his arms. Too brief. She'd mused on it, dreamed of it. When she saw him again, they would find some time to repeat those dizzying kisses.

He would call today, surely? He'd been so eager to speak. A cold chill went through Fenella at the pos-sibility that he'd changed his mind. But of course she didn't want him if he'd changed his mind. Except she did want him, desperately.

"There you are," her father said when she entered his room. "Where do you get to? I've been wanting to speak to you."

She'd been with him not half an hour ago. But he didn't remember such things these days.

"You must do something about Nora's temper, Mary."

He thought she was her mother. Fenella didn't even resemble her. Greta looked much more like their departed parent.

"She was screaming with rage in the stables," he continued. "Over some triviality about her pony. You must take steps to curb her. She was truly excessive."

Like you, Fenella thought silently. Many had noticed this similarity between her father and sister. She didn't remember this particular instance, but Nora's capacity for anger was famous. Or infamous.

"This is your area, Mary," he said. "You produced all these daughters. You must do something. Get them in hand!"

"I'm Fenella, Papa," she said. "Mama has been dead for eight years."

He blinked at her, eyes bleary. For a moment he looked frightened and confused; then his mouth tightened and turned down. "Of course I know that. Third daughter. Not the charm."

And so they were back to the somber present.

"A good shot though," he continued, to Fenella's surprise. "Greta wouldn't hold a gun, and Nora was too hotheaded to take proper aim. But you were a different matter. Used to tell them at my club how you shot the pip out of the ace of spades. Twice, so it wasn't a fluke."

Had he actually been proud of her skill? Fenella didn't remember him saying so to *her*. But it warmed her to know that he'd praised her to others.

"Had those two decks put away somewhere. What's become of them?"

Fenella had no notion. Had he actually kept them as proof of her marksmanship? She blinked back the hovering tears.

"It was almost like having a son," her father finished.

And thus he spoiled the moment, she thought. Why must he always do so?

He was frowning at her. "If you'd just been born a boy, all would have been well."

Something in Fenella snapped. "All?" she repeated. "What does that mean, precisely? Mama wouldn't have sickened and died so young? Nora would be meek as milk? Last year's grain harvest wouldn't have been spoilt by a hailstorm? You wouldn't be ill now?"

His head wobbled in a sort of half negative. His good hand twitched on the coverlet. Feeling guilty for her outburst, Fenella saw the thread of the argument leave him. His eyes grew vague. "Where's Chatton gone?" he said.

"He died last—"

"Not him," her father interrupted. "The younger one. His son. The one you were meant to marry. He was here." He gave her a defiant look, daring her to contradict him.

Fenella nodded. Her father's memory was erratic. He forgot so much, but then he remembered things one wished he would forget. Could he have sensed that her thoughts were full of Roger?

"I cannot believe you're making the same mistake twice," he went on in a fretful tone. "If you would just put forward a little effort, you could have him. He's out there for the plucking. Why not grasp your chance? You'd outrank your sisters as a marchioness. You'd like that."

Fenella was surprised. She didn't think he'd noticed the friction with her older sisters. She was even more surprised to find that the idea had an appeal. She almost told him that she thought she would marry Roger. But she couldn't quite give him the satisfaction after his criticisms about her sex.

"You're less stupid than I used to think," her father went on, destroying her impulse to confide in him. "Your grandmother did that much for you. And you're not bad looking." He surveyed her as if she was a brood mare. "Not as pretty as Greta or as lively as Nora, but well enough."

He'd always had an instinct for the low blow. Lively as Nora who shrieked at her pony? "I don't wish to talk about this, Papa."

"Why not? There's no impediment now. Everyone's forgotten that stupid story Chatton spread about. Saying you killed his wife by encouraging her to go out riding in a storm." He snorted.

She'd thought he hadn't heard that, shut up in his sickroom as he was.

Her father gazed at her. "You didn't, did you?"

"Are you seriously asking me that question, Papa?"

"You're right. Don't tell me."

"Of course I did not!" Fenella exclaimed. "I tried to persuade her not to go."

"Well, that was foolish."

How could this be her father, Fenella thought. Was he really advocating murder? This must be his illness speaking.

"It was too much to *send* her out into the storm," he continued. "I see that. But why argue with her? It wasn't your idea. Let the chit soak herself."

"Because it was the right thing to do!"

He made a derisive sound. "She was no great loss. Pretty, I'll give you that. Deuced pretty. But cold. Hoity-toity marchioness. She wasn't liked, you know."

"Please don't say such things, Papa." His attitude and tone saddened her. She'd thought him a better man than this.

"You always were a wet goose." He spoke with a kind of contemptuous fondness that grated on Fenella more than anger.

"Promise me you won't talk about this with anyone else," she said. "Not Simpson. Not anyone."

"I have no one to talk to," he complained.

She started to press him. But her father's promises held no weight these days. He forgot.

"You're doing this just to spite me, aren't you?" He picked at the bedclothes.

"Doing what?" Trying to keep him from ruining his reputation?

"You refuse to admit that I was right about Chatton. You'll throw away your future rather than do so. You're that stubborn!"

His mind drifted irresistibly back to his grievances. Nothing else stuck any more. Fenella looked at the prominent bones of his hands, the overly thin body under the bedclothes. Once, she'd wanted to prove her father wrong about many things. Suddenly, that seemed less important. She wondered if there was any chance of a better understanding between them before he was gone forever.

Fenella was diverted by the sound of horses through the open window. She went to look out. A carriage had arrived in front of the house. A footman had sprung down and was helping an older lady out. As she stepped onto the gravel, hoofbeats heralded a rider, and Roger came riding down the drive toward the front door. The lady turned. The footman handed another older female from the carriage.

Roger pulled up at the sight of them. He paused, spoke to the ladies, then turned his mount away and trotted off.

Fenella watched him go with a keen sense of disappointment. She needed to see him, for a number of reasons. Roger's expression, insofar as she could see it from this distance, had been odd. "I must go, Papa," she said. "We have visitors."

"To see me?"

Perhaps they had come to cheer her father, Fenella thought as another older lady emerged from the coach. She couldn't think of another reason for this group to arrive together. "I'll bring them up to you after a bit." She went to receive them.

Fenella found four women of her mother's generation in the drawing room, standing in a group that had the distinct feeling of a delegation. They included the leading female figures of her neighborhood. Colonel Patterson's extremely correct wife was there, and Lady Prouse, the spouse of the local baronet. Mrs. McIlwaine, whose husband was the largest landowner in the area after Roger, stood next to Mrs. Byrne. These latter two were the mothers of Roger's old friends. Fenella wondered that the vicar's wife was not among them. She usually formed part of their distaff cabal.

The callers looked serious when she greeted them and asked them to sit down. Fenella had ordered refreshment to be brought on her way downstairs.

"We felt it best to come and speak to you," said Mrs. Patterson.

"To me?" So they hadn't come to see her father.

"Because of something that has begun to happen in the neighborhood," said Mrs. Byrne.

Fenella tried to imagine what could it be. If the estate's cattle had broken loose and ravaged a farmer's fields, he wouldn't send these grand ladies to protest. If they wanted her help in some charitable endeavor, they'd send a note. And expect her to cough up a donation. Which she would. There was no need for a formal request. These ladies ran local society without her help.

"Some very strange letters have been arriving," said Lady Prouse. "Disturbing. Each of us has received one."

"Delivered by hand," said Mrs. Byrne. "Not by the mail."

"Anonymous letters," said Mrs. Patterson. "Which are a despicable thing."

Fenella stared at the four venerable faces confronting her. A tremor went through her suddenly. "What kind of letters?"

"Outrageous ones," replied Mrs. Patterson.

"Dreadful," declared Mrs. McIlwaine.

"Reviving that ridiculous story about the young marchioness's death," said Lady Prouse.

"Story?" But Fenella knew the answer.

"These letters claim that you egged her on to ride out in the storm," said Mrs. McIlwaine.

"And that you were well aware that she had weak lungs," added Mrs. Byrne. "And was particularly susceptible to chills. Had been all her life."

Was there a hint of relish in her voice, Fenella wondered. No, she was imagining it.

"Of course none of us ever believed you were at fault," said Colonel Patterson's stately wife. "Not to speak ill of the dead, but the young marchioness was a headstrong girl."

"Very *modern* manners," said the baronet's spouse. "No one imagined you could suggest anything to *that* young woman."

Yet all four ladies were looking at her, waiting for something. "Of course they're not true," said Fenella, humiliated by the need to deny. "I begged Arabella not to ride out."

"You went with her," said Lady Prouse.

"When I saw that she wouldn't be convinced, I did. To make sure she got home safely." Arabella had been in such a reckless mood that day. Fenella had worried about a fall from her horse.

Mrs. Byrne looked reluctant, but it didn't keep her from asking, "*Did* you know that she had a history of lung complaints?"

"I did not. She said something about it after she became ill." Did they not believe her?

"Miss Fairclough is not required to defend herself," said Mrs. Patterson. "We didn't come here for that. We all know her and admire her character." She met

Fenella's eyes with a grave glance. "We thought you should know, however."

Fenella supposed she appreciated the information. This was better than whispers behind her back.

"And decide what to do," said Mrs. McIlwaine.

"It's difficult to counter anonymous accusations," said Fenella. Indeed it was nearly impossible. There was no one to confront, no forum to declare the truth. Some would assume that the writer knew secrets. "But I've done nothing wrong."

"Of course not," said Mrs. Byrne.

"If there were a way to track down the source," said Mrs. Patterson.

All four ladies looked at Fenella. "I have no idea who would send such sneaking letters," she said. Hand delivery suggested they came from nearby. "The idea that a neighbor would do this is simply horrible." It made her want to cry.

There were murmurs of agreement from the others.

"We've inquired about how they arrived," said Mrs. Byrne. "But no one seems to have seen anything."

A silence fell. What did they expect her to do? Fenella wondered.

"It's just, the timing is rather awkward, as you and Chatton are...renewing your childhood friendship," said Mrs. McIlwaine.

The sentence descended on Fenella like a smothering blanket of fog. Of course people had noticed her outings with Roger. They had undoubtedly passed numerous unseen observers on their rides. *Clandestine* was not really a possibility in a small country neighborhood. Color flooded her cheeks as she wondered if anyone had seen them at the berry patch.

"We thought we might offer to help, as you have no mother of your own," said Mrs. Byrne.

"You'll tell everyone that the accusations are untrue," Fenella said.

Her callers nodded, but they didn't look satisfied.

"We could give Chatton a push," said Lady Prouse. "We're all well acquainted with Lady Chatton, of course. We could enlist her in the cause. An announced engagement would show this letter writer that his, or her, slanders were futile."

"I don't want—" began Fenella.

"And a fine match it would be," said Mrs. McIlwaine, speaking at the same time.

Fenella looked at her visitors, leaning forward, a cadre eager for action. What made them so ready to arrange younger people's lives? This was just what had happened to Roger before, when he'd been manipulated into marriage. That couldn't happen. She'd rather return to Scotland. "I would prefer to manage matters myself," she said. She needed to speak to Roger.

Her guests looked doubtful.

Fenella set herself to convincing them that she was quite able to deal with her own affairs. And after a good deal more conversation, accompanied by tea and Madeira cake, she thought she'd done so. The ladies departed with expressions of goodwill and promises of support. And at last Fenella was free to contemplate her situation in private.

A clandestine courtship had been a ridiculous idea, she thought as she went upstairs to her room. They weren't children any more, to be meeting by an oak tree and roaming the countryside. She'd let herself be carried away by Roger's enthusiasm. And more than that, she admitted.

In her bedchamber, Fenella looked in the mirror and saw the person her grandmother had called forth gazing back at her. Features firmed by intelligence and resolution. Eyes that saw reality. Which brought an ironic smile to her reflection's lips.

The last week had felt like removing a corset pulled far too tight. After so much denying and suppressing, suddenly there was no need to pretend she was indifferent to Roger. All sorts of memories and feelings had come bubbling up.

She'd been drawn to him all her life, she admitted now. She'd followed his antics as a child, admired his courage and sheer effrontery. She'd longed to be one of his cronies, careening over the countryside, wild and free. And when their fathers had first suggested marriage, right at the beginning, she hadn't been opposed. Here in the privacy of her room she admitted it to herself. She'd been seventeen! She'd concocted a brief, romantic fantasy of being Roger's wife and a marchioness, living in Chatton Castle, the neighborhood at her feet.

That had gone up in smoke at his reaction. "Sodding sheep," she said to the mirror. Of course she'd rejected him after that. She'd had some spirit, even then. She'd gone away, and then he had, and come home married to someone else. The past had to be buried. She'd had to do what was right. Fenella had applied a thick veneer of correctness, and avoided him.

And then to top it all off, Roger had blamed her for Arabella's death, loudly and publicly. Fenella frowned at the mirror. She'd understood some of what he'd felt, but that was no excuse. He'd created a wretched tangle, and no doubt inspired this sneaking letter writer who had popped up at just the wrong moment.

She turned away from her reflection. What to do now? She didn't think anyone had believed that she'd encouraged Arabella to ride out into a storm. But if she was sneaking out to meet Roger, some might wonder what they had to hide. Which was nothing! She'd done nothing wrong. She'd tried to be Arabella's friend, difficult as that had been. And in return she'd received a load of unpleasantness.

She wasn't suddenly free, Fenella thought as she left her room. That had been an illusion, born of an exhilarating gallop and some delirious kisses, and now destroyed by a few lines of malicious ink.

Eleven

As Fenella rode out the next morning, the August day promised to be hot. The house had felt stifling, though part of that might be due to the news she'd received rather than the weather, she thought. She went to the old oak in hopes of seeing Roger alone. She wasn't prepared to call at the castle just now, but she needed to speak to him.

She didn't have to linger long before he arrived. "It's so pleasant to find you here instead of James and Alistair and Donald waiting to plan some minor deviltry," he said as he brought his horse up beside hers.

"Is it?"

"The last time we four gathered, we decided to set a litter of piglets loose at the church fete."

"I remember that."

He looked down at her. The tenderness in his eyes rendered her momentarily speechless. The last time they'd been alone, they'd been drowned in kisses.

"Where shall we ride?" he continued. "It's going to be a hot day. I wish I could take you swimming."

"In the sea?" The currents made that a chancy

proposition, even if the shore hadn't been unaccept-
ably public.

"No, I know a little pond in a hollow on the side of
a hill. It's hidden by bushes and banks of reeds. Spring
fed, wonderfully cool on the hottest day. We boys
used to swim there."

"And we'd undoubtedly be caught by someone if
we ventured there."

"I don't think so. Did you ever hear of the place?
Years ago, I mean."

Fenella shook her head.

"So there is one secret we managed to keep."
Roger seemed inordinately pleased by the idea.

What a joy it would be to throw off her clothes
and plunge into cool water and consign all her worries to perdition! But she'd discovered a dreadful
thing in the night, alone in the darkness. Troubling
half dreams had plagued her. While she was not
asleep but drifting, she'd found that the advent of
these malicious letters had roused the timid girl she
used to be. Something about older ladies coming to
warn her—as her mother had so often scolded about
standards that she'd never seemed able to meet—had
pushed her back into the past. The disappointment of
one's parents was a heavy weight, she thought as she
and Roger set off across the field. And the sense of
being whispered about throughout the neighborhood
was as bad, or worse. The young, fearful Fenella was
urging caution, recalling old mockery and hurts. *She*
wanted to hide or run away, far from prying eyes.
It was mortifying to find that her weakness was
still there. She wanted to take bold steps, to dismiss

mean-spirited talk with a sweep of her hand, but she couldn't quite.

"We could go and look at it," Roger said. "I don't suppose we can actually swim."

What was he... Oh, the pond. "John seems to pop up everywhere."

"True. And Tom as well." Roger frowned. "If they find the place and blab about it—" He brightened. "They'll both be leaving soon. I'll swear them to secrecy."

Fenella had to laugh. "Would you really swim there now?"

"Of course. It's a marvelous spot. You'd love it, I promise. Let's go and see."

"Not today."

"What's wrong?" he said. He examined her face. "I can tell something's wrong."

"Can you?" If she told him about the letters, he'd be furious. If she didn't, he would hear anyway, probably after he made some embarrassing misstep. "Papa is declining. I can't stay out long."

"Is that all?" He held up a hand. "I don't mean it's a small thing, but he has been ill for a long time."

Of course she had to tell him. For all sorts of reasons, but mainly she didn't want to hide things from him. That never answered.

"Fenella?"

"Something's happened."

"Not good, I take it."

"No." Fenella took a breath and told him the bad news that the neighborhood committee had brought her.

Roger began to mutter well before she was done. Curses, she thought, though he kept them inaudible. He crushed his mount's reins in his fist. "Damn the infernal impudence," he said when she finished. He looked as if he'd very much like to hit something.

"So you see, this clandestine game you imagined isn't possible. People will begin to wonder what we have to hide. Indeed, I think we will have to stand back a bit and—"

"I'll fix this," he interrupted. "It's my fault. I'll make it right."

She was reminded of John's insistence on responsibility.

"I'll start at once," Roger added. He was appalled. "You may depend on me." In the future, he vowed, he would hold his tongue when he felt the impulse to place blame. It didn't matter how difficult words were for him, he *would* resist.

"I don't see what you can do. Contradicting anonymous letters is like trying to bat away fog." She grimaced. "People always quote Shakespeare about the lady who 'doth protest too much.' It's no wonder no one likes Queen Gertrude."

"Queen…who?"

"I think we'll have to avoid each other for a bit," she said. The thought of going back to their distant acquaintanceship made her sad. But it had worked.

"On the contrary, we'll announce our engagement. And let the insinuating coward of a letter writer go hang." Roger grimaced. "That went too fast. I meant to propose in form. Will you get down so I can kneel at your feet?"

Fenella was torn between laughter and tears.

"Macklin thought... What I mean is, you must know how ardently I wish to marry you."

"This news is pushing you to speak."

"No, it's not. I've been trying to do so for days." He rode closer and reached for her hand. "I was on my way to ask when those interfering busybodies came to call on you."

"They thought to help." Fenella imagined the storm of gossip an engagement would rouse in the wake of those letters. "We can't do it now."

"That doesn't sound like the intrepid woman I know. We can. We'll simply face them down."

Would she disappoint him now? Fenella wondered. As she had others. "It's easier for you."

"Are you saying that you don't wish to marry me?" asked Roger quietly.

"No."

"So you will? Once I make things right and prove myself worthy of your hand?"

"Of course you are worthy—"

"I will," he interrupted. "You'll see. I'll begin immediately."

Before Fenella could suggest that he take some care with whatever he planned, he was riding away.

Could she have done anything differently? She wondered as she rode home alone. Was there some action she could have taken, or refrained from taking, that would have improved their situation? She couldn't think of any.

❧

The following Sunday, Fenella stood in the churchyard after the service beckoning to John, who had
scampered off into the long grass of the graveyard. She
wanted to go, but her nephew had accorded that desire
as much attention as usual. It was as nothing compared
with the possibility of snakes among the headstones.

Her gaze strayed to Roger, who was talking ear-
nestly to a group of their neighbors a little distance
away. "He's telling them that you absolutely did *not*
encourage his late wife's disastrous ride in the rain,"
said a melodious voice at her side. "He's been telling
everyone this morning." Fenella turned to find that
the vicar's wife had joined her. "I'd forgotten all about
that ridiculous story," the woman added. Apparently
she still hadn't received any of those wretched letters.

Lady Prouse came over to them. "Chatton is
explaining how wrong he was to blame you for his
wife's death," she said to Fenella. "He's rather making
a point of it. Do you think that's…altogether wise?"

Fenella didn't. But she didn't see what she could do
about it just now. She hid a sigh. For all the traits she
admired in Roger, she could not accuse him of finesse.
If she'd known he meant to do this, she wouldn't have
come to church today. Of course that would have
roused another flurry of speculation.

"Did you tell him—" began Lady Prouse. She
glanced at the vicar's wife and fell silent.

She was glad Mrs. Cheeve hadn't been told about
the anonymous letters. The vicar's wife enjoyed being
excessively shocked. "Perhaps he's sorry for having said
it in the first place," Fenella said lightly, as if this was a
matter of indifference to her. She didn't see what else to

do. She shrugged, disavowing the vagaries of the male sex. "Excuse me, I seem to have lost my nephew."

John had disappeared, taking advantage of his first foray outside the Clough House garden walls in days. She needed to fetch him and depart. Fenella walked through the gate into the graveyard. There was no sign of him. She moved around the corner of the church. It was a relief to be out of sight of the congregation. "John?" she called.

Roger appeared, following in her footsteps. He looked for her, smiled, and strode over. "I've been contradicting that stupid story," he told her. He seemed proud of himself.

"Yes, and making everyone who'd forgotten think of it again," Fenella replied. She couldn't keep a touch of asperity out of her voice. "And wonder why you're bringing it up. And so someone will mention the letters."

Roger took a step back. When she put it that way… Well, he saw her point. He ought to have consulted Macklin before he began talking, he thought. Or his mother. Or both. He'd just been so eager to make amends.

"I must find John." She called. "John?"

The boy popped up from behind a monument on the far side of the graveyard. "I've found a gigantic toad!" he called triumphantly. He held up the animal, its body much bigger than the palm of his hand. Its long legs flailed in the air.

John brought the creature over to them like a prize. It looked like every other toad Roger had seen— warty gray-green skin, bulging eyes, gangling limbs.

He didn't want to discuss toads. He wanted to explain to Fenella. She was gazing over his shoulder now. Roger turned to look and discovered the vicar's wife, peering around the corner of the church as if searching for something.

"Show Mrs. Cheeve your toad," Fenella said to John.

John did so. The vicar's wife looked startled. She pulled back and disappeared.

A sound escaped Fenella. It wasn't quite a laugh, Roger thought. Not exactly a sigh.

"I wish I had a cage to put it in," said John. "I suppose I can hold it in the carriage."

"I think you'd better leave it," said Fenella, sounding harried. "It will be happier here."

John slumped. "Someday, I'll have a proper place to care for animals. With the right food and everything." Sulkily, he set the toad down. It hopped quickly away.

"We must go," said Fenella.

"When will I see you again?" Roger asked.

The vicar's wife appeared again. Arm in arm with Lady Prouse, she walked toward them. The sight seemed to alarm Fenella. "Come along," she said to John.

Roger's heart sank. He'd put his foot in it again. Perhaps he'd said too much. Or chosen the wrong bit to tell. It was so hard to judge about that. And now she was walking away from him.

He followed her to her gig, trying to find better words. Most people had gone. His mother's carriage wasn't there. The vicar's wife trailed after them for some reason. Macklin waited with their horses.

He handed Fenella into the gig as John jumped up on the other side. "I will come to visit your father."

"That would be kind, but he's not really up to visitors now."

She used a polite tone that made Roger want to grind his teeth. Yet when she looked at him, he thought her eyes brimmed with sadness. Could that be right? She drove away before he could think of a way to find out.

Roger stomped over to his horse and mounted up. Macklin followed suit, and they rode together toward the castle. Roger wrestled with his temper. Anger hadn't helped anything before. "You always say the right thing," he said after a while.

"Hardly," replied Macklin.

"No, you're known for it. Everyone says you're a master of conversation."

"An exaggeration."

Roger ignored the older man's humility. "I'm much more likely to say the wrong thing. I have a…a kind of genius for it. Words just pop out. And go on after I should stop. Because I don't realize until afterward, mostly."

"Are you thinking of some particular instance? Today?"

"I was trying to retract that stupid tale about Miss Fairclough that I was fool enough to start. Because… but I suppose you already know." Roger sighed. His mother was probably aware as well. She tended to know everything. Though in that case, it was surprising she hadn't mentioned the letters.

"Know?"

"About the letters."

"What letters?"

"You haven't heard?" Perhaps no one had dared bring the news to Chatton Castle?

"I don't know what you mean," Macklin said.

As they rode on toward his home, Roger explained. When he'd finished, Macklin looked angry. "Despicable. I hate a sneak."

"So you see why I was contradicting the story, but Fen—Miss Fairclough said I just made everyone think of it again."

"Ah."

"How can I deny the gossip without mentioning the circumstance?" Roger complained.

"You cannot, of course," said Macklin. "But a subtler approach might be warranted."

"Subtle!" Roger hated that word—that indefinable, unattainable state. Truthfully, he didn't believe anyone really knew what it meant. People lobbed the term at him like a smothering pillow. "Can you teach me to be subtle?"

Macklin gazed back at him with sympathy and great kindness. And possibly a tinge of amusement? Roger tried not to resent that. "I don't know, Chatton. Subtlety may be alien to your temperament."

"My temperament can go to perdition! It's been nothing but trouble."

Macklin bit back a smile.

"You may think it a joke," said Roger. "But from my side, it's not."

"I don't think it. And I would be pleased to help you. It seems to me that we need to find this letter writer and expose them. We can make them tell the truth. Anonymous writers are cowards."

"But difficult to root out." Roger wasn't optimistic about the chances.

"I may have an idea about that."

His confident tone gave Roger hope as they rode under the arch into the castle courtyard.

Several miles away, driving the gig though the gates of Clough House, Fenella fought an urge to cry. Last night, she'd dreamed of kissing Roger again. Very vividly. But then today the sidelong glances of her neighbors had rasped. Her inner landscape felt like a battleground, she thought, and blinked more rapidly. "Are you all right, Aunt Fenella?" asked her nephew.

If John noticed her turmoil, it must be blatant. "Yes," she lied.

"I can take the gig around to the stable, if you like."

More than anything, Fenella wanted the solitude of her bedchamber. She handed John the reins. "Thank you," she said, climbing down and striding into the house.

✎

In the predawn dark the next morning, Fenella was roused from her bed by her father's valet. "He's much worse, miss," Simpson said. Fenella pulled on her dressing gown and slippers and hurried to his room.

Her father lay limp, his breath an odd gasping rattle. His once-sturdy frame hardly raised the bedclothes, and his skin had gone ashen.

"I think this may be the end, miss," said Simpson, his lined face creased with melancholy.

Fenella had known her father was failing, but she found she still wasn't ready for this news. She'd thought he would hang on longer. Just yesterday he'd been arguing in his old fashion. "I must send for my sisters."

The valet shook his head as if to say they'd never make it in time. "Better have someone go for the vicar."

Fenella nodded permission for this errand. She had kept Greta and Nora apprised of Papa's deteriorating condition. She'd even urged them to come and see him, though she knew such visits would be full of friction. Her sisters had passed off her concerns as overblown, as if Fenella, who was here on the spot, knew far less about their father's capacities than they did. She'd send messengers south at first light. They must come now.

Taking her father's hand, Fenella sat down beside the bed. "Papa?" The ends of his fingers were cold. He was drifting away from life. Despite their disagreements, she felt a pang of grief. "Papa?" she said again.

His eyes opened, though they didn't seem to focus. "Mary?" he asked, naming her dead mother.

"It's Fenella, Papa."

"The stubborn one," he murmured and closed his eyes again.

This was all he had to say to her, when she'd tended his sickbed for months, picked up his responsibilities on the estate. But this was the way it had always been between them. Nothing about her pleased him. If anything threatened to, like her skill with a gun, he turned it into shortcoming.

His disparagement had shaped the timid girl she'd been. It weighed on her now, when she was struggling with more unfair accusations. If this was her last chance to talk to him, what did she want to tell him about the twenty-three years she'd been part of his family?

Fenella realized that he'd opened his eyes again and was looking at her. "Can you wait a bit, for Greta and Nora to come?" Not what she'd meant to say and probably a ridiculous question, she thought. But perhaps the idea would hearten him. "I know they would like to see you."

"Could have if they wanted to," he growled. "Not bothered to visit."

"They have a great deal—"

"Pack of ungrateful brats, all you chits."

Could he really feel this way about his daughters? Surely not. "Mama told me once that you were over the moon when Greta was born," she said. At the time this had been a bitter pill, since their father had been so disappointed by Fenella's birth. Now, she wanted him to agree. "You adore Greta." Certainly he'd always favored her.

His gaze had gone vague. It roved over the ceiling and the bed curtains as if he didn't recognize the room where he'd slept for thirty years. "Mary oughtn't to have left me with a dratted female on my hands," he said.

"She didn't want to, Papa."

"Settled," he said, as if he hadn't heard her. "The last one might have been. Wanted her settled."

This was a form of concern. She chose to see it that way. "I will be, Papa." It was time to release grudges. What did it matter if he gloated? She'd give him what he'd wanted. "Chatton and I may be married. After all." For now she would ignore the complications surrounding them.

"Wouldn't listen," he muttered. "Ran off and made me look foolish."

Fenella leaned closer. "Papa, I'm going to—"

"Impossible girl," he burst out, loud and angry. He lurched as if trying to sit up. But the effort was far beyond him. He fell back; his eyes closed.

His breathing hitched, paused for an ominous interval, then resumed. This happened again and again, the only sign of life. Then his hand went limp in Fenella's, and his breath stopped forever. The ticking of the mantel clock was suddenly the loudest thing in the room.

Fenella sat on by his bed. Her mother's death had been more sudden and shocking. Yet this prolonged decline turned out to be no easier, in the end. Death was irrevocable. And with this one she was an orphan. The weight of grief dragged at her.

And these were to be his last words to her, indeed his last on this earth. "Impossible girl." Full of anger. No regret or reconciliation. No benediction before the end.

She folded her arms over her chest and listened to the clock mark off the passing seconds. Perhaps she was impossible. She'd never fit into the mold her mother had ready for her. Her sisters had found her negligible. She'd certainly never satisfied her father on any count. If she'd told him about Roger earlier... But giving in to her father had never appeased him. There was always a new criticism behind the one she over-came, a demand she couldn't fulfill. Their relationship was a long history of her failures. At this moment, it seemed as if she could remember them all.

Simpson put a hand on her shoulder. Fenella hadn't heard the valet come in. "Vicar's here."

The Reverend Cheeve stood behind her. "My condolences for your loss."

Fenella rose. There was nothing to be done about the past. Papa would never approve of her. They hadn't found a way to resolve their differences. She had to go on from this empty place.

"I expect he made his own peace with God before the end," said the clergyman.

He hadn't made his peace with anyone, Fenella thought. But she didn't say so. "Thank you," she told him. She looked at the valet. "You'll take care of his...him."

"Yes, miss."

"I must write my sisters." Greta and Nora could come for the funeral.

Twelve

THE SUN ROSE. A NEW DAY BEGAN. AND FENELLA found that between one morning and the next, her life had changed. She'd been managing the household and the estate for more than a year, with few complaints and many marks of approbation. But it seemed now that her authority had rested on the presence of her father, upstairs, a tacit endorsement of her commands. Suddenly, the steward acted as if he wasn't entirely sure she should be giving him orders, and the solicitor who had handled her father's affairs put off all her inquiries with patronizing blandness. It was as if her status, indeed her very existence, had faded into obscurity with her father's death. She'd moved from forefront to background. On top of her loss, this made everything feel like a strange dream.

Fenella knew that her father's property was to be inherited equally by his three daughters. There was no title or entail to consider. He'd been a landed gentleman with a tidy fortune, not a peer. Fenella would become a woman of independent means, and though she was *not* glad that her father was dead, not in the least, the prospect was heartening. She would have decisions to make, once matters were settled. She expected the estate would be sold, and felt a pang at the prospective loss of her home. Yet it had never been a place of unalloyed happiness for her. She would find her own way when it came time to plan.

Neighbors called to offer their sympathy, Roger and his mother among them. Fenella was happy to see them. But even when Roger pressed her hand, gazed into her eyes, and said, "Please call on me for anything, anything at all," she couldn't find any words to reply. Her life had fallen into a kind of limbo—a floating existence plagued with trivialities that no one would allow her to resolve.

On the second day after her father's death, a post chaise arrived carrying John's father, Sherrington Symmes. Greta's thin, discontented-looking husband had brought Wrayle with him, and the latter's narrow smile implied that he had retribution in mind. A few hours later, another vehicle pulled up and disgorged Nora's husband, Donald Gissing. When Fenella asked about her sisters, she was given to understand that both of them were prostrate with grief at having missed their father's demise. Fenella was berated for depriving them of the chance to say farewell and informed that their husbands would *deal with her.* Whatever that meant. She wanted to argue with them, but she kept her tongue between her teeth.

In the course of the next few hours, the feel of Clough House changed completely. She wouldn't have believed that an alteration could be so quick or so disagreeable. But the place suddenly possessed two contentious masters. And their problem wasn't only Fenella. They didn't get along with each other either. Fenella had often thought it curious that her elder sisters had chosen such opposites for their mates. Symmes was slender and sour and sarcastic, a man who savored cutting remarks as another might a fine wine. Gissing was physically his opposite—large and blustery and untidy. He maintained, continually, that he was an easygoing fellow, while actually demanding his own way in every particular. They did have that in common, Fenella thought after a thoroughly wretched dinner. So maybe they weren't so different after all. She couldn't wait until they went away.

The reading of her father's will, which the solicitor had refused to disclose to Fenella, was held the following morning, and it was then that Fenella's world finished crashing down around her ears. Her father's estate was indeed divided into thirds, going to her and her sisters, as she had expected. But her portion was placed in trust until she married. Not until she attained a certain age—although twenty-three seemed perfectly mature to her—but until she married.

Worse, her two brothers-in-law had been appointed her trustees. They were charged with approving whatever expenditures she wished to make, as well as any marriage proposal she might receive. They were made, in effect, her guardians, even though she was of age and hadn't the slightest need of such a thing. Her father had found one last way to disparage her, Fenella thought as she struggled to control her anger at these provisions. Having watched her manage these last months, how could he have doubted her ability to handle her inheritance? And how was she to go on with trustees who couldn't agree on what to have for dinner, let alone more significant decisions?

The solicitor finished reading. He folded the document. "That seems in order," said Gissing.

"As we anticipated," replied Symmes.

They were disgustingly smug. Had they known about the trust before this? Fenella wondered. From their expressions, she suspected they had. She was so furious, she was afraid to speak. It was going to be necessary to get along with these men, for a while at least, until she could think of something. Difficult as that was to accept, she had to hide her outrage.

"You need have no worries about your pin money," Gissing said to her. "I don't begrudge a lady a few geegaws."

"Within reason," said Symmes.

"I've never been called clutch-fisted," said the other man, in a tone that implied his brother-in-law *had*.

"A term used by the profligate for those who practice reasonable economies," said Symmes.

"Like nipcheese and penny-pinching?" said Gissing with false cordiality.

Would she be able to play them off against each other to get what she wanted? Fenella wondered. The idea filled her with distaste. And she didn't think it would work for any large outlay. Her spirits sank farther. She wouldn't be allowed to make any important transactions. It felt like a prison sentence.

Symmes rose, his expression sour. "I believe we are agreed that the estate will be put up for sale? I don't know how long that may take. Have your maid pack your things, Fenella. You will return home with me."

Even before the categorical denial could escape her lips, Gissing said, "Or with me, if you like. I'm sure Nora would welcome your help."

The men gazed at her. She'd wanted a choice, and here was one. Two paths into an absolutely unacceptable future. She could never live with one of her sisters. Did they even know of these invitations? Fenella doubted it. Neither Greta nor Nora would *welcome* her. And their husbands were not inviting a valued relation into their households. Her new fortune was their real object. She could see it in their eyes.

They hoped to find a way to use her to enhance their own positions. And that meant arranging her marriage, which they had the right to approve. To one of their penurious cronies perhaps? And would they levee big charges on her estate for upkeep? Or were they simply enjoying the power over another that their new positions provided? Every feeling revolted.

Fenella struggled to control her tone. "I'd prefer to stay here," she said. "I can look after the house until we find a buyer." If she said *we*, would they begin to see that she was an equal in this matter?

"Oh, I think we'll close the place up," Symmes replied. "There's no need for the outlay, with no one living here. Wouldn't you say, Gissing?" The other man nodded.

Suddenly, she was no one. A person with no say in her future. Or perhaps not so suddenly. To these men, she'd always been a negligible figure. As she had been to her father. "What about the servants?"

Gissing shrugged. "Pension off the older ones, dismiss the others to find new posts."

As if that was easy, and not very important. She had no power to save their positions, Fenella saw. At most, she could provide letters of reference. Perhaps some neighbors had places open. But that wouldn't be enough.

"You may keep your personal maid, of course," said Symmes, like a monarch conferring a great favor.

Fearing she might burst into angry tears, Fenella retreated to her bedchamber. She could run to her grandmother in Scotland again. But that would mean giving up her fortune to these vultures. They would never let go once she was gone.

She could go to the law. Grandmamma might help her. But leaving an inheritance in trust for an unmarried woman was common practice. She would probably be told to be grateful that she had male relatives to look after her money. Fenella gritted her teeth. She had to get out of the house, breathe some fresh air. But when she'd put on her riding habit and gone to the stables, she discovered that the *gentlemen* had sent all but the cart horses off to be sold. Including *her own* mount, a gift from her grandmother, which was not theirs to dispose of. Without informing her!

When she taxed them with this transgression, they were unrepentant. "No sense keeping a stableful of animals eating their heads off" was Gissing's only reaction.

"No place for you to keep a horse," Symmes pointed out. "Didn't seem a proper mount for a lady in any case."

And then they gazed at her as if she was being dim.

It was all Fenella could do not to fly at them with her riding crop.

⁓

It was as if Fenella had disappeared from the neighborhood, Roger thought. He was longing to see how she was, to do something for her, but he hadn't been able to manage one private word. He'd called several times at Clough House. At first there'd been a mob of other callers on visits of condolence. And when they cleared out, he'd been received by her brothers-in-law, playing lords of the manor. He didn't know these gentlemen, and he hadn't taken to them. When he'd asked to see Fenella, they'd been as suspicious as dogs guarding a contested bone. He'd longed for a reason to punch the fleshy one—Gissing. The fellow had practically leered at him.

Fenella hadn't been riding either. Roger had lurked along her usual routes each day and seen no sign of her. The delay was driving him mad. And then, at last, more than a week after her father's death, he finally spotted her on a path by the sea. She was mounted on a rough-coated brown gelding rather than her gray. But she was here. He spurred toward her with eager relief. "There you are," he said when he caught up. "I've looked for you every day."

"I have not been able to get out until now."

"Has something happened to your gray?" She'd looked so at home on that spirited creature, as if they had a special bond. The horse she rode today wasn't nearly in the same class.

"Lightfoot has been sent off to be sold," Fenella

replied in a toneless voice. "Along with my father's other horses."

"I thought she was your horse."

"So did I. But apparently what's mine is now… not."

"What do you mean?"

"I had to borrow a mount from one of our tenants," she went on without acknowledging his question. She indicated the gelding. "He was kind enough to *humor* me. I had to have some air. I'll pay when I get home."

"Pay?"

"When my brothers-in-law learn I've been out riding alone, I'll get a lecture. Or worse."

Roger remembered her tart response when he'd made that objection, so long ago it seemed now. She seemed a different person today. Still as beautiful, but she looked weary and dispirited. Perhaps she was mourning her loss? That burden could grow heavier before it lightened. "I'm sorry about your father," he said.

"I am more than sorry. I am ruined."

"But surely he left you well provided for?" Roger wondered if Fairclough's affairs had been left in disorder. Was that why the horses were being sold?

"Some might think so," Fenella replied. "I do not. He left my portion in trust until I marry." She gritted her teeth. "To be overseen by my sisters' husbands. I believe you've met them."

Roger nodded.

"We have never been more than uneasy acquaintances."

He could understand that. They hadn't seemed the sort to be her friends.

"And now we are very likely to become bitter enemies." Fenella shook her head. "I expected to gain my independence. Of course I did not want Papa to die. I'm sorry he's gone. But to leave things like this! He might have noticed that I managed his affairs quite competently for the last year. That I can take care of myself. But no. My fortune is left entirely out of my control. Every move I make must be approved by two men I dislike, who hardly ever agree with each other." She made an angry gesture. "They've been given the right to approve any match I make. Can you credit it? They intend to make the most of that, I can tell. My only hope is that they won't be able to settle on one candidate. Of course I shall refuse."

Roger groped for words. It seemed that his thought of presenting himself as an official suitor would not do. Fenella's greedy relations would see that they'd gain no advantage with him.

"I have been ordered—ordered!—to live with one of my sisters. Most generously, I may choose which. Perhaps you remember how well we get on."

Her tone was bitter. Roger could see that she was devastated. But the fact that stood out in his mind, selfishly, was that she was going away.

"Can their husbands have failed to notice that Greta and Nora have very little regard for me? But why do I ask? What do the silly opinions of women matter to them?"

"I don't suppose you can fight the will," Roger said.

"For what cause? And what judge would side with me?"

It was true. A trust for an unmarried woman was thought to be a kindness. She would be cared for with no need to bother her head about business.

"I suppose I will return to my grandmother." Abruptly, Fenella looked wary. "Don't tell anyone I said that. They'd stop me."

"You have my word." Perhaps he could visit her there, Roger thought. And then flushed. *He* was not the one needing help here. She was.

"The idea of running back to her makes me feel like the frightened girl I used to be. Again!" She hit the saddlebow with her fist. "First those wretched letters and now this. It isn't fair."

"There must be something you can do."

"I don't have any *time*. They mean to hurry me away. And they keep me confined in the most insupportable way!" Fenella looked out over the sea, her expression deeply unhappy.

He had to do something. He couldn't stand seeing her this way. But what? An idea bloomed in Roger's brain. A tempting idea. Unthinkable? But he'd thought it, hadn't he?

"Grandmamma would be happy to see me, of course," she said as if trying out a theory. She grimaced.

How to put it? Macklin had said he should be subtler. Roger searched his brain for a delicate way to frame his admittedly outrageous suggestion. And then he chucked the idea. Subtlety would never be his strong suit. "Marry me," he said.

"They won't agree. And in any case, you mustn't be forced—"

"At once," Roger interrupted. "It's only four miles to the border. We can be married at the other end of the Coldstream Bridge. That's just as good as Gretna Green."

"Gretna Green!" She stared at him.

"Your fortune will be put into your hands as soon as the knot's tied. I swear it."

"If I elope! You imagine I am so lost to propriety as to make a runaway marriage?"

"It's not a matter of days on the road. And staying at inns, and so on." Roger had certainly not meant to insult her. "It's just an hour's ride. Less than that."

She gazed up at him from her smaller mount. "You're serious."

He nodded. "Absolutely."

"You married in haste once before."

"This isn't haste. We've been talking of marriage for—"

"Days," she interrupted with a thin smile.

"Before this change. I beg you to allow me to do you this service."

"Service?" she repeated in a constricted voice.

"Your fortune will be yours to command," Roger repeated. "I promise."

"So you're offering me a bargain?" she asked.

"If you wish to put it that way." He didn't care much for the word. But he wasn't going to dispute it.

"We marry. I fulfill the…obligations of being your wife. And you give me full control of my own money."

She said *obligations* a bit strangely. But this wasn't the time to quibble. "Yes," he said.

"But to elope! My family would kick up a great dust."

Was she wavering? Her tone suggested it. "I don't think they would, you know. Not once they were presented with a fait accompli. You'd be Marchioness of Chatton. They can't really object to *that*. Not with any cause that society would accept. Your father wanted it." Immediately, Roger wondered if that last remark had been a mistake.

Fenella gave a humorless laugh. "We could put it about that it was his dying wish. It actually was, in a way. His usual intractable way."

She was being pulled into the scheme. For once in his life, Roger managed to keep quiet. He would let her think.

Fenella frowned into the distance. "But is this really possible? How does it work? You don't need banns called or a special license?"

She was definitely wavering. "In Scotland you simply declare yourselves in front of witnesses, and it's a binding marriage. Any citizens will do. You don't need a clergyman. Though we can hunt one up if you like. We'll have a certificate as proof of the marriage."

"How do you know that?" Fenella asked.

"It's the sort of thing one does know."

"No, it isn't."

"No. Well, an acquaintance of mine looked into the all the ins and outs of the thing a while back. He knew I lived up here and wanted to bring this chit along and marry her. I refused, of course."

"Because eloping is a terrible thing to do?" she asked.

"Because she was sixteen, and her parents didn't like him. With some reason, I must say."

"What sort of friends do you have?"

"An acquaintance, I said. And not so much anymore."

She nodded, looking distracted. And perhaps hopeful? Even intrigued? Roger examined every line of her face, searching for clues.

"I'd have to find a way to sneak out. Which will be next to impossible now that I've done it once." She looked rueful. "They expect me to leave with them in a day or so."

"We could go right now," Roger heard himself say.

Fenella blinked. "Right now?" she repeated, as if the words were in a foreign language.

"It's just a few miles to the bridge."

"But I…I haven't anything with me."

"Buy what you need. And then you can send for your things. When you inform your brothers-in-law that you're married."

"Inform them," she murmured.

"And that they needn't trouble themselves about your money any longer," Roger added. "We'll send off a note as soon as the knot's tied."

"Needn't trouble themselves," Fenella repeated. She said it again, silently. Clearly, she liked this idea.

"Or anything else concerning your affairs," Roger added. "Which have nothing to do with them any longer."

Fenella smiled. She smiled at the horizon, and then she smiled at him. "I'd like to tell them *that*," she admitted.

"They deserve it," he replied, making common cause.

She gazed at him. Roger struggled not to say the wrong thing and ruin all. If only there was a way to tell what people were really thinking.

"I suppose I've gone mad," she said. "But…very well. I'll elope with you." She laughed.

Elation flared through him. He felt like shouting for joy. But not wanting to do anything that changed her mind, he simply nodded.

They turned their horses to the northwest.

Thirteen

SOME HOURS LATER, TWO IRATE GENTLEMEN ARRIVED at the gates of Chatton Castle. They were uninvited, though not altogether unexpected. Roger's mother received them. Arthur stood at her side, in his most impressive Lord Macklin guise.

The large fleshy one waved a piece of crumpled paper in their faces. "Are you aware of this outrage?" he demanded.

They'd had their own note with the startling news of Roger's runaway marriage and were prepared. But Arthur saw no reason to make it easy for these rudesbys. "Outrage?" he repeated, as if the word was a social gaffe.

The thin, sour fellow, whose face reminded Arthur of someone, glared at Lady Chatton. "Your son has behaved like an utter blackguard. Lost to all propriety, he has lured our sister-in-law into conduct unbecoming a lady."

"That really doesn't sound like Roger," said Arthur.

The larger man reddened. "They have eloped, sir! I rode up to Coldstream myself and confirmed the story. The idiots there had no idea where he's taken her off to."

"Somewhere comfortable, I'm sure." Arthur said it partly to goad the man and saw that he'd succeeded admirably.

Their uninvited visitor swelled and reddened further. "You are impertinent, whoever you may be. I don't see how this concerns you."

"You're not acquainted with Lord Macklin?" said Helena. Her manner was a consummate combination of surprise and pity. She turned to the earl. "These are the husbands of my late neighbor Fairclough's daughters. Mr. Symmes and Mr. Gissing. I met them at their weddings." Her tone implied they were the barest of acquaintances.

"Ah." Arthur nodded. "I see now. We did hear that Miss Fairclough had fulfilled the dying wish of her father and married Lord Chatton." He emphasized the title.

"We have no evidence of such a wish," snapped Symmes. "Fairclough left no instructions on that subject."

A fussy man, Arthur thought, realizing that this was young John's father. That was why he looked familiar. Fleetingly, he felt sorry for the boy. "Well, Miss Fairclough—or, I should say, the new *Marchioness of Chatton*—would know best about that." Arthur watched the title sink in. "As I understand it, she was eager to fulfill her father's dearest wish."

"By eloping? And causing a scandal?" asked Gissing.

He was a blusterer, Arthur noted. He probably got his way quite often, with people who were intimidated by a looming figure and a loud voice. Fortunately, there were no such people present. "Scandal?" Arthur repeated. "I believe they married privately in accordance with her father's wishes."

"Everyone hereabouts knows how he felt," Helena said. Her raised eyebrows emphasized that they were strangers in the neighborhood.

Arthur hoped they hadn't heard Roger's reckless talk about his first wife's death. Or about the letters. He had the sudden sensation of walking a tightrope over the lair of a couple of snapping beasts. He found he rather enjoyed it.

"You are condoning this outrage?" Symmes said to Roger's mother. "How can you?"

"I'm extremely fond of Fenella," she replied. "I think she will make an admirable marchioness."

Arthur approved her repetition of the young lady's new title. Surely the advantages of the match would sink into these fellows' hard heads soon? If they could care about anything but their own consequence.

"We'll disavow the thing," said Gissing. "A runaway Scottish marriage! We'll drag her back here and—" Seeing the others' expressions, he fell silent.

Helena drew herself up, the very model of a peeress depressing pretentions. "If *they* say they are married," she began. "And *I* say they are married, I cannot imagine who would question the fact. Or spread malicious gossip that might harm the marchioness's *whole family*. Who would be so mean-spirited?"

"One would be forced to contradict that kind of rumor," added Arthur. "And discredit anyone spreading it. Among the people who matter." He brought the full weight of his personality to bear on their unwelcome guests.

"I don't see what right you have to interfere," said Gissing.

It was difficult for him to give up blustering, Arthur noted. Intimidation was obviously a pleasure as well as a—usually—successful ploy for him.

But now Symmes plucked at his sleeve.

"Lord Macklin is a good friend of our family," said Helena. "He is certainly not interfering. Indeed we appreciate his support as he is acquainted with *everyone*." Her tone implied that her visitors, on the other hand, were not, and that they certainly *were* interfering.

"We'd better go," muttered Symmes.

"It is rather late," said Helena, adding a jot to their transgressions.

Gissing glowered at them. "You haven't heard the last of this," he growled. Turning on his heel, he stomped out. Symmes followed, with one uneasy look over his shoulder.

"Do you think Mr. Gissing will make trouble?" said Helena when they were gone.

"I think his colleague will convince him to let the matter rest. And Gissing will calm down once he has no one before him to bully."

"Attempt to bully," said Helena. "That was masterly."

"Your handling of your obstreperous guests, you mean?"

"Yours."

They exchanged a smile.

"What do you really think of this marriage?" she

asked him. Not for the first time. "The match and the…imprudent way of it," she added.

"I think it has every possibility of success."

"And yet a distinct danger of failure," she said.

"We must see if there is anything we can do to prevent that."

"Which would be?"

"There are these letters. They should be dealt with."

"Yes."

"Our recent visitors don't seem to have heard about them."

Helena nodded. "With no friends in the neighborhood, they had no one to tell them."

Arthur nodded. "Still, best to put a stop to it."

"But can we?"

"I have an idea we can try."

Helena gazed up at him with admiration. "You really are the most complete hand, aren't you, Lord Macklin."

He laughed at her use of this uncharacteristic expression. "Let's wait and see how I do before we say that."

❧

Fenella and Roger shared a supper of roast mutton and vegetables at an inn on the banks of the river Tweed. They drew no sidelong looks or whispered comments, as Fenella had half feared. No one took any particular notice of them. "We're married," she said to Roger.

"We're married," he agreed.

"Actually." She looked at the ring on her finger. Roger had purchased the gold band from an enterprising jeweler near the Scottish end of the Coldstream Bridge. Apparently others arrived at the border without this important item. But did they also lack so much as a hairbrush, she wondered. Perhaps so, as she and Roger had found a shop offering personal necessities as well. It had been embarrassing and rather thrilling to stock up.

"My...not-friend researched the matter thoroughly. Definitely a binding marriage."

"So I have eloped. I am married. And I've stolen Mr. Larraby's horse." Emotion bubbled in Fenella's chest, struggling to escape in a laugh. She was...glad? Or perhaps this was what insanity felt like.

Roger smiled at her. "Borrowed, surely? We'll have the animal taken back to him."

"Or shall I purchase it, out of sentiment?"

He looked a question.

"The mount that bore me to my wedding. To live in my stables ever after."

"Well, if you like," Roger began.

Fenella's laugh burst out. "No, no, he must go back to Mr. Larraby. He's a perfect slug, I'm afraid."

"We'll find out where they've taken Lightfoot and buy her back for you."

Her throat grew tight at the fact that Roger had remembered her loss and at the idea of having her favorite mount back again. She had to clear it before she could speak. "I'd like that. Thank you." She heard hoofbeats outside and couldn't help pulling back from the window. "I'm sure Gissing came after us. He wouldn't have been able to resist. I hope he won't find us." She would defy him if he did, of course. But she'd prefer not to. She'd had enough of his bluster to last her the rest of her life.

"He'll find no one to tell him which way we went," said Roger.

"But several people saw us ride out of Coldstream. You spoke to them."

"To provide each of them with a liberal encouragement to forget our existence."

"You bribed them?" Fenella cocked her head. "You're rather good at this, aren't you? Perhaps a bit too good? One would almost think you'd eloped before."

"Not me."

"Your nefarious nonfriend?"

Roger spread his hands and shrugged. "I had no notion what a loose fish he was until that incident. He had a plan all written out, including the bribes, and at the end, a list of what he would do with the girl's money when he got his hands on it."

"Clearly you were right to save that young lady from his clutches."

"No question. Why did he think I would help him?" Roger shook his head as he refilled their wineglasses. "That was one of the most offensive things about his scheme." He sipped his wine, set down the glass. "Ah, it's probably best to stay up here for a few nights."

"So my brothers in-law can recognize that I'm properly ruined?"

"Adjust to the fact that you're married, say," he replied.

The reality of her situation had come home to her when she said it out loud. Fenella put her hands to her reddening cheeks. "What will Reverend Cheeve say?

He always joked about presiding at my wedding. And Mrs. Cheeve? She will…wallow in being shocked."

"Had a thought about that," said Roger.

"About the vicar's wife? Oh, and Mrs. Patterson. She's such a model of rectitude. What will she think?" Fenella let her hands drop to her lap. "We'll have to face the colonel at that wretched pageant. And the stares of the whole neighborhood." She rested her head on her palm, weighed down by this vision. "We'll be a regular raree-show. After those letters, too."

"I've thought of something we might tell them. The whole pack of gossips."

Fenella looked up. "What?"

"That we came up to Scotland for the wedding because of your grandmother. As she's your favorite relative. Not saying outright that we were married at her place. No lies. Just talking of her and letting people assume that we were. She'd have to agree, of course."

"But my sisters' husbands will have been ranting about an elopement. Gissing especially. He doesn't care who hears when he starts ranting."

Roger nodded. "That's a ticklish bit. We'd have to shrug it off without directly contradicting. Awkward bit of family friction. Don't care to speak of it. That sort of thing."

"The servants at Clough House will certainly corroborate *that*," she said.

"Or anything else you'd like them to say."

"True. Oh, I'll be able to look out for them now."

"Certainly you went to your grandmother before. Did it again."

"My invariable habit," said Fenella dryly. "When

in doubt, run away." But as the idea sank in, she grew more and more enamored of it. "We'd have to go and see Grandmamma."

"Right." For the first time, Roger looked apprehensive. "Don't suppose she'll be pleased with me."

"Or me. But when she hears the whole story, she'll…understand. I think she will. I don't say she'll approve, but she has always been ready to help me." Fenella marveled that she hadn't thought of this plan herself. She'd been too unsettled by the changes in her life. "You are brilliant." She reached out and put a hand over his on the tabletop.

He turned his hand over and laced his fingers with hers. Their eyes met and held.

They'd grown so accustomed to suppressing any feelings about each other, Fenella thought. It had been a matter of honor, and quite right, too. She'd been careful not to acknowledge so much as a spark of interest, and she knew he had as well. Caution had become habit.

That wasn't necessary any longer. Indeed, it wasn't advisable. They were married. She could let her hand rest in his. She could look at him, admire the strong lines of his face, meet his eyes and not immediately glance away. She could kiss him, as she had at the raspberry thicket. And more. A shiver of excitement shook her. She could let go. Not here in the inn parlor, of course, but…later.

A different kind of heat rushed through her, a flush of attraction, not embarrassment. Or perhaps both. The change was new, to both of them. It made her head spin. Unless that was the desire in his gaze, seeming to tremble in the air between them. The skin of his hand was hot under her fingertips.

"I've, ah, engaged two rooms here," he said finally.

"Have you?" He would get tangled up in words now, Fenella thought. As he did. She decided to let him. For a while. The muddle was so endearing.

"So that you don't... I wouldn't want you to... This was all very sudden... That is, of course there is no pressure for you to—"

Fenella took pity on him. "I understand you."

He looked relieved. "We can wait as long as you wish. Naturally."

"We're married." Her sisters liked to mock her ignorance of physical passion, though of course she knew the mechanics from the farmyard. Their sly insinuations made her believe there was much more to it than *that*. There was the matter of legality, too. She wanted no questions about the validity of the marriage. But that wasn't the main thing, Fenella thought, noting the yearning in Roger's eyes. He was remembering their flurry of kisses in the grass. She had no doubt about that. Because she was as well. His touch had made her tremble. "We should stay together."

"Are you certain?" He wanted to take her assent and sweep her off to the bedroom. That was obvious. His longing practically scorched her. But he was too chivalrous.

She couldn't resist teasing him a little. "If you would rather stay in two rooms—"

"No! I was simply—" He stopped, visibly gathered his wits, smiled. "I wouldn't rather. Not in the least."

They went upstairs together. The bed took up most

of the space in the inn chamber. They were left standing close together near the door.

All her life, a woman was told never to be alone with a man, Fenella thought, not to allow herself to be touched or compromised in any way. And then, between one day and the next, after a brief ceremony, all those strictures flew out the window for the sake of *one* man. She was directed to be freely intimate with him, with no practical experience of what to do. If the woman was lucky—and here Fenella considered herself very lucky indeed—she had some clue that she would welcome her husband's caresses.

Roger bent his head, then went still, as if poised for a signal of her wishes. Fenella looked up to meet his lips. The kiss began tentatively, lengthened, melted into heat. They relaxed into it, drew back, then resumed. He slid his arms around her and pulled her closer. She felt the contours of him all along her body. His kisses, the touch of his hands, seemed to vibrate through her entire being.

When they parted the next time, they were breathing faster. Fenella's clothes felt unbearably constricting. She untied her stock and tossed it aside, unbuttoned the bodice of her riding habit. Roger shed his coat and neckcloth in one swift motion. He looked strong and handsome in shirtsleeves. "Shall I pull off your boots?" he asked.

It was odd how one became more polite as a situation grew more awkward, Fenella thought. She sat on the bed and held out a foot. He removed one riding boot, then the other. "Thank you," she said. She stood as he sat down to tug off his own footwear.

Fenella unfastened her long skirt and let it fall. Her petticoat followed, and she stood in her shift, not certain where to go from there. She had no night-gown, and she was not ready to stand naked in the inn bedroom.

Roger had slipped out of his buckskin breeches. His shirttails were almost as long as a nightshirt above his bare legs. He went to pull back the coverlet and sheet, then extended a hand as if he offered to help her into a carriage rather than a bed.

She took it and climbed in. He joined her. For a moment, Fenella hesitated. It was so new, to lie here with only two thin layers of cloth between her and a...husband. He was her husband. Between one day and the next. Then Roger bent and kissed her again, and the flame of sensation drove all thoughts right out of her head.

Their last garments were soon discarded. Through long, fiery kisses, Roger's hands explored the contours of her body. Fenella enjoyed his touch. She urged him on with somewhat inexpert caresses of her own. Knees and elbows were negotiated. She opened to him and moved from maid to wife.

And yet part of her held back. She was happy to be married to him. She didn't believe she'd done anything wrong in agreeing to their scrambling wed-ding. It wasn't that. She didn't regret her choices. She certainly didn't wish herself back home. She didn't understand what plagued her. She only knew that something kept her a little separate, detached, not wholly there. Was it because she'd made a bargain with her vows? Or because her wedding had been so different from anything she'd ever imagined? No new gown, no celebration, no family present, and she'd had scarcely an hour's preparation to grow accustomed to the change in her circumstances. Among strangers.

All except Roger. She gazed at his sleeping face beside her, envying his easy slumber. She cared for him. She liked him. She enjoyed his touch. This feeling would pass off with time, she told herself, and closed her eyes in hope of sleep.

The following morning they sent off three more notes—a longer one to Chatton Castle, one rather vague epistle to be rushed ahead of them to Fenella's grandmother, and another to Fenella's maid, asking her to pack some of Fenella's things and come with them to her grandmother's estate. Knowing her brothers-in-law, Fenella enclosed a banknote in the latter to pay for the journey. And let Symmes and Gissing make what they liked of that, she thought as they rode north once more. They would certainly recognize her grandmother's name. In any other set of persons, that might be a signal to keep quiet and await further news. Her brothers-in-law were unlikely to exhibit such discretion, however. They'd shown no signs of having any. But with her grandmother on their side—and Roger's mother, too, she trusted—she and Roger would brush through this without scandal.

Not too fast, Fenella added silently. She was *almost* certain that Grandmamma would accept her unconventional marriage and aid them, but it would be fatal to take anything for granted.

Fourteen

KNOWING THAT WORD OF ROGER'S UNEXPECTED wedding would inevitably leak out, with Symmes and Gissing ranting and complaining over at Clough House, Macklin and Roger's mother decided to share the news themselves. The couple's last letter from Scotland had given them promising phrases to use, implying that Fenella's grandmother was part of the whole marriage scheme. Trusting Fenella to gain the support of that formidable old woman, they agreed that it would be wise to tell certain sociable neighbors, so that their version of the story would be the one the gossips spread.

"Oh, I'm glad they paid no attention to those dreadful letters," replied Mrs. McIlwaine when the dowager marchioness conveyed the tale over tea the following day.

Arthur glanced at their hostess. Seeing uncertainty in her gaze, he decided to pretend ignorance. "Letters?" Things one had heard nothing about often seemed less important.

"No one told you?"

Mrs. McIlwaine's expression was familiar. She was one of those who reveled in knowing more than anyone else, Arthur thought. Not necessarily malicious, but overeager. He made a noncommittal gesture.

"I expect Chatton didn't want to upset you." Mrs. McIlwaine directed her comment at Roger's mother.

"And what would have done that?" asked Helena calmly, following his lead.

"Several of us received the horridest anonymous letters," the other lady replied. "Repeating that silly rumor blaming Miss Fairclough—Lady Chatton, I should say now—for her, er, predecessor's ride out in the storm."

Arthur kept his expression bland. If neighbors were talking of this insult so openly, something really must be done.

"Several of you," said Helena evenly.

The visitor mentioned names. "And Mrs. Cheeve had one yesterday. She was excessively shocked."

The vicar's wife would have been, Arthur thought. Or would have wanted to appear so. Both, probably.

"Particularly as Chatton was talking of the story again last Sunday," continued Mrs. McIlwaine. "It might have been better to ignore it." She shook her head. "Difficult, though, when one is angry at the injustice."

Not malicious at all, Arthur concluded.

"I'm so glad they didn't let it stop them from marrying," the visitor added.

"Why should they?" asked Helena. Clearly, she was angry.

"Exactly so," answered Mrs. McIlwaine. "One mustn't give such a vile person the satisfaction. It's so lowering to think that one of our own neighbors would be so sneaking and spiteful."

"Neighbors," said Helena.

"Well, they were delivered by hand, you know. Dreadful to imagine that creature writing them nearby." Mrs. McIlwaine gathered her shawl, eager now to go and spread her juicy news. They said their farewells and waited a few minutes until they heard her carriage depart.

"You said you had some idea what we might do about those letters," Helena said then.

Arthur nodded. "Find out who is sending them," he replied.

"How will you do that?" Her voice was clipped with annoyance.

He didn't blame her. "By watching for the messenger. Someone local has been enlisted, and no doubt paid, to carry them. They will be more flush with cash than before. And perhaps prone to boasting."

Helena frowned. "We can't wait in the lanes or the village tavern for this person to appear."

"No, but I have someone who can. Tom is a keen observer." Arthur noted her doubtful expression. "He's proven his ability to discover information when we needed it. You may trust me on that."

"Well, of course I do. It's just…this is rather important. I can't bear to have more of these letters arrive. What a horrid welcome to her new home for Fenella."

"We will treat it so," said Arthur. With a courteous salute, he went out.

After a moment's thought about the best way to arrange a private conversation, he went up to his bedchamber and rang for Clayton, who was dispatched to find Tom. The lad turned up a few minutes later, bright and inquisitive. When the problem was explained to him, he said, "I can do that. Likely this messenger is spending his new wages around the village."

"That's what I thought," Arthur said.

"He may be itching to tell about his good fortune as well. Most do. But even if he's not, there'll be summat to notice."

"And then you must follow him to the source," Arthur reminded him. "Without being observed yourself."

Tom nodded.

"After that, we will root them out," the older man added. "There's nothing worse than poison-pen letters."

"Ha, poison pen, that's a good name for them," said Tom.

"Descriptive of the effect they can have."

Tom turned toward the bedchamber door. "I'm right pleased to have something to do," he said. "That Wrayle fellow has got John shut away at Clough House, and I've been back to walking about the fields on my own."

~

Roger pulled his horse up beside Fenella's and joined her in gazing at a cascade of water foaming over a tumble of rocks and into a stream by the side of the road. They had decided not to hurry their journey north. They might have reached her grandmother's house in two days, but they were taking at least three.

Fenella's horse wasn't as good as his, for one thing. Mr. Larraby's hapless animal was plodding and stubborn. He took advantage of any opportunity to pause and crop grass, as he was doing now. And he objected strenuously to long treks into unknown territory.

Also, Roger was balancing concern about facing Fenella's formidable grandmother with the inconvenience of having no change of clothes. He'd bought a few necessities in Coldstream, so they weren't without a hairbrush and tooth powder. But they had little else. The cash he'd had with him when they fled was running low. He told himself that it would suffice.

"It's beautiful, isn't it?" said Fenella.

The most beautiful thing in Roger's view was his new wife, but he didn't say so. Sometimes she appeared to enjoy a compliment; other times praise unsettled her. He hadn't learned the difference, whatever it might be. "The scenic route," he replied instead.

This won him a smile. "I promise you I know the way," she said.

"I'm counting on it." They had veered off the main road onto a track that Fenella promised would show him striking views of the countryside. Roger suspected that his valet and her maid might well reach their destination before they did.

Fenella tugged on her horse's reins, addressing the animal's reluctance to move on. "Come along, sir. You will have better fodder when we stop for the night, as you might very well understand by this time."

The borrowed mount snorted and fought her control, straining toward the grass. She got him moving with difficulty.

"I'd gladly ride him for a while," Roger offered, not for the first time.

"I couldn't inflict him on you," she replied as before.

The day waned as they rode on. The track grew more overgrown. It seemed to Roger that little traffic had passed this way in some time.

"I was certain there was a small inn about here," said Fenella. "Yes, there it is."

But the building at the side of the road was empty, clearly abandoned. A thick plank had been nailed across the front door. The roof sagged in the middle. And the small stable at the back was partly burned.

"Oh dear." Fenella surveyed the place. "I was through here only... I suppose it *was* two years ago. I didn't stay, but...I suppose they didn't have enough travelers to keep going."

Roger thought it very likely. "We'll have to break in. There's rain coming. Unless you know of some other shelter nearby?"

She shook her head. "Not for miles."

"Right." Roger jumped down and handed Fenella his reins. "I'll check for other entrances first." He walked around the building. There was a back door, but it was secured with several planks. The mullioned windows looked too small to crawl through, even if he managed to open one. It would have to be the main entry.

Back at the front door, he found a sturdy tree branch and slipped it between the plank and the panels. By prying at first one end, then the other, he finally got the board off. Throwing it aside, he tried the door. "Locked. I'll have to bash it in." The darkness was deepening, and the wind definitely promised rain. He looked around for a suitable rock.

"Just a minute." Fenella dismounted. She pulled two pins from her hair and knelt before the lock. In a few minutes, she had the door open.

"Where did you learn to do that?"

"My cousin Rob taught me," she said.

"Rob?"

"My mother's brother's son. You'll meet him. He lives near Grandmamma."

Roger had never heard of this fellow before. He felt a twinge of jealousy. "Sneak thief, is he?"

Fenella laughed. "He's the current laird."

"So that means yes, if I know my Scotsmen."

"We're making a family visit, not a border raid," she teased. "You will remember that we're going to enlist Grandmamma's help?" She stepped through the door.

"Help, not a raid," repeated Roger with a smile, following her.

It was damp and chilly inside the small building. The rooms were empty; everything had been taken away. But a wide stone fireplace remained in the largest chamber, and it appeared the roof would keep out the rain, at least on the lower floor. Roger doubted that it did upstairs.

They went back out to collect wood. The surrounding vegetation was green and damp, but they found some dry scraps in the ruins of the stable, along with shreds of old hay for tinder. "I'll bring the horses in here," Roger said. "There's enough cover left to shelter them. I'll pull some grass for them."

"I'll help you."

"No need. Take the wood in." He handed her the flint and steel he always carried in a pocket on his saddle. "You could check the kitchen for food. Not that there will be any from the looks of things."

"Women's work?"

"Kitchen maid's work, while I do the ostler's." Roger gave her a smile as he went out. Rain was indeed starting. He led their mounts into the upright part of the stable and unsaddled them. Mr. Larraby's horse voiced running complaints about the nature of the accommodations. Even a handful of the grain they'd purchased along the way didn't mollify him.

When Roger returned, he found Fenella seated cross-legged on the floor before a crackling fire, holding her hands out to the flames. She'd fetched water, too. Whoever had stripped the place had forgotten to take the bucket from the well, fortunately.

Fenella turned and gestured at the meager results of her search, lined up by her knee. "Some salt in a twist of paper," she said, pointing to the first object. "Left in the back of a cupboard. A broken paring knife. A few beans, well chewed over by what I believe is a rat living under the kitchen floorboards."

"I suppose I could try to catch it for our dinner."

"I am not *that* hungry," declared Fenella. "And I'm sorry."

"For what?"

"Suggesting this diversion in our route. It's far more rustic than I remembered. I do think more people used to come this way."

"One day without dinner is no great hardship," he replied, sitting down next to her. "And we are out of the weather." Rain had begun to beat against the window. Certainly the sagging roof would leak, Roger thought. But they should be all right if they stayed down here. Fenella looked melancholy. He searched for a diversion. "Tell me more about your grandmother. So that I'll know how to ingratiate myself with her."

As he'd hoped, this made her laugh. "I can't wait to see that."

"Is she such a fierce Scot?"

"Actually, she's the daughter of an English duke and his French émigrée wife."

"What?"

Fenella nodded. "She met the laird of Roslyn during a hunting party. It was in Northumberland, actually. She was visiting the North, and he'd ventured a bit south. Voilà, they fell madly in love."

Her voice had an odd inflection at the end. Roger couldn't interpret it.

"It was a fine match, except that she was a Sassenach and his family deep-dyed Scots. Her French blood helped persuade them."

"Why was that?"

"Mary, Queen of Scots?" she answered. "The Stuart Pretenders living in Paris? There's been a link for centuries." She held up a hand. "By the way, don't call the Stuarts 'Pretenders' while we're up here. Should the topic arise."

"I can't imagine why it would," Roger said. "That was ages ago."

"I have a great-uncle who remembers the Battle of Culloden as if it was yesterday. Or claims to." She considered. "Though he can't have been more than five in 1746. Ha, to hear him you would think he'd cut a bloody swath through the enemy ranks."

"Was that the one where the Hanovers defeated the Stuarts once and for all?"

Fenella shook her head. "Never say it that way up here. It isn't so very long since then."

"A good long lifetime," said Roger.

"There aren't many left who were there," she agreed. "But live up here for a few years, and you'll hear about it." She gazed into the fire. The rain pattered outside.

They still weren't completely comfortable being alone together, Roger thought in the silence. This wasn't what he would have planned for a honeymoon journey. "What is your grandmother's house like?"

"Elegant," Fenella replied. She frowned. "Will your valet have packed evening dress?"

"For a country house visit. Of course."

"Yes. Good. Grandmamma is a stickler on some things, and then liberal about others." She smiled. "She despises the sidesaddle, for example. She'll be sorry to see mine. While I lived with her, I had a riding habit with split skirts and rode astride. As does she. I didn't bring the habit home with me because I knew Papa would object." A shadow passed across her face. "Would have."

"I hope you'll bring it along when we return."

She looked at him. "You're not afraid of scandalizing the neighborhood?"

"Not in the least."

Her blue gaze was steady. And perhaps speculative? "I will then."

"Splendid." Roger yearned to fold her in his arms, capture her lips, and sink into the pleasures that had illuminated their nights together. But the floor was dusty, and there was a smell of mold from the back premises. Hardly a spot for romance. He endured another pause, then said, "What sort of place is Roslyn?"

"The town is pretty. About seven miles south of Edinburgh, on high ground, near the North Esk River. There's an ancient chapel." Fenella yawned.

"You're tired. You should rest."

She looked around. "We must sleep on the floor. I looked upstairs. There's nothing here."

"I'll spread my coat for you to lie on."

"Nonsense. You'll be cold."

"The fire will do." Indeed, the room was warmer.

After another glance at the dirty floor, she accepted his offer. She lay down with a look toward the moldy kitchen. "Do you suppose the rat comes out at night?"

"I'll keep watch and feed the flames. That will discourage any visits."

"I should take my turn."

Roger nodded, not wishing to argue. But she looked so weary, and so lovely curled on the wooden floor, that he did not wake her. Instead he waited until light showed at the windows and then roused her to ride on, to the surly indignation of Mr. Larraby's horse.

The rain had stopped, and they went faster than before, both having had enough of their cross-country trek by this time. Early in the evening, they crested a small rise and looked down on their goal—a substantial mansion of stone and slate.

Fenella set her heels to her borrowed horse, whose

quirks had filled her with an irredeemable disgust for him, and moved down the incline.

Five years ago, she'd arrived at this house seeking refuge, Fenella thought as she rode. And she'd received it in full measure. Now she was looking for safety of another kind. A shield from scandal. What would Grandmamma have to say about that?

Her grandmother's home was the same, with ranks of windows throwing warm light into the growing dusk. Fenella trusted her own judgment, and she didn't regret her actions. But her grandmother had a lifetime's more experience and a wealth of wisdom. She would be glad to hear her grandmother's opinion. And of course to gain her approval and help. Fenella hadn't realized until this moment how very much she wanted the former.

They were ushered into the lady's presence without delay. As usual, she looked polished and elegant, making Fenella wish she'd been given a bit more time to prepare. A gown of lilac satin perfectly set off Grandmamma's white hair and emphasized the wretched state of Fenella's riding habit, crushed and stained by the night on the dusty floor. The lines in the old lady's face seemed designed to emphasize its timeless bone structure.

Fenella saw Roger looking back and forth between them. "The resemblance has been remarked upon," she said. Many observers had told her that her grandmother showed what she would look like at seventy. She hoped they were right.

"Well, what have you to say for yourself, young man?" said Grandmamma.

"I think I'm a very lucky fellow," Roger replied with a bow that acknowledged them both.

"Ha."

Fenella hid a smile. Her grandmother didn't mind a little flattery, if it was judicious.

"I received your letter." The old lady's tone was dry. "And your servants, who arrived this morning." She looked them up and down. "Fortunately," she added.

Fenella was relieved to hear that her clothes had come. Grandmamma didn't care for an untidy appearance, which she certainly presented just now. She didn't have to voice a criticism for Fenella to be aware of it. "As I had no way of predicting the time of your arrival, you have missed dinner," she finished.

"We'll behave much better tomorrow, Grandmamma." That won her a smile, so Fenella followed it with "I didn't know the little inn south of here had closed. We spent last night on a hard floor, so I'm rather tired."

The sympathy Fenella had hoped for showed in her grandmother's blue eyes. A short time later, they were settled in a comfortable set of rooms, supplied with hot water for bathing and a savory meal. As a favorite with the staff here, Fenella was showered with greetings and small attentions. She reveled in the luxury, well aware that a searching conversation with her grandmother had only been postponed, not avoided.

And indeed Fenella was summoned to her grandmother's private parlor as soon as she was up and dressed the following morning. She waved aside Roger's concern when it was made clear that she was to come alone. If Grandmamma wanted to scold her, she would, and Fenella preferred to face that on her own. She was just glad she had a proper gown to wear and freshly washed hair.

When she stepped into the comfortable room, she remembered how she'd admired this chamber when she first saw it. Her grandmother had created a very personal retreat with books, flowers, keepsakes, and soft furnishings. Her parlor was a bower of color and ease. Fenella had envied it fiercely five years ago. A thrill went through her as she realized that she would be able to create a place like this for herself at Chatton Castle. She had her own home now, and the power to arrange whatever retreat she wanted.

Her grandmother sat in an armchair by the window. "Are you more rested?" she asked.

"Yes, thank you."

"So now we can talk." The old lady gestured at the chair opposite.

Fenella sat down. "Of course. Oh, first of all I must send back Mr. Larraby's horse."

"Larraby?"

"A tenant of ours." Fenella grimaced. "Of the new owner of Clough House, I should say. Which is no longer any concern of mine. That has been made very clear."

"Do I hear bitterness?" asked her grandmother, eyes searching her face.

"A bit," Fenella admitted. She told the story of Lightfoot's sale, which made her grandmother frown, as the horse had been her gift.

"Upstarts," said the old woman. "But I hope you didn't think to pay back your family by eloping.

Because that would not be a good reason for such a rash action."

"No, not pay them back," she answered. "Escape their control in one fell swoop, yes." She set her jaw. "I'm going to buy Lightfoot back, too."

"Fell swoop? Are we in the midst of a melodrama?"

"A bit," Fenella said again, with a smile this time.

Her grandmother didn't smile back, but her expression eased. She summoned a servant and gave orders about Mr. Larraby's horse. When this was done, she turned back to Fenella. "I intend to take a hard look at this young man you've married, and if he is not worthy of you, I can end this hasty match. I have influential friends, and I could manage that for you."

"I don't want to do that, Grandmamma."

The old lady's eyes narrowed. "You came running to me five years ago because you wouldn't marry this very man. Now you come running because you *have* married him, in the most scrambling way. You do see the irony in that? Does it sound like sense?"

Fenella was rather tired of having their history thrown into her face. "That isn't exactly how it was then. And I'm not running."

"What *are* you doing?" Her grandmother sounded genuinely curious.

"Staging a strategic pause," said Fenella. "Negotiating an important...alliance."

Finally her grandmother smiled. "With me?"

"My sisters' husbands wouldn't dare oppose you. Any more than Greta and Nora would."

"But I don't understand why the issue would arise."

Fenella explained the terms of her father's will,

and the attitude of her brothers-in-law. "Roger has promised me that my inheritance will be under my control."

"And you believe him?"

"Yes." Fenella had no doubts in that regard.

Her grandmother accepted her opinion. "But this is the man you described as rude and insufferable and—what was it?—vile. Yes, I believe that was the word."

Fenella laughed. "And so he was, five years ago. He has changed."

"People don't often do that."

"I did."

The old lady acknowledged this with a nod. She considered briefly. "There are those who will say you married for rank and fortune."

"Gossips must always be saying something."

"I can see you are determined on this marriage." She sat back in her chair, looking dissatisfied. "It all seems very convoluted. It wasn't like that when I met your grandfather."

"You fell in love all at once. I remember you told me." Fenella shrugged. "Not everyone has it so easy."

"Easy? I don't believe I've ever said it was *easy*."

"You were madly in love."

"Oh yes." Her grandmother looked wistful.

"And so was my grandfather." Fenella remembered him as a fierce Scot who had no patience for fools. Even her sister Nora had been frightened of him.

"Do you think that makes marital bliss automatic? Not at all. I think it may heighten the disappointments that inevitably come, from time to time."

"I thought you were happy together," said Fenella.

Disillusionment stirred in her. She'd set up her grand-parents' marriage as an ideal in her mind.

"We were. Because we worked at it. Love makes you *want* to agree. It doesn't mean you will, or solve every problem that comes along. Like some sort of magic wand." She snorted at the idea.

As Fenella took in this nugget of wisdom and stored it away for future reference, she felt the beginning of a broad relief.

"Well, let's get this husband of yours in here and see what he's made of," said her grandmother.

It was a thrill to hear Roger called that, even as she worried about the coming encounter. "I hope you won't bully him, Grandmamma."

"Would he let me?"

"Well, no, but—" She didn't want them to wrangle.

"Then we have no problem."

Roger was summoned. He stood before them with his hands behind his back, a bit like a schoolboy brought before the headmaster, Fenella thought.

"Tell me about yourself," said her grandmother to him. "How do you describe yourself to a new acquaintance? A gentleman acquaintance, that is. None of the namby-pamby stuff you'd tell a female."

"Wouldn't," said Roger. "I'd be a dead bore *describing myself*. We'd talk about whatever we were doing. Who introduced us. That sort of thing."

The old lady showed no particular reaction. "What are your favorite pursuits?"

"Riding, shooting. Dancing. I'm fond of a hand of cards with skilled players."

"What do you despise?"

"Cruelty," Roger replied promptly.

"What would your mother say if I asked her about your character?"

"Well, good things, I expect. She *is* my mother. Macklin might be a better reference if I require one. He's a very honest fellow."

"Macklin?"

"The Earl of Macklin. He is—yes, I think I can call him a friend of mine, though I just met him this year."

"An older man?" asked Fenella's grandmother.

"About fifty, I believe."

"Ah, it must have been his father then."

"What must have been, Grandmamma?" asked Fenella. The conversation was going better than she'd expected, if not predictably.

"The previous earl. He was a suitor of mine, long ago."

"Really?" said Roger. "The current Lord Macklin courted my mother. In London, years ago."

"Indeed."

"She thought he might be again, when he came to stay with us. But now they say they're friends. Do you suppose that's all right?"

"I beg your pardon?"

"Didn't mean to say that," said Roger. "That's something else about me, you may as well know. If I'm describing myself. Sometimes words just…won't do what I wish them to. They pop out, or stay in, at the least opportune moments."

Fenella's grandmother looked amused for the first time. "Do they?"

He nodded glumly. "Bane of my existence."

The old lady hid a smile. "Bane?"

"Phrase I spotted in a newspaper once. It seemed apt."

"I see. So what was it you wanted to ask me?"

"Never mind. I shouldn't have said anything."

"No, I'm interested to know."

Roger hesitated as if determined to get this right. "I just want to be certain my mother is all right. They claim to be friends, and all *seems* well. Macklin said that as people grow older, they understand the importance of friendship."

"And since I am *older*, I must know the truth of this?" asked Fenella's grandmother.

Roger blanched. "I didn't mean—"

"As it happens, I agree," she added. "This Macklin sounds like a sensible man. Is your mother a sensible woman?"

"Yes."

"Then I don't imagine you have anything to worry about." She waved a dismissive hand. "You may go now."

Roger hesitated, then bowed out of the room.

"All right," said Fenella's grandmother when he was gone. "I'm inclined to stand with you on this marriage."

"You like him?" She hadn't acknowledged how very much she valued her grandmother's opinion until this moment, Fenella realized.

"I think I do. I want Rob's opinion."

"What can my cousin tell you? He isn't acquainted with Roger."

"He has the male perspective. And he might have heard things. Men gossip like washerwomen among themselves, you know. They put a bluff face on it, but they indulge just the same."

"There is nothing disreputable to hear."

"Splendid. We will simply have a pleasant family dinner together."

"Do you promise?"

"Go along with you, impudent girl."

Fenella gave her a hug, then hurried after her husband. She found him in the corridor outside. "That felt like an interrogation," he said.

Fenella wondered if she should apologize. It wouldn't be honest. She wasn't sorry. His answers had been fascinating. "Grandmamma is extremely forthright."

He smiled at her. "An understatement. But answering her was interesting. I hadn't thought about some of that before. And I'm determined to prove myself to her."

"For my sake."

Roger nodded. "And for my own. Clearly, her respect is a thing worth having."

Fenella nodded.

"Nearly as much as yours."

"My respect?"

"I hope I may earn it eventually."

Fenella looked into his eyes. During the talk with her grandmother, a new idea had suggested itself to her. Perhaps there was madly in love and then there was…gradually overtaken by love? Could that be a hope? "You do have it," she said.

"That means a great deal." He took her hand and held it. The tenderness in his eyes made Fenella tremble. It was marvelous to know that she hadn't made a mistake.

The current laird of Roslyn joined them later that day. Stocky and dark-haired, he didn't resemble his grandmother, or Fenella. As Roger acknowledged the introduction and met the other man's shrewd brown eyes sizing him up, he wondered how much of the current situation had been conveyed to him. He didn't have to wait for an answer. "Eloping with my cousin, man?" said the laird. He looked grim.

"Rob," said Fenella.

Roger didn't blame him for wanting to protect his cousin. But that role was his now, and he didn't intend to be supplanted. "It wasn't what we planned. I'd asked her to marry me before Mr. Fairclough's death threw all into confusion," he said.

"Took all my choices away from me," said Fenella. "Even my horse."

The laird glanced at their hostess. Some silent communication passed between the two. "Let us go in to dinner," said Fenella's grandmother.

They settled at table. Food was served, wine poured.

"I met Fenella when she was running up here to Scotland as a lass," said the laird then. "Found her lost and cowering under a holly tree like a little mouse."

"I was sheltering from the rain," Fenella protested. "I might have been a bit lost, but I was *not* cowering."

"'Wee, sleekit, cow'rin, tim'rous beastie,'" he replied mysteriously.

"Do not begin with your Robert Burns," said Fenella's grandmother. "A most improper person," she told Roger.

"But a right proper poet was Robbie," said the laird.

"If you are partial to low comedy."

"Aye, and so I am," he answered, a teasing gleam in his dark eyes. They went cool again as he turned to Roger. "She was running from you then, if I recall correctly."

"Well, you don't," said Roger. He'd had enough of the fellow's mistrust. And he wasn't accustomed to feeling so left out where Fenella was concerned. "Our fathers were pressing her. Not I." He met Fenella's warm gaze. "Because I was... I didn't." He ran out of words, maddeningly.

Her lips moved. Did they silently form the phrase *sodding sheep*? Surely not. "We will leave history out of this," she said. "Circumstances are quite different now, and there is no need to rehash all that *again*. Anyway, what I choose to do is not your affair, Rob."

"Not even if you bring scandal down on our family? Of which I am the head, I might remind you."

"Not of the Faircloughs," she replied. "That would be...who? My father's cousin Gerard? Oh, what does it matter. I'm not a Fairclough any longer. I'm—"

"Marchioness of Chatton," interrupted Roger, thinking it was time to remind them of that point. He wasn't some skirter or half-pay officer.

Fenella smiled. "So I am. Watch your step, Rob, or I'll overawe you with my consequence."

The laird examined her face. He turned to survey Roger. He exchanged another long look with his grandmother. Then, for the first time since he'd arrived, he laughed. "The first week Fenella was in Scotland, she challenged me to a bout of marksmanship," he told

Roger. "Shot the pips out of a playing card and beat me all hollow."

"And how you hated that," Fenella said. "You would not believe I'd actually managed it until I'd shredded half a deck."

"Well, a crack shot wasn't exactly usual among the girls I knew."

"I was nothing like them. I'm still not."

"True enough. Best mind your manners, Chatton, or she'll lob a bullet past your ear." He seemed only half-joking.

Roger had never seen Fenella sparkle so with a stranger. He'd known her only in their small neighborhood with gentlemen they'd been acquainted with all their lives. He was captivated anew, and just a bit jealous. He kept wanting to mention that he was her husband. But for once he managed not to blurt out an inappropriate remark.

"*He* has nothing to fear," said Fenella. "You, however, could use a setdown."

"Shall we go out and try a few rounds? You must have some pistols about, Grandmamma."

"I'm out of practice," said Fenella.

"So you admit that I'd best you now."

Fenella hesitated, and for a moment Roger thought she was going to jump up and accept the challenge. He looked forward to watching her trounce her cousin. But then she nodded. "I expect you would, Rob."

"Really? You concede?"

Their grandmother made a small sound.

Fenella and her cousin turned to her like plants

stirred by the wind. "We need to talk about averting a scandal," the old woman said.

"Just tell everyone that you're behind the match," replied the laird. "Who'd dispute it? Or dare to argue?"

"No one," said Fenella with a fond smile for her grandmother.

"Well, I suppose that is the plan, more or less. With a few refinements." Their hostess turned to Roger. "Your mother will add her approval?"

He nodded. "She's very fond of Fenella."

"And I of her."

The old lady nodded. "Your sisters' husbands are gabsters."

"Shoot 'em," said the laird.

This earned him a stern glance. "You are not to have any more wine," said his grandmother.

"Yes, ma'am." He pushed his glass away. "Only joking."

"They must be brought around."

"I'll speak to them," said Roger.

His tone made the others turn to gaze at him.

"They won't cause problems," he added.

Fenella's grandmother and her cousin offered respectful nods. The look Fenella gave him sent a wave of heat from Roger's head to his toes.

Fifteen

THE MARQUESS OF CHATTON BROUGHT HIS NEW MAR-
chioness home to the castle a week later, to a warm
and lively welcome. He found that his mother had
already moved back to the dower house, a pleasant,
roomy residence half a mile away across the park. Lord
Macklin remained and was soon exercising his genius
for keeping out of the way when he wasn't wanted.

Roger was delighted to install Fenella as the new
mistress of the household. The servants knew her, of
course, but not in this role. And if, now and then, a
thread of worry nagged at him, he was able to push it
away. There must always be a period of adjustment in
the early days of a marriage, he told himself. His life
with Fenella was pure bliss compared to his first foray
into matrimony. She would soon settle and regain
her spirits. Not that she moped or drooped, he hastily
amended to himself. She was happy. He was nearly
certain she was happy. He had no reason to suppose
that there was some spark missing. Probably, she was
still worried about her father's legacy. That could be
easily remedied.

The next morning, he prepared himself to visit her former home and settle the matter of her inheritance.

"I should go with you," Fenella said. "Though I must admit I don't really wish to see my brothers-in-law."

"Symmes and Gissing will expect me to handle the business," he replied.

"Oh yes. What could a mere female have to say?"

"An idiotic attitude. You know I don't share it. But I would be delighted to do this for you."

She bowed her head. "Thank you."

Roger rode over on the familiar lane and was admitted to the Clough House by a doleful-looking maid. He found that a very different atmosphere had descended over the place since he'd last been inside. What had been a warm, well-run establishment now felt slipshod. There was dust in the corners. Tension showed in the set of the maid's shoulders as she took him upstairs.

Fenella's brothers-in-law, when he was brought to them in the drawing room, scowled at him. "This is the height of effrontery, showing your face here," said Gissing, trying to use his bulk to loom.

Macklin had warned Roger about the man's habit of bluster. "We are married to sisters," Roger replied, trying with his tone to suggest that it was best they get along.

"Now that Fenella has money," replied slender, satirical Symmes, openly mocking. "When you refused her before."

Roger's temper flared, but he suppressed it. He wasn't going to be baited or pulled into side arguments.

"And you've caused a scandal," said Gissing. "An outrage!"

Roger raised his eyebrows. This couldn't be allowed. "I beg your pardon?" He outranked them, and he offered Fenella every advantage. Though he didn't enjoy the process, those points had to be made. The brothers-in-law had no worldly reason to object to the match.

"Running off to Scotland," said Gissing. "Disgraceful. Not to mention inconvenient. Kept us hanging about this wretched place far longer than we planned."

"You might have gone home," said Roger.

"With this scandal hanging over us?" asked Symmes. "I think not."

"I really don't know what you mean. We have been staying with Fenella's grandmother, her favorite relative. Are you acquainted with Lady McClaren?" He knew that they'd barely met her. They didn't move in such exalted circles. Pretension was tiresome, but these two deserved a setdown.

"*She* is part of this?" said Symmes.

"Our marriage, you mean? Of course." And if this suggested that she'd known in advance, well, Fenella's grandmother had agreed to the plan.

"We are looking into having this runaway marriage set aside," said Gissing. "There is a case to be made."

Pure bluster, Roger thought. Macklin was right. Gissing was accustomed to getting his way by intimidation. Still, Roger couldn't believe he would dare hint at annulment. That was out of the question. He hated the very idea. He gave the two men his coldest, hardest stare. "If you try, you will be very sorry. Your wives will not appreciate the results."

"Do you dare threaten us?"

"I defend my own," replied Roger. "With every resource at my command." He didn't need to say that these were considerable. Here, in the neighborhood where his castle dominated the countryside, this was obvious.

The two men looked as if they'd tasted something foul.

"Perhaps we could get to business?" Roger continued. "And put the rest of this nonsense behind us." He didn't like them, but he didn't *want* to be at odds. They were the ones fomenting trouble.

"We have no—" began Gissing, but Symmes silenced him with a gesture.

"You'll receive Fenella's portion of the estate," said the latter sourly. "Most of that will come once this place is sold."

"I might take the lead in that," Roger offered. "I'm right here and know the local values."

Gissing scowled at him. "We've already written to a top fellow in London," he said. "Handled the sale of Rivington last year."

"We should get a good price," Symmes added. The thought seemed to lighten his mood. "I've ridden about the land. It's in good order."

Roger couldn't resist. "Fenella did a superb job managing it throughout her father's illness."

"Did she say so?" Gissing's laugh was patronizing. "I expect that was the steward. Already living under the cat's foot, are you, Chatton?"

He meant it as an insult, but Roger didn't care. It was a step toward accepting their marriage, and that was all he wanted from these two. Along with an honest accounting of Fairclough's legacy, which he would see that they got. Beyond that, he and Fenella would let some time pass, and then they'd see them only at family gatherings now and then. He would do his best to get along with his new in-laws, if it was humanly possible.

      ❧

She would have preferred that her husband did not return to a shouting match in his drawing room, Fenella thought with a mixture of amusement and irritation. Surely her sisters' husbands would have provided him with enough friction for one day? But here was Roger back to find a sullen, near tearful John Symmes refusing to hear that he could not come to stay at Chatton Castle without consulting his father.

"Mebbe your dad would be glad for you to make a visit," said Tom, who had, reluctantly, reported John's presence to Lord Macklin, who had brought both of them along to Fenella. It seemed that her nephew had tried to persuade Tom to go back to his rambling life and take John along. And when he could not, he'd tried to convince Tom to hide him at Chatton, like a stowaway on a great ship.

"He won't be!" said John. "He doesn't care about anything I want. He brought Wrayle, who's been prosing on and on about all the things I do wrong. They'll drag me home and shut me up in my room until school begins. With Wrayle there *persecuting* me." Hands tightly clasped, he gazed up at Fenella. "I'm to be in the pageant next week. I promised. With the mud and all. Can't you make him let me stay?"

"I doubt he would listen to me," she had to tell him. "He's rather angry with me just now."

"Because you got married? Why does he mind about that?"

Fenella tried to form an answer that John would understand. She wanted to help him, but she was certain that his father would refuse requests just to spite her at this point. And Greta would go along with him because apparently she always did. She hadn't gotten rid of Wrayle, for example, despite Fenella's warning about him.

While she was still searching for a reply, John turned to Roger. "Couldn't you ask him, Lord Chatton?"

She watched Roger ponder the problem. He was so kind; he'd try to find a way. But there wasn't one. "What about Colonel Patterson?" he asked.

Everyone gazed at him in surprise.

"He's overseeing the pageant," Roger went on. "He's got John all prepared for his part. He won't want to lose him. And he's a hard fellow to refuse."

"A highly influential man," said Macklin. "In London and the country. Far more than his military title suggests. Any sensible person would be glad to do him a favor. A good idea."

If Sherrington Symmes saw an advantage, he would jump to take it, Fenella thought. She caught Macklin's eye. "But will John's father know this?"

"Someone will have to drop a word in Symmes's ear," the earl replied. "I can attempt it, if you like."

The adults in the room exchanged doubtful looks. Symmes was not pleased with Macklin after their earlier encounter. He was unlikely to listen to any of them.

"Ought to hint about it to that Wrayle fella instead," said Tom. "He likes to winkle things out. Secrets, like. And then tattle about them to his master."

John, who had been looking back and forth anxiously, nodded. "He does. Better than anything."

"Very clever," said Macklin. "Could you find an opportunity to speak to him, Tom?"

"Easy. He comes 'round the village tavern, poking and prying, asking what's happening up at Chatton. Driving the barmaid distracted." Tom looked disapproving.

"But how would you bring the talk around to Colonel Patterson?" Fenella asked.

"People must be discussing the pageant," said Macklin.

Tom nodded. "I could say as how I'm in it, and everybody praises the colonel."

"I will give you some details that might be mentioned," the earl added. "And would definitely impress."

It was agreed that Tom would foster an awe-inspiring image of Colonel Patterson in Wrayle's mind. And that Roger would ask the colonel to intervene. The plan was explained to John, who hadn't followed all of it. "We're supposed to go in two days," he objected. "There's no time."

"I'll find Wrayle today," Tom said. "Right now. Go over to the house and hang about the kitchen if I have to."

"And I'll go and see the colonel later," said Roger.

Fenella wondered if the older man would fall in with their scheme. He seemed a high stickler and was not acquainted with her brother-in-law, as far as she knew.

On the other hand, he was militant about the success of the pageant. He treated it like a campaign over which he had been given command, and did not intend to lose.

Tom took John away, the younger boy having promised that he would go home. Macklin soon followed them, saying he had letters to write. Roger sat beside Fenella on the sofa.

"Is it right to hope this works, I wonder?" she asked. "I should wish, rather, that John was happy with his family. And we could find a way to reconcile him and his father."

"That may well happen on its own. Fathers and sons butt heads and then reconcile."

"Do they?"

"My father and I certainly did. Yet we got along rather well most of the time."

"I often envied his pride in you," Fenella said.

"It's part of a father's job to be proud and encouraging."

She made a soft sound, like a puff of skepticism.

That remark had been inept, Roger realized, remembering occasions when he'd overheard Fenella's father express disappointment in her. Fairclough had been a fool in this area, failing to see the gem in his household. "That's what I think, at least," he said. "A father can support the spirits of his children. I hope to be such a father."

Fenella gave him a startled look. His point appeared to sink in as she held his eyes for a moment. She looked down. "I'm sure you will be." She bit her lip. "It's such a responsibility, becoming a parent. I sometimes wonder what sort of mother I will make."

"You'll be an exemplary mother."

She gazed at him again. "You're quick to compliment, but why should I be? I've had no mother to emulate since I was fifteen. Even before that, we had so many disputes over my want of conduct. Greta and Nora may remember her as a kind parent, but I do not. I've never been around children. Until John, this summer. With his snakes." She gave a half laugh, though her expression remained worried. "Can he be a representative example?"

"You'll be a fine mother because you're kind and sensible." Roger wanted to add *loving*, but they hadn't spoken of love. Somehow he couldn't say the word.

"That hardly seems enough."

He hadn't known of this doubt in her. She'd appeared so strong and confident since her return from Scotland.

"Of course we have your mother nearby to help," Fenella added. "She's a wonderful model of motherhood." The idea seemed to comfort her.

He'd seen Fenella as beautiful and spirited and sometimes annoyingly stubborn, but never so vulnerable. "Mama and I have had our disputes."

"Really? You always seem in harmony."

"I don't think that's true of any family. Not *always*."

The word seemed to startle her, as if it had struck her before in some conversation. "I suppose not." Suddenly, she smiled. "Grandmamma used to ring tremendous peals over her son. And he was a fierce Scottish laird! Yet I know they were extremely fond of one another."

Having experienced a hint of that lady's disapproval,

Roger didn't envy her progeny. But he said, "There, you see?"

Fenella looked at him. "See what?"

Roger was lost in her blue eyes, which had regained their lovely spark, and for an instant couldn't remember the subject. "Not always harmony," he managed finally.

Her smile widened. "I wager I could learn to shout like Grandmamma. She certainly had a marked effect on you."

"Please don't!"

"No." Her smile faded. "I couldn't carry it off."

He took her hand. "Are you happy?"

"Of course."

He thought she spoke too quickly, and then chastised himself for being over-nice.

"Things did go so very fast," she added, making Roger's heart sink a little. "We'd barely acknowledged that we…were drawn to each other, and then we were eloping. We were so pressed by circumstances." She frowned at him. "Where would we have ended up, if not for Papa's death?"

"There's no way of knowing, but—"

"Exactly. Were we forced into a false position?"

She'd cut him off before he could insist that they would have been wed in any case. "You think our marriage is false?"

"No, of course not. I didn't mean that!" She squeezed his hand. "Our situation is so new. I expect that adjustment takes time."

Though he'd had the same thought, Roger wasn't satisfied with this. But he didn't want to probe farther for fear of hearing worrisome revelations. He longed to kiss her, but felt this might be the wrong moment. He was certain of his choice of wife. Did she feel the same?

❧

Their scheme with Colonel Patterson was successful, and John came to stay at Chatton Castle when his father departed. But they were forced to accept Wrayle into their household along with the boy. Fenella saw it as a sort of punishment from her sister's husband. Wrayle's smirking presence was a constant reminder of Symmes's disapproval. That did not mean that the valet would be allowed free rein, however. Fenella took the man aside before he had even unpacked and said, "If I find you've spoken inappropriately to any of the maids—"

"You'll what?" he interrupted. "You can't send me away this time. I shall do as I please." His arrogance was insupportable.

"I'll order William to stay at your side," Fenella replied. Another reason to be glad she'd been able to hire all the Fairclough servants who couldn't find other positions when the house was closed up, she thought. With Roger's mother in an establishment of her own, they'd needed additional help. "At all times," she added. "It would be quite a tedious duty for him. And put him in a foul mood, I expect." Actually, the tall footman enjoyed the role of protector. And he was itching for an excuse to floor Wrayle.

"I'll appeal to Lord Chatton," Wrayle sputtered.

Fenella shrugged.

The valet regained some of his sly insolence. "He

won't want the neighborhood to hear that he's under the thumb of a managing female." He smirked. "There are other things I might tell about your affairs as well, *Lady* Chatton."

Tell or fabricate, Fenella thought. Certainly he would have gotten an earful about the elopement. But she doubted that he'd be limited by the truth. How did a person become so unpleasant?

"And I daresay people may wonder why a hulking footman is required to keep me silent." Wrayle clearly thought this was the coup de grâce of his argument. He waited for her capitulation with his familiar smirk.

There was no reasoning with the man. "William will join you directly," Fenella replied, and left Wrayle with his mouth open in surprise.

As she walked downstairs to speak to the footman, she knew that William would gladly play his part for the few days until John and Wrayle departed. And he would prevent Wrayle from spreading his venom both in the house and out of it. There was no danger that the young footman would be swayed by Wrayle's stories. The man's treatment of William's friends among the maids had hardened his, and the whole household's, opinion against him.

Symmes and Gissing left the neighborhood. The last August days lazed past, with only the approach of the festival on Lindisfarne to vary the household's routine. John settled in, irritated by Wrayle but companioned by Tom. Fenella enjoyed her role as mistress of Chatton Castle, creating the beautiful, cozy retreat she'd imagined for herself when she first saw her grandmother's.

There was, naturally, widespread curiosity about

their hasty marriage, and a few spiteful remarks were an irritant or a hurtful disappointment, depending on the source. The anonymous letters had sown malice that would take time to fade. Nothing to be done about that but show people the truth of her character, Fenella knew. It helped that there had been no sign of letters since their return. Fenella told herself that they'd stopped. She even hoped that perhaps the writer regretted sending them.

When she said as much to Roger as they were going up to bed one night, he said, "I'd like to think so. But I don't believe the sort of person who'd write them is likely to be sorry."

"I suppose not."

"Too occupied with making trouble and gloating over the havoc they cause," he added.

At this description, a thought struck Fenella. "I wonder if it could have been Wrayle?"

"That valet fellow Symmes foisted off on us?"

She nodded. "He's exactly the sort of person you just described. And he has a grudge against me."

"You?" Roger looked offended at the idea. "Why should he?"

"Because I won't allow him to creep about the maids, and I keep his bullying of John to a minimum."

"Why do we have such a servant in the house?"

"Well, I don't wish to, but John's father insisted, as a condition of allowing John to stay. You needn't worry. I've given William the task of watching Wrayle. He won't let him go beyond the line."

"And rather enjoy it, if what I've seen of William is anything to go by."

"Precisely." Fenella sat down at the dressing table and began to pull pins out of her hair. She'd taken to dispensing with her maid at bedtime. She and Roger had evolved some more...delightful routines.

"Anonymous letters would be precisely Wrayle's style," she said. "He is a pernicious snoop and underhanded."

Roger's voice came from the dressing room off the bedchamber. "Didn't the letters begin before the fellow returned to the neighborhood with Symmes?"

Fenella ran over the timing in her mind. "Yes. That's true."

"So he would have had to find someone to deliver them."

"He could have paid someone."

"Right. Would he have known the...sorry tale well enough?" Whenever the topic of the letters came up, Roger sounded guilty.

"He makes sure to hear everything." But William had reported that Wrayle wasn't much more popular in the village than in the castle. Would anyone have passed along a stale bit of gossip, which was what the story had been before the letters revived it? It didn't seem very likely. Fenella was disappointed to see the holes in her theory. She would have liked to place the blame squarely on Wrayle rather than one of her neighbors. "Well, if it was him, he won't be sending any more. William won't give him the opportunity."

Roger came out of the dressing room in his shirt-sleeves and stocking feet, and Fenella was distracted by how very handsome he looked. "Macklin's lad Tom is still on the track of the letter carrier," he said. "He's certain he'll find something."

"Tom is a kind boy and seems intelligent. I like him. But"—she sighed—"best just to get on with life, I suppose. It's not as if I have nothing to do."

He bent to kiss the back of her neck. "And you are doing it all splendidly. You are a superb mistress of Chatton Castle, as I knew you would be."

Fenella met his gaze in the mirror. "Why? What made you think that the girl I was, or even the woman I became, would be *superb*?" There was a hint of challenge in her voice, as if the accolade was inappropriate.

She never quite seemed to see what a marvel she was. Roger didn't understand that. It seemed so obvious to him. And she wasn't easily fobbed off with empty compliments either. On the one hand, that was good, because he could never think of any empty compliments. On the other hand, it presented difficulties, because he had to find a way to put her wonderful qualities into words. That would require a speech, as she had so many, and the chances of him saying it right were slim. Perhaps a distraction? He held her eyes in the mirror as he undid the top button of her gown. A small smile curved her lips, as if she knew what he was doing and didn't mind in the least.

Roger undid another button. Together, they'd developed a glorious nighttime ritual, an undressing game that drove both of them wild. Slowly, and deliciously, until they couldn't wait a moment longer to leap into bed. He undid another button. The sleeve of Fenella's gown fell off her shoulder, and he dropped a kiss on the bare skin. He heard her breath catch and reveled in it, as he did every time he was able to make that happen.

Roger was making a study of his new wife's body, on a quest to discover everything that brought her pleasure. It was the most enchanting study he'd ever undertaken. And he felt he was doing rather well—certainly better than he ever had in school, he thought with a smile.

Another button. The bodice of her gown slid down. Fenella rose and let the garment fall to the floor. Now there were lacings and a petticoat and stockings, in an escalating pattern of arousal. Her fingers went to the fastenings of his shirt. Which had to be taken slowly, in concert with his efforts. Because when she moved on to the breeches, well, that was usually where the game broke down and they tumbled into bed.

They'd found their way to a heady combination of breathless need and tenderness and shattering release. Roger reveled in it, and he was pretty certain she did as well. She seemed to have dedicated herself to a similar sort of study from her side. He was undoubtedly a very lucky man, he thought, before a flood of desire wiped all thought away.

Sixteen

"A FRIEND OF MINE IS ARRIVING IN THE NEIGHBORHOOD tomorrow," Macklin told the assembled party at dinner the following evening.

Roger's mother had joined them for the meal, as she often did. It was another boon of his marriage that she and Fenella liked each other so well, Roger thought. "Indeed?" she said. "A happy coincidence."

"She's taking part in the pageant at Lindisfarne," Macklin replied. "Giving a reading from *Macbeth*."

"You know the famous London actress who's performing?" Fenella asked.

The earl nodded.

"How…unexpected."

"That I should know an actress?"

"Well, yes. And call her a friend."

"I was acquainted with her husband first. He's a prominent banker. My banker, in fact." Macklin smiled. "Mrs. Thorpe is a respectable married lady, despite what some may think of her profession. I seem to say that each time I mention her."

"I thought the actress coming was called Simmons," said Roger.

"She uses her maiden name for the stage."

"And her banker's name for society," said Fenella.

"Precisely," replied the earl.

"Where is she staying?" asked the dowager marchioness.

"An inn near the island, I believe."

"No, no, she must come and stay with me," replied Roger's mother. "It will be so amusing."

"She would be a charming guest," said Macklin.

Roger wondered if he should object to this plan, but he couldn't see why. Which was fortunate because he was sure his mother wouldn't listen to him.

Mrs. Thorpe was duly contacted, invited, and installed at the dower house. The next evening she joined their company at dinner. An impressive lady in her middle years, she carried herself with immense dignity. Her voice was musical, with a note of command that Roger thought must be helpful in her profession. If he hadn't known she was an actress, he would have assumed she was a grand lady of the neighborhood. Watching her converse with his mother and his wife, Roger for some reason thought of Fenella's grandmother. If she ever had a set-to with Mrs. Thorpe, the confrontation would rival the epic bare-knuckle match between Gentleman Jackson and Daniel Mendoza, he thought. He wouldn't want to predict the outcome. And what had put such a bizarre idea into his head?

"Yes, I am rather known for my Lady Macbeth," Mrs. Thorpe said in answer to Fenella's question. "I'm past the age for girlish parts."

The idea didn't appear to disturb her.

"Indeed, I'm thinking of retiring from the stage," she added.

"That would be a great loss," said Macklin.

Mrs. Thorpe smiled benignly at him. "Knowing when to withdraw gracefully into the wings is the mark of a truly great actress. I've done more than I ever hoped I could when I was a girl." She looked pensive. "Though not more than I dreamed."

"Have all your dreams come true?" asked Fenella in a curious tone.

"The important ones. But then those *would* be the most likely."

"Why do you say that?" Fenella seemed quite interested in the new guest.

"Because that's where I worked the hardest," replied Mrs. Thorpe. "Except—"

The others at the table waited, transfixed by her voice and presence. Mrs. Thorpe smiled at them. "Marriage came to me as a gift. When I least expected it and with very little effort on my part. Mr. Thorpe surprised me, I admit. And asked only my whole heart."

"Perhaps you were a dream of his," said Macklin. "Indeed, from what I know, I'm certain you were. And are."

Mrs. Thorpe turned to gaze at him. She looked moved, her perfect facade for once undone. "I like that. Thank you."

They saw less of his mother and Macklin after Mrs. Thorpe's arrival, and Roger had the feeling they were having a lively time over at the dower house. He might have envied them, but he had his wife, and they found plenty of diversions of their own as they settled into their partnership. And so Roger was simply glad that his mother had interesting companions to amuse her.

❦

At a knock on his bedchamber door, Arthur looked up from the writing desk and bade the person enter.

Tom came in, his homely face showing satisfaction. "I'm fairly certain I've found out who carried those letters," he said.

"Good work," replied Arthur. He set aside the missive he'd been writing and gestured at the armchair by the window. Tom sat down.

"I can't say for sure," the lad went on. "Seems there haven't been any letters just lately."

"I haven't heard of any."

Tom nodded. "So I couldn't follow the messenger. Had to do a bit of a nose about instead. Talking to this one and that one. Piecing bits together. I found there's a girl, daughter of the miller, coming up on nine years old. Seemingly she's been where she oughtn't to be, and then not shown up where she's supposed to be, a deal of times this last month. Enough so's people noticed. And all of them places where she wasn't meant to be were houses where letters came."

"A girl," said Arthur. "Not what I expected. I would have thought a boy less likely to be noticed." He wondered what this might reveal about the letter writer.

Tom nodded again. "The thing about Lally—this girl—she's just a bit dim. Or mebbe that ain't the right word. I don't know. Folks say she's generally lost in a daydream, pays you no more attention than a songbird. And she wanders. I reckon someone took advantage of that."

The earl frowned. "She doesn't sound like the best choice to carry secret messages."

"Not who I'd pick. But then mebbe I'd be wrong."

"What do you mean?"

Tom settled deeper in the chair. "I've been thinking on it," he said. "We figured somebody was being paid to take the letters. And that we could give him more money to tell us where they came from. 'Cause that's what he'd be interested in. The pay."

"Right," said Arthur.

"But if the person weren't doing it for money." Tom spread his hands. "Then we'd look all nohow."

"Why would they be doing it then?"

"I talked to Lally." The lad smiled. "Couldn't really call it a conversation. She talks about what *she* wants, not what a person might want to know. But I'd swear she has a secret. Right pleased about it, she is. Hugging it to herself, like. And she won't be telling."

"If I spoke to her parents?" Arthur asked.

Tom shook his head. "They'd want to help you, most likely. There might be shouting. But Lally won't care. I'm thinking people shout at her a good bit."

He wasn't going to bully a dreamy child, Arthur thought.

"Another thing is, I reckon that girl knows every nook and path hereabouts. Even if she thinks that fairies live in the mounds. She could slip about easy."

"Perhaps we can keep an eye on her. See where she goes. She might visit the letter writer."

"I got a few boys doing that," Tom said.

"They won't plague her?"

"I picked out some good fellows. Those with a bit of heart. Said as how her folks were worried about her, didn't want her getting hurt."

"Well done."

"And we are paying *them*," Tom added with a shrug.

"Do you need money?"

"I will, by tomorrow."

Arthur fetched his purse and opened it, offering Tom a five-pound note.

Laughing, the lad waved it away. "Coin, my lord. We ain't making their fortunes here. A handful of sixpences, by choice."

"I'll ask the housekeeper for change and get them to you." Arthur replaced the banknote.

Tom rose. "I'll keep my eyes open as well."

"On your rambles in search of snakes?" asked Arthur with a smile.

Tom grimaced. "There's no more of that. That Wrayle fellow's keeping John to his books. Only way he can get at him, with William hovering about."

"Who is William?"

"Footman." Tom face showed sly enjoyment. "Her ladyship set him on Wrayle, seeing as how Wrayle ain't got no manners belowstairs." Having explained this, Tom still lingered.

"Was there something else?" Arthur always enjoyed Tom's point of view.

"Well, I *was* wondering, my lord, what's the point of Latin? John says he's got to learn it, no joke, and that there's six different ways to write each and every word." Tom shook his head. "But nobody speaks

Latin any more, seemingly, haven't for hundreds of years." The lad's homely face was creased in puzzlement. "I like learning myself, my lord. You know that. But I don't see the point of knowing a language that ain't around any longer."

It was always interesting having Tom about, Arthur thought. The lad's curiosity allowed him—or goaded him—to delve into matters Arthur had never considered before. Was he to justify English pedagogy now? "Our own language developed out of Latin," he said. "Partly, at least. So knowing Latin can help one work out the meaning of words one doesn't know. Also, there is the heritage of the Roman Empire. Their history and literature and so on were written in Latin. All the best schools teach it." Immediately Arthur hoped that last point wouldn't wound a boy who'd had minimal opportunities for schooling.

Tom nodded, showing no sign of chagrin. "It's not just Wrayle bullying John then. That's good." He grinned. "And that's why Wrayle keeps twitting me for not knowing a single bit of Latin."

"Do you need me to speak to this Wrayle?" Arthur didn't like the mention of bullying.

"Naught for you to worry about, my lord."

"Very well." A thought came, and Arthur wondered if Tom's sense of mischief was rubbing off on him. "I could teach you some Latin tags."

"Tags?"

"Common phrases that people use."

Tom considered. "Nah. I expect I couldn't carry it off. And John and me have an idea brewing for Wrayle."

"Do I want to know what it is?"

"Best not." Tom's grin was impish.

Arthur had learned, over the course of their acquaintance, to trust Tom's instincts. The lad wouldn't do anything beyond the line. And from what he'd heard from Clayton as well, this Wrayle deserved a setdown. So he asked nothing more, letting Tom go on his way. Arthur was due at the dower house for tea and conversation that was certain to be delightful. He set aside his letter and prepared to walk across the Chatton Castle property.

It was a positive joy to see these two ladies side by side, he thought a little while later. They presented a picture of mature beauty and dignity. Mrs. Thorpe's black hair was immaculately dressed, as always. Of the two, her clothes obviously came from the more fashionable modiste, being the height of the current London mode. Her face was a bit pale, but nothing could detract from its classic bone structure. Her blue eyes gleamed with sharp intelligence. In contrast, the dowager marchioness's blond hair gleamed in a shaft of sunshine from the window. She was more slender, her gaze softer but with equal acuity. Arthur was happy that the two women had found much in common and was pleased to have given Helena another new friend. They'd been making plans for her to go to London and see a play of Mrs. Thorpe's in the spring.

When they had settled their arrangements, Mrs. Thorpe turned to Arthur and said, "You haven't asked me about my visit to Shropshire."

"True," he replied. "I await your report."

"Report?" Helena looked interested. "What does that mean? Is this part of your campaign of helping?"

"Yes," said Arthur. "The last bit of it, in fact. Mrs. Thorpe was making a visit to a friend in the area where the young man lives, so I sent her on a reconnaissance mission." Somehow, Arthur could never bring himself to use Mrs. Thorpe's first name. It simply did not feel appropriate, even if he had been given leave, which he had not. A completely different case than Helena somehow. Of course he and Mrs. Thorpe hadn't been friends in their youth.

"Reconnaissance." Mrs. Thorpe smiled at the label. "It did rather feel like that. Alberdene is a curious place, practically in Wales, and like something out of a Gothic novel."

"Ruins and bats and spiky towers?" asked Helena.

"Not far off, particularly the ruins part."

"May I ask who lives there? Or is it a secret?"

Arthur didn't see why it should be. He'd confided other things to his hostess, and he trusted her. "The young Duke of Compton. I'm looking forward to seeing this ancestral pile."

"It very nearly is a pile," said Mrs. Thorpe. "It looked like it might subside into a heap of stones at any moment."

Helena was looking at Arthur. "You're going soon then?"

"I've stayed a long while," he replied. "When I was never invited here in the first place."

"It's been lovely to have you. I shall miss your company."

Arthur noticed Mrs. Thorpe's raised eyebrow. "We are old acquaintances and now have agreed to be firm friends," he said.

She surveyed them with a shrewd eye, and accepted this.

"And what will you do in a pile of stones in Shropshire?" asked Helena.

"I don't know yet," he replied.

"And that is a great part of the attraction," she said.

Once again noting her keen understanding, Arthur had to nod. "There is a certain excitement in not knowing."

"Be sure to pack your woolens," said Mrs. Thorpe. "It was already growing colder when I was there, and Alberdene did not appear well heated. Or indeed well anything. The owner is really a duke?"

"He is."

"Well, I suppose even dukes fall on hard times. I beg you will not ask me to take part in any schemes you hatch there."

"Have you helped with others?" Helena asked.

"My nephew's case," said Arthur. "I told you about him."

"A most happy outcome," said Mrs. Thorpe, with the satisfaction of one who had supported the endeavor. "I wish you good fortune in Shropshire."

"On my own hook," Arthur said with a smile. "Granted. I will stay for your performance here, of course."

"You have seen me as Lady Macbeth before. More than once, I think."

"But I haven't seen Chatton as a marauding Viking."

"Or the bishop as St. Cuthbert," put in Helena. "I understand he finds the robes sadly plain. And they chafe."

"How do you know that?" Arthur asked.

"And where precisely do they chafe?" asked Mrs. Thorpe.

"That I *don't* know," replied Helena with dancing eyes. "But the vicar told Mr. Benson, and he told me. I suppose the bishop must have complained to Reverend Cheeve. *He* took that as a sign that he should be been given the role. He is still exceedingly bitter for a clergyman."

He would miss her company, too, Arthur thought, but the pageant would mark the end of his visit. All seemed to be well here, and he felt his work might be done. If it weren't for the lingering question of the anonymous letter writer. But that abject individual would probably fade into obscurity, as such people most often did, nursing their malice in small, mean corners.

Seventeen

FENELLA TOOK A DEEP BREATH OF THE SUMMER AIR moving past her cheeks and enjoyed the view over a stretch of low hills. It was restful to drive a gig along a country lane—a much finer gig than she'd had at Clough House—and think her own thoughts. The Chatton Castle household operated with more pomp and required more attention than her old home. She was happy in her new role, but she was also glad to be away for a brief time. So she'd slipped out to make her visit to Mrs. Dorne, which had been put off by John's antics at Lindisfarne and then a positive rush of events.

She sat with the old lady for nearly an hour, eating one of the cakes she'd delivered and discussing the merits of the liniment she'd brought, as well as the doings of Mrs. Dorne's various offspring, some of whom were stationed in the outermost reaches of the British Empire. By the time she started back, Fenella was considerably refreshed and looking forward to being in her own house again. Her own house. She repeated the words silently. A few weeks ago she'd had no notion that she'd soon be mistress of Chatton

Castle. And a wife. Perhaps before long a mother. As her horse ambled along the familiar route, Fenella's thoughts drifted off into the various pleasures that her change of status had brought.

A hissing sound startled her out of her daydream. It was followed by a sharp blow to her left arm, just below the shoulder. Fenella looked down in astonishment. An arrow had passed through the skin on the outside of her arm. It stuck there, quivering, the reddened head behind her, the fletching in front. Blood welled up and flowed onto her shawl, pinned in place by the missile.

The pain came then, sharp and dizzying. Fenella bent under the onslaught.

Another arrow passed over her head with a hiss like a hunting cat. That one would have pierced her chest if it had found its mark.

Crouching even lower, Fenella slapped the reins on the horse's back. "Go!" she shouted. "Run, Dexter!"

Startled, the horse surged forward. Fenella slapped the reins again, urging him to greater speed. The pain in her arm spiked as the motion caused the arrow to wobble and shift. This grew worse with every bump in the road. "You will not faint," she commanded through clenched teeth. "You will not!" If she slowed, the archer might catch her. If she fell, she'd certainly break bones, or her neck, at this speed.

At least one more arrow arced toward her, but it passed well behind the gig. After that, Fenella wasn't certain. She didn't see any more. But the ride had become a haze of teeth-gritting pain. Her attention narrowed to urging Dexter on each time he tried to slow.

Which was often. Dexter was accustomed to gentle
rambles, not desperate races down winding lanes.

After what seemed an eternity, Chatton Castle
appeared before them. Fenella slapped the reins again,
and they hurtled up to it. The gig careened under the
arch and slewed around into the stable yard. A surprised
groom came out to receive the vehicle. At his shocked
cry, others appeared. "My lady, what's happened?"

"Someone shot at me."

Horrified exclamations rose around her.

"From a clump of trees." She tried to remember the
moment of the attack. "Near the turn to the village."
Fenella swayed in the seat.

"Hold that horse, nodcock." The head groom came
to Fenella's side. "Let me help you, my lady."

"Yes, I should—" But when she moved to step
down, the arrow shifted and the pain made her cry out.

"Fetch Mrs. Burke," said the head groom to his
minions. "And his lordship. Run, cloth head!" He
reached up and lifted Fenella to the ground. "Rafe,
you ride for the doctor. Sharpish, go!" He offered his
arm to Fenella. "Can you walk, my lady? Or shall I
carry you?"

"Yes, of course I can walk." But Dexter shied, jerking the gig sideways. The carriage caught the head of
the arrow, knocking it sharply. Fenella cried out. She
reached for support, noticing that her whole arm now
ran with blood, and fell into darkness.

❦

Roger sat beside his wife's bed as Mrs. Burke bound
up her arm with a length of cotton bandage. He'd

cut the head off the arrow himself and eased it gently out even as he went quietly mad. Someone on his own land had shot at Fenella. Which was impossible, insane, because no one would. This didn't make sense. He was on good terms with all his tenants. She'd been driving along a common lane. She hadn't been creeping through the woodlands, where she might have been mistaken for a deer. By an idiot! And no hunter would use a bow and arrows. Nobody had for years and years. Snares, firearms, yes. But not this. A poacher? Perhaps. But none of that brotherhood would be lurking by a traveled lane. Still less would one risk a shot across it. Roger's thoughts bounced from one impossibility to another. And yet Fenella lay there, wounded and pale. He held her hand as Mrs. Burke took away the bowl of bloody water and felt as if his heart might burst out of his chest.

Fenella opened her eyes. She looked around her bedchamber, confused. "I told myself not to faint," she said.

"You didn't do so until you were home. You did splendidly." Roger squeezed her hand and tried to keep the frantic note out of his voice. "I don't understand what happened." He needed more information so he could catch her attacker.

"It makes no sense," she said, echoing his thought. "I was driving along the lane—"

"Alone."

"Yes, Roger, as I often have." She held his gaze until he had to look down. "And suddenly an arrow went through my arm." She looked at the bandage as if she still couldn't believe it. "I would assume it was a bizarre accident, but there was another when I was bent over."

"What?"

"It flew right above my head. If I hadn't crouched down, this would have been much more serious."

Roger couldn't sit still. He had to get up and pace. "This is unbelievable."

"And there was one more shot after that. At least. Then Dexter ran. That's all I saw." She frowned. "Someone was aiming at me. One arrow might be a mistake, but not three."

"If I had been with you—" he began.

"What? You would have caught the arrows with your bare hands?"

Of course he couldn't have done that, though he might have wished he could. "Why would anyone do this? How did they dare?"

Fenella shook her head. "I don't believe I have enemies. Now, if my brothers-in-law had not left the neighborhood, I might suspect Gissing."

"This is not a joking matter!"

"I know that." She put a hand to her wound.

"Are you in pain?"

"A little. Some."

"The doctor will be here soon."

"I'm not sure that's—"

"He will look at it!"

"Very well."

"I didn't mean to shout." He sat down beside her again and took her hand. "I've been so worried about you. And I am far more concerned now that I hear what happened."

She looked down at her bandage. "This isn't too bad."

"But it very nearly was, apparently. You will take a closed carriage from now on, should you go out. And have servants with you. We must withdraw from that scene in the Lindisfarne pageant obviously, and—"

"Roger," she interrupted.

He couldn't stop. "No one can touch you within these walls. I've never been so glad to live in a fortified castle. You will stay at home and be safe."

"Forever?"

Her dry tone on this one word brought him up short. His hand tightened on her fingers. "For a while."

"We must look into this incident and find the person responsible," she answered. "We will investigate, discover if anyone saw something, and bring the archer to justice. But I won't hide. I won't have my life so narrowed."

He started to object.

Fenella held up a hand. "I agree to use a closed carriage and not go out alone." She sighed. "I suppose I can't ride either, for now. But I won't be made a prisoner in my own house."

"Aren't you afraid? Because I'm terrified."

His vehemence caught her full attention.

"When I saw you lying there covered in blood and thought perhaps I'd lost you…" He had to swallow a tremor of fear. "I was desperate. I don't know what I'd do without you. Now that I've understood how very much I—" His voice broke on the words he needed to say to her. He mustn't get tangled up in them now!

"There is one person who hates me, seemingly," said Fenella.

"What?"

"The one who wrote those letters," she added. "They wanted to hurt me. And when the letters didn't work, perhaps they decided to do more."

"People who send anonymous threats are cowards," said Roger. His brain jittered from his curtailed declaration to fears for her to the knowledge that they'd never found the earlier culprit.

"So they say. But I suppose some might be different." She looked at him. "I can't think who else it might be, Roger. I've lived in this neighborhood most of my life and never made any enemies. Well, except you."

"Don't joke about that!"

"I'm sorry. But you must agree it's the most likely explanation for this." She indicated her bandaged arm.

"Perhaps."

"The only one that makes sense."

"All right." Roger tried a smile. He wanted to pour out eloquent speeches about his love for her, and to hear her say that she felt the same way. Particularly the second part, perhaps. He yearned for that, his throat tight with emotion. Wordless, of course. The frustration compounded his worry.

Fenella smiled back at him. She looked drawn and weary. This wasn't the time to press her.

"And so you must promise to take care," he said.

"I will."

The doctor arrived, putting an end to their private conversation. After an examination, he agreed with Mrs. Burke. Fenella had received a nasty, deep scratch, which would require time to heal. But it did not threaten her life. The wound should be kept very clean, and she should rest. Other than that, he was simply outraged by the incident. "What numbskull fires an arrow across a public lane?" he asked Roger. "Something should be done."

"Indeed. And it's worse than you know." Roger threw caution to the winds and drew the doctor out into the corridor to tell him the whole story. He wanted it spread through the neighborhood as rapidly as possible, in case anyone had seen the attack and could supply information. On this or any part of the tangle.

The doctor exclaimed and deplored and went away ready to tell everyone he encountered. Roger returned to the bedchamber to find Fenella drowsy from some potion he'd given her. The time for tender declarations had passed. For now.

Roger went downstairs to his study and sat down to write out the tale, so that it could be conveyed to his neighbors. But before he finished, he wondered how to send the messages. Fenella's theory was probably right. He had accepted that as the logic sank in. But it was barely possible that she'd been the victim of some lunatic archer. Was anyone who ventured out of Chatton Castle open to attack?

Roger shook his head as he scattered sand over lines of ink. Highly unlikely. Yet if so, even more reason to send out warnings. When he had produced a sufficient number of copies, he went to consult his head groom about danger to his staff. The man scoffed and assured him that his lads could manage the task.

"They're champion at sneaking about," he said. "The times I've gone looking for one or the other and found them gone." He shook his head. "They know the countryside better than anybody, too. They won't be caught out."

And so Roger sent off his notes, with a request at the end for any information the recipients might be able to gather.

And then he waited and longed for action.

Oddly it was Macklin, a stranger to the neighborhood, who finally brought him results. "Tom has found out something about the attack," the earl told him the following day when he found Roger in his study.

Roger came to his feet at once. "What? Where is he?"

"In the kitchen."

"Have him come—"

Macklin held up a restraining hand. "He has a way he wishes to do this," he interrupted.

"A way?" Roger frowned. "What does that mean?" He felt a spark of resistance. Tom was a pleasant lad, but this was Roger's problem.

"A method he thinks will produce the best results." Before Roger could protest, Macklin held up his hand again. "Tom is often wise beyond his years or background."

"What then?" asked Roger impatiently.

"He's brought someone to speak to your wife."

"No, she's not seeing anyone," Roger pronounced.

"A little girl," Macklin continued as if he hadn't spoken. "About nine years old, I believe. The daughter of the local miller."

"What has she to do with anything? Did she see something? Get her up here, and let us find out." Roger nearly shot off to the kitchen to find out for himself.

Macklin leaned a little toward him and spoke with quiet emphasis. "Tom thinks she's much more likely to tell a lady what she knows. She's an odd little creature, apparently."

"What, you think I'd frighten her?"

"You are, rightfully, agitated about this matter."

Silently, Roger admitted it. He was ready to shake information from the very trees. A little girl probably would find him intimidating. He would curb his impatience. "I'm coming along to listen," he said.

"Of course."

Ten minutes later, their strange delegation entered Fenella's bedchamber. She was sitting with a book open on her lap, but Roger didn't think she'd been reading. He knew she'd had her fill and more of *resting*.

Fenella examined the group as they spread out before her. She'd been prepared for their arrival, and she was curious about the little girl. The child was thin, with large, dark eyes and black hair that straggled as if she'd recently pushed through a thicket. There were thistles stuck in the hem of her gown and a bright feather at the bodice. She had a palpable, untidy charm. Tom stood protectively next to her. The two tall men hovered at the back. "This is Lally Graham, my lady," said Tom.

"Hello, Lally," said Fenella.

"You're her ladyship," replied the girl.

"Yes."

"The lady of the castle."

Fenella nodded, not certain where this was going.

The child turned to look at Roger. "But he's not the Sheriff of Nottingham."

"No, he's the Marquess of Chatton."

Lally frowned as if this didn't make sense. "What about the other one?"

"He's the Earl of Macklin," said Fenella.

"Like I told you," said Tom to the girl. When Fenella raised her eyebrows, he added, "I promised her this Nottingham fella wouldn't be here."

Lally caught sight of the arrow that had wounded Fenella. Macklin had told them to display it for this interview, and she had complied. The little girl stared at it. "It looks just like hers," she said.

Fenella saw Roger start. He took a step forward, but Macklin caught this arm and held him back. She approved. She suspected that this was a delicate moment, and she understood that she was to be the questioner. "Hers?" she asked.

Lally examined her, looking torn. "Did she really shoot you?"

Despite being struck by the female pronoun, Fenella merely pulled back her shawl and showed the bandage. "Someone put an arrow through my arm as I was driving along in my gig. On my way home."

"When you wouldn't stand and deliver?" asked Lally.

Did the girl think it had been a highwayman? Fenella wondered. That didn't make sense on a seldom-traveled country lane. There'd be too few people to rob. Even if a witless highwayman decided to use a bow. "No one asked me," she said. "I didn't see anyone. Only the arrows. Two other shots missed me."

Lally frowned as if this was puzzling. Fenella could see that Roger was itching to push her, but she stopped him with a look.

Whatever struggle Lally felt appeared to resolve itself. She stood straighter. "It's true," she said. "That looks just like one of Maid Marian's arrows."

"Maid Marian?" Fenella looked at Tom, who shrugged.

Lally nodded. "I met her in the wood. The Greenwood she called it."

"Maid Marian did." Fenella held the girl's eyes to keep her attention off the men's incredulous frowns.

"Yes. She was practicing with her bow and arrows like that." The child pointed at the broken missile.

"Archery?" Fenella glanced at the others to warn them to stay silent.

"Yes." Lally showed a hint of enthusiasm. "Robin's band has to be good at it, you see. All of them. Even Maid Marian. Especially her, because she can't fight with a sword."

"Are you talking about Robin Hood?"

Lally nodded. She looked oddly proud.

"And she gave you some letters to take about?" asked Tom.

Fenella couldn't tell if he already knew the answer or was guessing.

"To plan Robin's forays," agreed Lally. "Forays." She visibly savored the word. "He steals from the rich and gives to the poor." She looked around the room. "You're rich, I reckon."

"But he doesn't hurt people, does he?" Fenella put her hand on the bandage. "If I hadn't bent over right after this happened, the second shot would probably have killed me."

Roger jerked as if someone had stabbed him with a hatpin. He never liked hearing that part.

"And no one tried to take my money," Fenella added.

"That ain't right," replied Lally.

"No. So we would like to speak to Maid Marian and find out why that happened. I expect it was a mistake." As soon as she said this, Fenella worried it was a lie. Still, it was nothing compared with the tale the archer had told the little girl.

Lally frowned.

"Do you know where she lives?" Fenella added.

"In the Greenwood," the girl said, as if this was obvious. "In a secret hidey-hole. She can't tell anyone where it is. That would risk everyone." She shook her head. "It's like a fairy mound, I reckon. I couldn't find no sign of it anywhere about."

This from a child who undoubtedly knew every corner of the nearby forest, Fenella thought. Which proved that her assailant was not living in the woods. "What did she look like?" she asked.

"She couldn't let me see that," answered Lally, as if this was obvious. "What if I saw her unexpected when the sheriff's men were about and gave some sign? Not that I ever would!" Lally brooded over this for a moment. "She wore a hood, like."

"A cloak?" asked Fenella.

"Nobody could shoot a bow in a cloak," replied

Lally scornfully. "It was just a hood. Separate." She shaped her hands around her head. "Came down low about her face. I'm going to make myself one."

"Could you show us where you met her practicing archery?"

Lally turned to look at the men. "Are they going to arrest her and turn her over to the sheriff?"

"I only want to find out why I was shot." Fenella was aware that this was a partial answer. But she wanted to find this woman—madwoman?—who had deceived a gullible child and used her for malicious purposes. That felt almost as objectionable as the attack.

"I guess I could. I haven't seen her there for days and days." Lally drooped a little. "She said mebbe I could join Robin's band. She was going to ask and see. But I don't think she did. I think mebbe she fooled me." Pale lids dropped over her big brown eyes.

It was like seeing the curtain drop on a rather melancholy play, Fenella thought. One returned to reality with a brush of heartbreak when those eyes opened again.

"Let's go and have some of Cook's cakes," said Tom to the girl. "I reckon they're out of the oven by now. She said you could lick the icing spoon, remember."

Lally turned to him with a forlorn dignity. "I am very fond of cakes," she said.

Tom escorted her out, giving the group a nod as he passed through the door.

"I must find something to do for that girl," said Fenella.

"You don't think she's…a bit touched?" Roger replied.

"She's beset by an oversized imagination," said Macklin.

"Yes." That described it exactly, Fenella thought.

"And a lack of judgment?" asked Roger.

"Perhaps." The older man shrugged. "The same might be said for some of our finest artists. And a great many *rational* adults as well."

"She's only, what, nine years old," said Fenella. "An adult who really wanted to might have fooled any of us at that age."

Roger looked dubious. "She gave us a clue at least. We can begin to track down this demented woman." His expression was fierce. "I'm trying to remember if any neighbor of ours is a skilled archer. Can you recall anyone, Fenella?"

"Sara Haskins liked it. But she has lived in Devon for years." Watching Roger's face, his intense concentration, Fenella thought how much she loved him. She ought to tell him so. As she certainly would, as soon as she found the right moment.

"She hasn't been back?" Roger shook his head. "I would have heard. And what reason would Sara have to do any of this?"

"None," said Fenella. "What reason does anybody?"

Roger's response was near a growl.

Later that day, Lally led a party from the castle to a patch of forest in the area. They found signs of activity and a tree that had been pierced by many arrows, but there were no clues to the identity of the inexplicable Maid Marian.

Eighteen

AND NONE WERE FOUND AS THE MONTH CAME TO AN end, and the day of the historical pageant on Lindisfarne arrived, with scudding clouds and breezes that held a taste of autumn. The last of August was near the turn of the season this far north, and the occasional sharp gust foreshadowed winter storms.

The pageant now represented a running dispute for the newly married pair. Roger continued to argue that they should withdraw. But Fenella insisted that they not be intimidated into hiding. They would be surrounded by friends and members of their household. No one would dare shoot arrows into a crowd, and anyone who tried would be seen and captured at once. Her arm was much better. And they had promised to be a part of this neighborhood effort. In the end, Roger gave in. But he arranged to post a party of men from his estate to watch for threats.

The Chatton household set out early, so that all those who had roles would be in place well before time. The timing of the pageant had been arranged around the tides that could make passage to the island treacherous, allowing everyone to come and then go at the lowest ebb. Those attending expected to make a day of it, and people had come from far away to see the pageant. Many had employed small boats, Roger noticed as they arrived, which would free them from the demands of the sea.

They found everything arranged around a wall of the ruined priory on Lindisfarne Island. One side of the line of vacant stone arches was set aside for spectators. Macklin and Roger's mother staked out a perfect spot for viewing, and the servants who'd come along furnished it with rugs and chairs, hampers of food and sunshades.

The performers were gathering on the other side of the ruined wall, where a large tent had been set up to serve as dressing room. Mrs. Thorpe was received with acclaim and led away to her own curtained corner. The others were directed to the separate areas for men and women to put on their costumes.

As Fenella donned the long skirt, heavy tunic, and cloth headdress that marked her as a Saxon matron, she wondered about the whereabouts of her attacker. Was the sneaking *Maid Marian* nearby? It was lowering to think the archer might be lurking in the shadows, burning with inexplicable malice. Not because she feared another assault. Fenella truly did not believe that would happen here, where the woman would be caught at once. She'd been so careful to avoid exposure. It was the idea of hatred aimed in her direction, perhaps by someone she knew, that depressed her spirits. Adjusting the last details of her costume, she determined to shake the feeling off.

The series of scenes and tableaus began with establishment of the religious center on the island many centuries ago. John's part came early, and he seemed very much to enjoy being slathered with mud from head to toe. He received the homily from St. Cuthbert with commendable humility, as well as the bucket of water poured over his head—partly hygienic and partly baptismal. When his bit was finished, however, he veered into the audience. As people edged away from his filthy, dripping figure, he rushed up to Wrayle and threw his arms around the valet.

He might have been a child overwhelmed by the attention and seeking comfort. Indeed, when Wrayle pushed him away with a disgusted exclamation, some parents in the crowd frowned. But Fenella suspected that this was a prank her nephew and Tom had planned to pay Wrayle back for some of his spite. When she glimpsed Tom's smirk, nearly hidden by the hood of his costume, she was certain. And she couldn't say that Wrayle didn't deserve it. Thwarted by William's continual presence, Wrayle had been doing all he could to make John's stay at Chatton Castle a trial.

The day progressed, and history moved forward, the scenes shifting smoothly from arch to arch.

The Viking Age came fairly soon, rife with shouting men waving swords and axes. Fenella wielded her broom with enthusiasm and was carried off by her dear, familiar marauder. Their scene was well received, with cheers and a few hoots and whistles. Out of sight of the crowd they laughed together, in relief that it was done and that no intrusion had marred the occasion.

Monks wound through the arches, chanting. A

melee with sword and axes was roundly cheered. A speech very like a sermon was not. The Normans arrived and recited bits of local history. Henry VIII's troops came to abolish the monastery and make it into a naval store before building a castle. After that it was chiefly the Scots and the English grappling over the border. Both sides had partisans in the audience.

Finally, as the sun neared the horizon, it was time for Mrs. Thorpe's contribution. Her recitation was not strictly chronological, as Macbeth had lived in the eleventh century. She came last because everyone had envisioned her recitation as the crowning moment of the show, a professional performance to cap the sprawling drama. Fenella found a good spot to listen at the far side of the audience just under one of the arches. She was still in her costume, awaiting the end of the pageant when all of them were to line up and be acknowledged together. Roger, sitting with Macklin and his mother, beckoned, but Fenella stayed where she was.

A deep drumbeat began out of sight. The sound gradually drew the attention of the crowd. There was a pause, building anticipation. Then Mrs. Thorpe drifted into a vacant, candlelit archway like a phantom. She wore a simple black gown and a peaked headdress. Such was the power of her presence that stillness spread out from her position over all the people present. Only when all was quiet and every eye had turned to her did she speak, in a ringing voice that reached the far edges of the gathering.

> *"The raven himself is hoarse*
> *That croaks the fatal entrance of Duncan*

Under my battlements. Come, you spirits
That tend on mortal thoughts, unsex me here,
And fill me from the crown to the toe top-full
Of direst cruelty! Make thick my blood;"

Fenella was transfixed. The power of Mrs. Thorpe's voice and expression was undeniable. One couldn't look away. Her gestures were small and subtle, but riveting. She commanded attention.

"Stop up the access and passage to remorse,
That no compunctious visitings of nature
Shake my fell purpose, nor keep peace between
The effect and it! Come to my woman's breasts,
And take my milk for gall, you murdering ministers,
Wherever in your sightless substances
You wait on nature's mischief!"

"Yes, exactly that," hissed a woman's voice in Fenella's ear. A loop of thick cord fell over Fenella's face and down around her neck, quickly tightening until it was painful. The cloaked and hooded figure beside her leaned close and pressed the barrel of a pistol into her side. Fenella had thought this person was part of the pageant, one of her fellow actors. Now, the cord was jerked, forcing Fenella to move out from under the arch into the gathering darkness behind the ruined wall.

The cord dug into her neck, choking her. Fenella tried to get her fingers under it and pull it loose. But the cord was too tight. The pistol's barrel came up and banged against her temple, leaving her momentarily dazed. Her captor dragged at the cord again. Fenella gagged and stumbled along in her grasp as Mrs. Thorpe continued.

> *"Come, thick night,*
> *And pall thee in the dunnest smoke of hell,*
> *That my keen knife see not the wound it makes,*
> *Nor heaven peep through the blanket of the dark,*
> *To cry 'Hold, hold!'"*

"Oh yes, a woman can kill," her captor muttered as she forced Fenella along. "You know it. You lured my poor gentle daughter out into a storm so that you could take her place."

"Daughter?" Fenella tried to say. It came out as a croak. She couldn't speak.

"Inflammation of the lungs," the woman growled, jerking on the loop of cord. "A broken heart more like."

Could this be Mrs. Crenshaw? What was Arabella's mother doing here? And *what* was she doing?

"She wrote me that you were her friend, you know. 'I've found one friend here,' she said. Poor deceived lamb." She stumbled, and the cord loosened a bit.

"I did try to be her friend," Fenella managed, her voice barely above a croak. "I tried to keep her from riding out that day."

The pistol struck her again, painfully, as the cord tightened. "Don't give me your lies! My cousin heard Chatton say it, out loud at White's club. Thought you'd rid yourself of my Arabella and take him for yourself, but I'll see that ended tonight."

They'd come to a dip in the ground, well past the

end of the ruined arches. Fenella could hear the sea streaming over pebbles nearby. Mrs. Crenshaw jerked at her, and they both nearly fell. But she recovered and pulled Fenella downhill.

Fenella clawed at the cord and stumbled over rocks. Water poured over her ankles. And still her captor yanked her on. Fenella felt a trickle of blood where the cord had cut into her neck.

At last, when a larger wave made her captor sway, Fenella got hold of the cord and managed to loosen it. "Help!" she cried. Her voice cracked. She doubted it could be heard over the sound of the surf.

Mrs. Crenshaw hit Fenella with the pistol again, a ringing blow that left her reeling. Grasping Fenella's tunic with her free hand, she dragged her into the sea, releasing the cord for a moment.

"The tide hasn't gone out," Fenella croaked. "We can't leave the island now."

"Leave?" The older woman's laugh was grating. "Depends on what you mean by that." She wound her free hand in Fenella's hair and twisted as the waves surged around their knees.

"We'll both go under."

"You think I care if I die?" The woman's eyes burned into hers as she tightened the cord again. "I deserve to die! Arabella was my only child, my darling, and I wanted a grand title for her. And so I thrust her into this terrible place of plotting killers."

She thrust her face closer. It was twisted with hate. "My poor mite! She wanted to marry a mere mister, and I dissuaded her. Pointed out the young man's faults, said her papa would cut her off, described the perils of poverty as if they'd be living in a hovel. As if he didn't have a penny when he was well enough to pass."

Fenella felt even sorrier for Arabella, that she'd been subjected to this woman's manipulations. And then she concentrated on getting the cord off her neck, while Mrs. Crenshaw was distracted by her remorse.

"If I'd left well enough alone, my baby would be alive now. Living near London! I might have grandchildren."

Fenella dug her fingernails under the cord and pulled with all her strength. She panted and strained, and at last the cord eased. With one sudden twist, she yanked it out and up and tossed the wretched thing into the sea. Her captor screeched and twisted her free hand in Fenella's hair.

"You don't know—" began Fenella. She put a hand to her hair, trying to pull free. Her eyes watered with the pain.

"Don't speak to me!" Mrs. Crenshaw hit her again with the pistol, so hard Fenella hoped it would go off and attract others. But it did not. "I may have made a mistake," her captor continued. "But you killed her."

"No." Her denial had no effect. Fenella doubted the other woman heard.

"I won't see that worm Chatton happy while Arabella lies cold in her grave! They say he cares for you. Now he'll see what it feels like to lose someone he loves."

Fenella's gown dragged at her, growing heavier with each wave that splashed over them. She clawed at the other woman and struggled to break her grip.

"What are you doing?" called a ringing voice from the shore behind them. Mrs. Thorpe stood there, staring.

"Get help!" answered Fenella. Her voice, still affected by the maltreatment of her throat, didn't carry over the sound of the sea.

But Mrs. Thorpe could see what was needed. "Help!" she cried much louder.

Mrs. Crenshaw shrieked and threw the pistol. It spun through the air and struck Mrs. Thorpe on the temple. She stumbled to the ground.

Then, with a grin worthy of a corpse, Mrs. Crenshaw threw both arms around Fenella and fell backward into the sea.

Cold water rushed over Fenella's chest and face, tried to go up her nose. The sudden immersion took her breath away. A receding wave pulled them away from the island. Mrs. Crenshaw let it, her grip frighteningly strong.

Fenella kicked and writhed. She managed to get her head above water and drew in a deep breath. They were already yards from shore. The ebbing tide was carrying them out with ominous power. She shoved with all her strength in the cold water, raising her knees and using her legs as well as her arms. Finally, she escaped the gripping hands. Arabella's mother lunged for her. Fenella lurched away. And then they were separated. She let the current pull her away from her attacker. In only a few minutes, Mrs. Crenshaw was well out of reach, and then she was gone, hidden by the waves' chop.

Fenella was free! But her heavy clothes were a death trap, a sodden weight dragging her down. She pulled her knees up again and dragged the sodden tunic up over her hips. It resisted, and a new wave swept over her, filling her mouth with seawater and turning her head over heels. She gagged, spit, and managed another lungful of air.

Wriggling, tearing, she slipped out of the tunic. The fastenings of her skirt resisted, but finally she undid them and shoved the swath of wool down and away. It swirled in a small whirlpool and then was sucked away as if by the inhalation of a giant.

Fenella kicked off her shoes. She was lighter now, in her shift. It was possible to swim. But she was also colder. The water sucked the heat from her body. She raised her head to get her bearings. She was well away from the island and rapidly being borne farther, out to sea, toward death. She saw no sign of Arabella's mother.

The strength of the frigid current was terrifying. It was like being pulled along by a racing carriage. She couldn't fight it. No one could have. Trying to swim against the tide would be futile. But Fenella had heard local fishermen discuss what to do if they fell from their boats into a riptide. She bobbed up again to judge the angle of the shore and started paddling slantwise, partly using the strength of the sea to move across the direction of the current.

⤚❦⤙

Roger moved through the pageant crowd, growing increasingly frantic. Fenella hadn't appeared for the ending of the performance when they were all sup-posed to take a bow. And now she didn't seem to be anywhere in this infuriating mass of people sitting, chattering, eating, and drinking. She had to be here, and yet he couldn't find her. The fear that had been with him since she was shot roared to life.

Cries from the dimness behind the arches set him running. He found three men bending over a woman on the ground. He rushed to join them and found not Fenella but Mrs. Thorpe being helped to her feet, holding a hand to her brow. "She threw that pistol at me," the actress said, pointing to a weapon on the earth. "And hit me, too, which is quite difficult."

Macklin rushed up with several others. "What's happened?" he asked. "Are you hurt?"

"Not badly," replied Mrs. Thorpe. "I'll have a bruise." Before Roger could consign her bruise to perdition, she added, "Someone, a woman, pulled Lady Chatton into the sea."

"What?" Torn between learning more and rushing into the water, Roger was frozen.

"She had hold of her hair. I saw her hit Lady Chatton with the pistol, too." Mrs. Thorpe watched as one of the men bent to pick up a gun. "She wore a hooded cloak, so I couldn't see her face. I think she must have been mad."

"Maid Marian," said Roger. He didn't care that all of them turned to stare at him. "I begged Fenella not to come tonight. But she wouldn't listen." He ran to the water and waded in, scanning the darkening sea, looking for any sign of swimmers.

Footsteps splashed behind him. "Which way does the current run?" asked Macklin.

"Out," said Roger, straining, examining every wave crest, every irregularity in the surface. "Like a millrace at this point in the tide. To open water, and Denmark, eventually." He saw nothing. Despair threatened to engulf him.

"Not directly," said the older man. "We saw that when the boys came up here. There are crosscurrents and rips." He turned toward shore, calling, "Fetch boats."

In a short time, a flotilla of volunteers had rowed out to search for Fenella, pulling against the draw of the sea.

Sometime later, there were shouts from one of the little vessels, indicating that they'd found a body. Roger plunged into shock and terror as he helped propel his boat over to it. But when they reached it, he discovered that the sodden bundle they'd pulled from the water wasn't Fenella. Relief warred with horror and astonishment as he gaped at the pale face and recognized Arabella's mother.

The boat holding her moved toward shore. His own began to follow. "What are you doing?" Roger demanded. "We have to keep searching."

"It's grown too dark, my lord," said the boat's owner. "We can't see properly. Might miss something. We'll wait and head back out at first light."

"Lend me the boat," said Roger. "I'll keep going."

But when they reached the island, all the mariners held the same opinion. It was no use going on in the dark. No one said that by this time the cold water would have sapped a swimmer's strength and most likely pulled her down. They didn't have to. Roger knew it. He'd lived his life by the North Sea. These waters were unforgiving.

They carried Mrs. Crenshaw up to the tent and laid her body on a rug. Roger, his mother, and Macklin joined the others standing over her. "What was she doing here?" said Roger's mother.

"Can she have been the archer?" asked Macklin. "Maid Marian?" His tone was dubious. The soaked middle-aged woman before them didn't look adventurous.

"Yes." Desolation dragged at every word Roger spoke. "She was a keen archer as a girl. Arabella mentioned it once. I'd forgotten. Her mother wanted her to learn, but she didn't care to." He ought to have remembered. He ought to have suspected. But how could he have imagined Mrs. Crenshaw would do such a thing? She must have gone mad.

"But," began his mother. "Why?"

"She blamed me for Arabella's death," Roger said leadenly. "And I…like a damned fool, I blamed Fenella. This was revenge. On her. On me. I've done this."

"No, you have not," said Macklin. He pointed at the dead woman. "She did it, and no one else."

"She promoted your marriage," said Roger's mother. "Arranged it even, you told me."

It was true. Roger's guilt lifted just slightly. He would not have married Arabella, and she would not have died, perhaps, if Mrs. Crenshaw hadn't pushed the match. She had much to answer for, wherever she might be now. Then this momentary feeling of respite collapsed. Fenella was gone. Just when he'd found her after so many years, he'd lost her again. And he hadn't told her he loved her. That cut so deeply that he nearly bent double with regret. He'd meant to.

He'd tried to. But his wretched tongue had betrayed him yet again, and so she'd never heard him tell her how very much he cared. If he could be given the chance—Roger prayed for a chance—he would say it every day, every hour for the rest of his life.

They went out to a murmuring, firelit island. Groups of people stood or sat exchanging wild stories about what had happened when they had no actual idea. What was he going to do? Roger wondered. How was he going to live now?

He wanted to snatch up a claymore and rage against an enemy, wild and invincible as a berserker. But there was no one to fight. And so little grounds for hope.

Nineteen

WEAKENED BY WHAT SEEMED LIKE AN ETERNITY OF paddling and the cold water, which leached strength from her body moment by moment, Fenella struggled on against the terrible power of the sea. The tide constantly fought her lateral course across the direction of the current. It wanted to carry her out into the depths. She was just another fleck in the vast flood moving away from shore and then back again, hour by hour.

But finally, finally, the pull seemed to lessen a little. She swam on and gradually confirmed the feeling. She'd broken out of the main rush of the current. It no longer gripped her so strongly. She could go a bit faster.

But night had fallen by this time, with low clouds, and she couldn't see very well in the dark. She moved on by feel, praying not to stray back into the tidal reach. A sound caught her attention. Was that waves breaking? She turned toward it, daring to hope.

A few minutes later, one of Fenella's feet brushed solid ground. Hardly daring to hope, she felt about with her toes. Yes, the sea bottom was shelving upward! She lurched upright and pushed forward—staggering, tripping, floundering, crawling finally—and at last dragged herself out of the water. She dug her fingers into packed wet sand, profoundly grateful, and collapsed onto it.

For a while she simply panted. It was an unutterable luxury to lie still, not to have to fight for her life, not to crane her neck to stay above water and catch a full breath. She could ask for nothing more.

Slowly, she revived a little. Her breath slowed. She pushed up and sat on the sand. Judging by the sound of lapping waves and dim outlines in the night, she decided that she'd reached an islet, hardly more than a sandbar. She couldn't see the real shore. She needed more light for that, to decide how she might truly escape the sea. This place was a temporary refuge in the ebbing tide. At high tide, it might not even exist.

Fenella shivered. She was freezing in her soaked shift. Her wounded arm hurt, as did her head where Mrs. Crenshaw had hit her, and her throat where she'd choked her. She almost laughed. A regular litany of pains. The relief of being out of the sea made her giddy. She'd survived. But she had to do something more now, or she would perish of cold.

Shifting to hands and knees, Fenella crawled slowly around the perimeter of her refuge. She came across no bushes or trees, no rocks, just wet sand, confirming her opinion that this speck of land was covered at high tide. It offered no shelter from the wind that was chilling her skin and making her shudder.

But at the far end of the bar she did find a sizable pile of seaweed, coughed up by the waves. "Beggars can't be choosers," she muttered as she yanked the bundle of fronds away from the water toward the center of the islet. There she scraped a shallow depression in the sand, pushed some of the seaweed into it, curled up on top, and arranged the rest over her. The fronds were cold and slimy, but they did cut the wind. Fenella pulled her knees up to her chest and nestled her icy hands in the space between. Slowly, she grew a little warmer as the heat of her body filled her bizarre cocoon. This wasn't comfort by any means, but it did mean survival. She rubbed her hands together to encourage circulation.

The waves repeated their lulling rhythm. The wind sighed over her dark burrow. She fell into a state that wasn't quite sleep, yet wasn't true waking either. Drifting in a kind of dream, she found the unexpected events of the last few weeks—the revolution in her existence—floating through her mind. She'd been the target of sly malice and curious whispers, lost her last parent, eloped, been shot, swum for her life. She put one hand to her wounded arm with its damp bandage. The catalog seemed fantastical. Yet it had all happened, like a trip through a labyrinth where one couldn't see what came next on the twisting path.

She'd also found more happiness with Roger than she'd ever known before. No one in her family, not even her grandmother, who genuinely loved her, had made her feel so cherished. All the tender moments she and Roger had spent together passed through her memory. She was so fortunate, blessed as she had never thought to be. The difficulties were as nothing to this gift. Despite her current predicament, a pulse of joy ran through her, a heady mixture of pleasure and gratitude.

But she hadn't told Roger how much she loved him! She'd meant to, but somehow she'd never come to the point of speaking the words. If she didn't see him again…but she would see him! She'd escaped the sea. She would reach home. Tomorrow. And when she did, she would let him know how much he meant to her. Every day, from now on. Because disaster could descend at any moment and make that forever impossible. On this firm resolve, Fenella sank into restless sleep.

Light came with a splash of cold water, dripping through the nest of seaweed that now admitted thin rays of sunshine. Fenella lifted her head and saw that the tide was rising, and her refuge was losing inches with each incoming wave. She sat up, pushing off the seaweed. It left brown slimy trails over her shoulders and arms. Her bandage looked filthy.

A larger wave broke, running along the sand toward her knees. Fenella pushed herself up and stood. It was time to go. The rest had helped. Yes, she was still cold, and very thirsty. Her muscles were stiff from her efforts yesterday, and she had painful bruises from the attack. But she was alive and ready to go on.

She turned in a circle on her sandbar, evaluating her position now that she could see the landscape. The tide had carried her away from the Lindisfarne priory, and her sideways swim had taken her around a higher spit of sand, so that she couldn't see the holy isle from this low vantage point. The closest bit of shoreline was south, judging by the sunrise, a promontory thrusting out into the channel. The tip didn't seem so very far away. She could see ripples that promised strong currents, however.

She didn't want to go back into the sea, Fenella acknowledged. Perhaps ever. She longed to sit here and wait for someone to come for her. Surely they were searching. She was confident that Roger was searching. If a boat appeared, she could wave them down. If only she could light a signal fire. But there was nothing to burn and not much time before the sandbar was engulfed. Which would put her in the water anyway. "Spineless and shivering," she said aloud, and was surprised by the croak her voice had become. She couldn't wait for rescue.

Still, she had to lash herself to enter the waves. Their touch on her feet made her shudder. At least the tide would carry her in the right direction this time, toward shore.

Fenella waded into the sea. The water reached her knees, her hips, her chest. She began to swim.

The tide did pull at her, but the journey was easier in the light. She could see her goal ahead, growing closer with each stroke. She swam harder. Her lungs began to pump and her pulse to pound. Slowly, painfully slowly, the spit of land neared.

The water grew shallower. The effort lessened. Fenella found purchase for her feet near the end of the promontory and started to stand up. A morass of sand sucked at her, eager to pull her down. She flopped forward and floated, propelling herself along the bottom with fingers and toes until the water grew too shallow. She tried rising again. This time the sand was firm. She hurried on and at last reached dry ground, sinking to her hands and knees and breathing hard.

Shivers brought her to her feet again. She wasn't

done yet. The narrow peninsula was empty of all but scrub. She had to find her way to help.

She walked along the crest, dipped down to cross a small channel running with water up to her ankles, and finally reached the mainland proper. She could see grain fields ahead. There would be people about surely. She hoped to come upon them soon because she was freezing in the early-morning chill. She pulled at her shift, clinging damply to her body. Not the way she would wish to meet countrymen, but she had no choice.

⚬⚭⚬

Roger rowed because he felt just slightly better when he was doing something, rather than sitting and scanning the empty sea and shore as their small boats crisscrossed the waters around Lindisfarne. He could feel the opinion mounting among the searchers—that Fenella couldn't be alive now, that the strong currents must have overwhelmed her, that the cold water would have leached her life away. And the moment he stopped moving, he might have to accept that. So he wouldn't stop, because he refused to give up hope. There was still a chance. Until the tide returned her body, he would go on. He realized that the other oarsmen in his boat had eased off.

"There's nowhere else to look, my lord," said the vessel's owner. "We've been all over."

"Down the coast," said Roger. He looked out to sea. "Farther out."

"We can't take boats this size far into open water," the man replied. "And out there—"

Roger knew the end of this sentence, and he didn't

want to hear it. Why were they talking? They should be rowing.

Movement caught in the corner of his eye, and he turned eagerly. But it was a line of dark clouds boiling up in the east, promising a squall. He glanced at the faces of the local men who had turned out to help. They looked sympathetic, pitying, but not sanguine. None of them believed they would find Fenella alive. Their eyes showed their fearful respect for the riptides and sadness for the losses any village of fishermen endured.

The owner of the boat was frowning at the approaching weather.

Roger couldn't endanger them, no matter how much he needed them to keep searching. "Very well." He would pace the shoreline from which she'd disappeared, he decided as they turned back toward the island. No, he would keep one boat, purchase it if necessary, and row out on his own. He would find her!

A choking despair loomed, telling him what he would find. He fought it off.

Another boat came closer. Macklin sat in the bow wrapped in a wool cloak. When they'd come alongside, he reached out and put a hand on Roger's shoulder. "I think we must go in," he said. "There's a storm on the way. I'm sorry."

"I can't leave her out there, struggling in the water." Roger choked on that unbearable picture, which was still better than the alternative—that all struggles were done.

A shout from one of the other boats drew their attention. A rower there leaned out and pulled a bundle from the water.

A stomach–clenching mixture of fear and hope shot through Roger. He grabbed his oar and nearly overset the boat with the strength of his shove.

They'd found the tunic Fenella had been wearing for the pageant. Roger recognized the pin fastening the neck. He snatched it from the man who'd retrieved it and held it to his chest despite the water that ran over his clothes. His mind felt perfectly blank. For a few minutes he didn't even notice that the boat was moving again.

Then he looked up. The chop of the waves was increasing. Clouds flowed across the sky. Macklin was directing the whole party toward shore. Roger wanted to argue, to convince them to turn back, but words had deserted him, perhaps forevermore.

They had to lift him from the boat. A man on either side escorted him to the waiting horses, and Macklin persuaded him to mount.

◦∾◦

Fenella trudged along a lane, trying to avoid stepping on sharp stones with her bare feet. So far, she'd seen no sign of people. The fields on either side had been harvested already, and the golden stubble was empty. The workers had moved on to others. Her hopes of coming across a cart to carry her were waning, and the cold of her damp shift and weariness dragged at her. She'd had a spurt of energy when she reached the shore, but now the efforts of last night were taking their toll. Still, there was no choice but to keep walking, one foot in front of the other.

Movement caught her eye. A gowned figure

emerged from a clump of bushes some way down the lane. Fenella raised her arm and waved. "Hello," she called. Her voice caught and rasped like a rusty hinge, the lingering effects of maltreatment with the cord. She tried again, forcing a louder shout. The figure turned and looked in her direction. "Please help me!" cried Fenella, waving again.

The person started toward her. When she came closer, Fenella was astonished to recognize the girl Lally. "What are you doing here?"

"I live up yonder."

Following the little girl's pointing finger, Fenella saw a stream tumbling down the incline toward the sea. She could just see the crest of a roof above its lip. This must be the mill.

"Are you dead?" Lally asked. "'Cause if you're a haunt, I ain't speaking to you." She made a banishing sign with extended fingers.

"I'm alive." It hurt to talk. And Fenella's mouth was parched with thirst. Her whole body yearned toward that stream.

"They said you was drowned. Like Maid Marian was. I saw them carry her from a boat up to the tent. Never knew she was so old." Lally looked anxious suddenly. "Don't let on I told you. Dad said I wasn't allowed to go to the pageant. On account of what I did." She looked as if she didn't understand her transgression completely, and as if this was a familiar experience. "I sneaked over when my dad thought I was in my room, 'cross the sand." She grimaced. "Which I'm also not meant to do. You won't tell?"

Fenella shook her head wearily. "I got out of the

sea," she said. "She tried to pull me under." Memories of the dark sea made her shudder. Or perhaps it was just the breeze on her wet shift. She wrapped her arms around her torso for warmth.

Lally frowned. "Pull you under the water? After she shot at you? I don't understand what she was about." The girl looked frustrated.

"Let's go up to the mill and find your parents." With a stop at the stream for a drink, Fenella thought.

"My dad," the girl corrected. "My mum's dead."

"I'm sorry."

Lally shrugged. "I don't remember her." She eyed Fenella. "You've gone all bluish."

"I'm very cold." Fenella started walking again. The girl fell into step at her side.

"Did somebody steal your clothes?" asked Lally. "Some boys did that to me once when I went swimming."

"No, I had to take them off in the sea, so that they wouldn't drag me down when I swam across from Lindisfarne."

Lally looked shocked. "Nobody's supposed to swim in that channel. You're like to be carried away by the tides."

"I very nearly was. That's why I need your help now, Lally."

The girl's face shifted. She seemed to take in Fenella's plight for the first time. Her dark eyes filled with sympathy. "I'll fetch a cloak," she said and ran off before Fenella could reply.

With a sigh, Fenella trudged on. She veered off the lane to a loop of the stream and half knelt, half fell to drink from the rushing water. The cold liquid was a balm for her bruised throat as well as her raging thirst. But it chilled her further. Really, she had never been so cold.

She had just struggled to her feet again when Lally came running back with a heavy cloak. Gratefully, Fenella draped it around her shoulders. The cloth dragged on the ground. She gathered it closer. Wool was a marvel, she thought, as she felt the first touch of warmth. "Does your father have a horse and cart?" she asked. Surely a miller would need such a thing.

Her heart soared when Lally nodded, then sank when she said, "Dad's gone out in it with a load of flour. Be back before supper, he said."

"He left you all alone?"

"Mrs. Fisk's here," answered Lally. "She didn't like me taking the cloak. Tried to snatch it away. You'll tell her I was helping?"

Fenella nodded as they started walking up the hill. They would just have to see what could be done. It might be hours before she could reach home, which was a disappointment. But she was here, and warmer, and she could see her way to a solution. Pulling the cloak closer around her shoulders, Fenella was overtaken by a giddy sense of astonishment. She'd done it. All on her own, she'd thrown off a murderous assailant and battled her way to safety. "I fought the very tide," she murmured. "And won. Unlike King Canute."

"Who?" said Lally.

"An old king who challenged the sea," said Fenella. She realized that she'd gone quite dizzy with relief.

"Only he didn't really. People get the story wrong. He was demonstrating the power of God to his courtiers."

"His who?"

She'd been young and timid once, Fenella thought, and for a while it had seemed that limitation would be with her always. But it wouldn't. She could take on anything after this. She would never again doubt her own competence. She skipped a step, and another, despite her fatigue.

Lally gazed up at her. She shrugged. "Don't know what you mean," she said. "But lots of times I don't. Dad reckons I never will. Says I'd best get used to it."

Fenella was filled with a desire to do something for Lally. She didn't deserve the way she'd been treated by Mrs. Crenshaw. "Is there anything you would like?"

The girl's brown eyes were both hopeful and wary. "Reckon I won't be joining Robin Hood's band."

"No, that was a lie."

She nodded as if she'd expected this, and perhaps heard similar things before. She trudged on at Fenella's side.

"I could give you some books about Robin Hood," Fenella offered.

"I'm not much for books. I don't read very good. And you have to sit still inside and take care not to spill."

Of course books weren't it. Fenella tried to think of something else. She wished she could find Lally a fairy mound or troop of merry, harmless outlaws.

"I'd like some flowers," said Lally.

"Flowers?" Did she mean a bouquet?

"Dad said the garden at the mill was a sight to see before my mum died. All sorts of flowers. But he didn't keep it up. He's sorry about that, but he was right busy and the plants were finicky."

This last sounded like a quote.

"I love flowers, and I could take care of them." The girl nodded as if she expected an argument. "I could. Water them and all. I've pulled the weeds."

"I'll have plants brought to you," said Fenella, delighted the request was one she could grant. "By someone who can tell you all about how to care for them." She'd have the castle gardener find just the right person to talk to Lally.

"Where will you find them?"

"In the gardens at my house."

"That castle?"

"Yes."

Lally made an astonished sound. "You really will? Even though I took those letters for Maid Marian?"

"I promise."

The girl's answering smile was brilliant.

Perhaps they could do more, Fenella thought. They might settle a small pension on her in the future. Or some such arrangement. She'd ask Roger. Fenella's heart soared. Soon she would see Roger and throw herself into his arms. After that, well a good bit after that, she would ask him. She laughed.

Lally joined in. The girl put her hand in Fenella's, and they walked side by side up the hill to the mill.

Twenty

A SLANT OF LATE-AFTERNOON SUN ILLUMINATED THE rows of leather-bound books in Chatton Castle's library, but Roger didn't notice. He was here because he never sat in this room. Neither had Fenella, and so it reminded him of nothing in particular. Not that this stopped the rush of tender memories, which hurt more than anything he had ever experienced before. Part of him simply refused to believe that she wouldn't walk through the door in another minute and ask him what in the world he was brooding about.

His mother and Macklin had herded him home. He hadn't wanted to come. But even he had been forced to admit that lingering on the shore opposite Lindisfarne—in the stinging rain of a squall, when everyone else had departed—was doing no good. Fenella was gone, such a short time after he had understood, at last, that she was just the woman for him. No one survived a night in the North Sea.

If only he had realized the truth sooner. If only he'd had more sense. If only… His mind teemed with regrets. None of which made a particle of difference. All was disaster. He couldn't really see where his life would go from here. Onward in numbing routine, he supposed, all his plans in ruins. He'd thought he had a second chance. This had turned out to be a cruel illusion.

Every bit of his attention was occupied by mourning. He didn't hear a cart arrive outside, and when the chamber door opened quietly, he didn't turn around. "Go away," he said to anyone who might imagine he could be comforted.

"Very well. I just wanted to tell you I was home," replied a woman's voice, familiar and yet altered by a rasping croak.

Roger whirled and leapt up so quickly that his chair tipped over and tumbled onto the carpet. *Fenella! Could it be?* Or had he gone mad and begun conjuring phantoms?

Her red hair was a wild snarl. There were dark smudges under her eyes, and she was wrapped in a bulky cloak. He ran over and swept her into his arms. She was reassuringly solid. He whirled her in a great circle. "I can't believe it! You're really here. I thought you were dead." He remembered his promise to himself. "I love you," he blurted out.

"I love you," said Fenella at the same moment.

"I meant to tell you," they said in unison.

Then spoke together yet again. "I'm sorry."

Fenella giggled. Roger couldn't laugh. In a little while he would, when this miracle had sunk in. But not yet.

The cloak came loose, revealing the top of her salt-crusted shift. He noticed bruises on her neck, scratches on her hands. "You're hurt!"

"Well, I have been through a bit of an ordeal. I'll tell you, in a moment. It's so very good to be home." She swayed in his arms.

Rather than berate himself for not noticing her condition, Roger sprang into action. He half carried her upstairs, scattering orders among the servants who lined the corridors for a bath to be filled, food and drink to be brought. Fenella's half-laughing protests were ignored as he piled on command after command. He was only just able to leave her in the hands of her maid as cans of hot water began to arrive from the kitchen.

An hour later, they sat together in her boudoir, surrounded by the results of Roger's demands, along with other treats added by Mrs. Burke and the cook. His mother had sent her delighted congratulations. Macklin had added a kind word, as had Mrs. Thorpe. Now they were finally alone. Wrapped in a warm dressing gown, with her feet up on an ottoman, Fenella had told him the story of her battle with the sea. She looked tired but content.

Roger couldn't let go of his wife's fingers. "I shall never allow you to swim again."

She raised her eyebrows at the word *allow*, but said only, "I don't want to just now. That's certain. We will see about the future." Fenella sipped hot chocolate with her free hand, one of the many delicacies that had been produced for her. Trays were crowded with small sandwiches and cakes and sweets. "Lally said they found Mrs. Crenshaw in the sea," she said.

Roger nodded. "I don't wish to say I can't forgive her, but...I haven't yet."

"She created a domestic tragedy with her schemes."

"Two," said Roger. "First for Arabella and then very nearly for us."

"'Very nearly' isn't the same," said Fenella.

After a moment he acknowledged this with a nod. "She was sorry for what she'd done to Arabella."

"Not as sorry as others," he had to say.

"No. Her daughter, and you, bore the brunt of her mistakes." Fenella considered. "And Mrs. Crenshaw herself, in the end. She was dreadfully unhappy."

"That doesn't excuse her."

"No. She was broken by grief, I think."

"*I* was desolate when I thought you dead," Roger objected. "But I didn't plot to kill anyone."

Fenella nodded. She sipped her chocolate. "How could she do it?"

He addressed the literal part of her question, as the philosophical was beyond him. "She was staying in a cottage on an estate north of the island. The owner who let it was at the pageant, and he recognized her when she was taken from the sea. She arranged the visit from London with a false name. Corresponded with the fellow's wife and gained her sympathy with a tale of being widowed and wanting to get away from home. Told them she was fond of history and meant to look around the area, ending with the performance on Lindisfarne. They lent her a horse to use, but never noticed that she had a bow." Roger realized he was babbling. Relief had set in. His brain felt as if it was fizzing.

"People don't take much account of an older woman if she dresses plainly and keeps to herself," said Fenella. She set down her cup and stretched. A soft groan escaped her. "I'll be stiff for days, I suppose."

"We will wait on you hand and foot."

Fenella smiled at him. Fatigue was making itself felt after the excitement of reaching home. She would crawl into bed soon.

"I keep thinking if only Arabella had—" Roger clamped his lips together, as if he had to prevent further words from escaping. "No," he said.

"No, what?"

"No trying to blame Arabella." Roger passed a hand over his forehead as if he felt a pain there. "Part of the horror of this day was how much sorrier I felt about your death than hers. She deserved better of me, and the world."

Fenella squeezed his hand. "Our children shall do as they please," she murmured.

Roger returned the pressure of her fingers. "We will have those years together. You're not gone. We will have a family." He bent to rest his head on her forearm. "I do love you so. I am resolved to tell you that every day. Possibly several times."

She caressed his bright hair. "I made the same resolution when I was lying on a freezing sandbar in the darkness. We will make a positive spectacle of ourselves." She found she didn't care. "I think perhaps I've loved you most of my life," she added.

He looked up. "The wretched sprig I was? With my rudeness and the sodding sheep? You can't have. You have much better taste than that."

"I do." Fenella smiled again. "And yet."

"Yet?"

"I think I was enchanted by the wild, fearless boy you were."

He looked touched, and a bit guilty. "I can't say that I—"

"Of course you didn't feel the same. I was... in hiding. It took an extraordinary goad from my father and a force of nature like my grandmother to release me."

"If I'd had any sense, I'd have seen the truth."

"Nonsense. I didn't know myself."

He leaned forward to embrace her gently. "I mean to strive for the rest of my life to deserve your regard."

Fenella gave him a saucy look. "That should be quite satisfactory, my lord marquess."

∾

Lord and Lady Chatton bade farewell to all of their houseguests on the same day in early September. John departed first, in the company of Wrayle. But he didn't seem to mind the man's presence quite so much as before, to the valet's evident chagrin. John was on his way back to school, of course, where there existed a sympathetic master who kept preserved specimens of various fascinating creatures in jars in his classroom. John had realized that this teacher might well know how a fellow prepared himself to lead expeditions of scientific exploration, and would probably be glad to impart that information. "The study of snakes is called herpetology," John told Tom through the window of the post chaise. "I looked it up in the library."

"Herpetology," repeated Tom from the courtyard, with his customary appreciation of a new bit of knowledge.

"I will write to you."

"Tell me about herpetology," replied Tom agreeably.

"Will you write back? About what you are doing? I expect it will be much more interesting."

"I don't think it will be, actually. I reckon you're bound for great things."

John basked a bit in the compliment. "But you will write?"

"That I will. When I have the chance."

"I suppose you'll forget. Or be too busy off in Shropshire. Why are you going there again?"

Tom ignored the last question. "Not I. I promise."

"It is past time for us to be off," said Wrayle from the far side of the carriage. The whine that often entered his voice was more pronounced. He leaned out to speak to the postilions. "Will you go!"

They signaled the horses. John was still hanging out the window and waving when the vehicle sped out of sight.

Not long after this, Lord Macklin's comfortable traveling carriage was brought around to the front door, a mound of luggage tied up behind. The earl, Tom, and Mrs. Thorpe got in. They were traveling together for a good part of their journey, before Macklin turned west and Mrs. Thorpe continued on south to London. All of them welcomed the company, not least Tom, on both sides of the conversation.

Their farewells were even warmer than the previous ones, the marquess, his wife, and his mother expressing their sadness at seeing the visitors depart. They stood waving at the castle entrance as the coach pulled away.

"A visit with you feels rather like being part of a traveling theater company," said Mrs. Thorpe to the earl when they had passed under the archway in the wall and out into the countryside. "The play is over, and we move on to the next place on the tour. Not that I'm going this time."

"'Our revels now are ended,'" quoted Macklin. "'These our actors, as I foretold you, were all spirits and are melted into air, into thin air.'"

"You do have a hint of Prospero about you now and then," she replied.

"Who's that?" asked Tom, with no fear that his inquiry would be resented.

"A magician in one of Shakespeare's plays," Mrs. Thorpe answered. "*The Tempest.* Prospero moves the other characters around like a puppet master until he settles everything just as he wishes."

"I make no such claims," said Macklin.

She raised her eyebrows. "Indeed? You managed another successful union. You should hire yourself out to the matchmaking mamas at Almack's. I will give you a reference."

The earl laughed. "No, thank you. The thought makes my blood run cold. And I don't do very much really. Just stand about and hope, it seems to me sometimes."

"More than you realize." Mrs. Thorpe shook her head. "And you'll need all your skills for the next one, if I'm any judge."

"Why do you say so?"

Tom leaned forward, clearly interested in the answer.

"People in Shropshire seemed to think your young duke was a bit cracked," continued Mrs. Thorpe.

"He seemed sensible enough when I met him in London," Macklin replied. "A little anxious perhaps, but the circumstances were odd."

"You would know better than I," she said. "I'm only repeating what I heard."

"And I appreciate your reconnaissance. I'm happy to have any preparation. Did they say anything else?"

"That he was a kind young man, for all his quirks, and they wished him well. Unlikely as they predicted that to be."

"Why?"

"It seems his family, these Rathbones, are dogged by ill luck." Mrs. Thorpe held up an admonitory finger. "But I may have fallen into the clutches of a local wag. There is a distinct possibility of that. He was very fond of the sound of his own voice. He even tried 'the curse of the Rathbones' on me, until I made it clear I thought the idea nonsense."

"I'll have to see for myself," said Macklin, nodding.

Silence fell in the carriage. When it had lasted long enough to show that this bit of conversation was complete, Tom leaned forward again. "Tell me more about this Prospero fella," he said.

❧

A good many miles away from Macklin's cozy carriage, Peter Rathbone, Duke of Compton, set a moldering implement beside his plate at the dinner table—an open wooden paddle strung with a grid of sheep's gut. The thing was ancient, as was just about every item great-great-grandfather agreed to sell. But he went back on his word. I found the agreement in our archive room." He gave Roger a triumphant glare.

So it seemed that Fairclough, not his father, had started the troubles, Roger thought. "I didn't know my great-great-grandfather, of course."

"Doesn't matter," the old man barked. "Debt of honor. Blot on your family escutcheon."

"Escutcheon?"

"It's an expression."

"I know."

"A shield, isn't it?" said Fairclough. "Like the old knights used to carry. Wouldn't want a blot on there. Bad *ton*, eh?"

It seemed to Roger that they were wandering from the point. "If you have a signed conveyance of the land…" he began. But he couldn't have, Roger realized. If he did, the courts would have ruled in his favor at once.

"There was an agreement," Fairclough replied. "A *gentleman's* agreement. The land to be sold. For twenty guineas."

"Twenty guineas! That's a ridiculous figure."

"That doesn't matter."

"It dashed well does. The land is worth far more than that."

"So was a guinea, back then." The old man's eyes, though reddened by illness, gleamed.

"That sum was paid then? To my great-great-grandfather?"

Fairclough's gaze shifted, and Roger saw another flaw in his argument. "It wasn't, was it? So an that he possessed. Ancient and useless and falling apart. Some ancestor of his had used it to play bouts of tennis with Henry VIII. And if the fortunes of the Rathbones were anything to go by, he hadn't had the sense to lose. It was no good for any sort of game now, but Peter found it convenient for another purpose.

Conway, one of the two aged footmen he employed, tottered in with a tureen of soup. He ladled some into Peter's waiting bowl, releasing an enticing aroma on a wisp of steam. Peter picked up his spoon. No one could fault his cook at least. She might never ask him what he would like to eat, or pay any heed if he tried to express a preference, but every dish she provided was delicious.

Before he managed to taste, a bat swooped into the dining room, as they continually did, everywhere in the house, no matter how often Peter sent workmen to examine the roof. They couldn't seem to find any holes in the slates, and yet there were always bats.

Peter lifted the paddle, moving slowly so as not to spook the animal. He sighted on the creature's trajectory, and when it passed close to him, he gave it a sharp rap. The bat fell to the floor. He was expert at knocking them senseless, had been since he was eleven years old.

Conway bent and picked up the small body with one gloved hand. He wrapped it in a napkin from the sideboard, a necessary measure in case it awoke and began flapping.

"Out to the battlements as usual," the duke told him.

His footman sighed audibly.

"I know it will probably fly right back in," said

Peter. "Or, all right, it certainly will. But I really can't bear to be killing them day in and day out, Conway."

"Yes, Your Grace." The footman carried the small bundle out of the room.

Peter ate his savory soup. Sitting at the long table, in the large, silent, empty house. The last Rathbone. He winced. He could just about manage to keep going if he refused to think about that. And so that is what he would do.

Keep reading for a sneak peek at the exciting reissue
of Jane Ashford's much-loved Regency classic

The
RELUCTANT
Rake

Coming October 2019 from Sourcebooks Casablanca

One

SIR RICHARD BECKWITH EMERGED FROM HIS ELEGANT town-house on a chilly spring evening wearing a black silk domino over his dark gray pantaloons and long-tailed coat of dark blue superfine. Any one of his friends would have been astonished to see him in this guise, still more to see him out of evening dress at nine o'clock. Had they known that a pocket of the domino held a black mask, they would have been dumbfounded.

None of Sir Richard's exclusive circle was likely to see him tonight, however. When he hailed a hackney cab and climbed in, he directed it to a part of London little frequented by the *haut ton*. If certain of its men from time to time made their way through these unsavory streets, they did not mention such excursions in polite society.

A cold mist rose from the greasy cobblestones, enlivened here and there by hoarse laughter and singing as the hack rattled past some gin mill or bawdy house. One victim of blue ruin went so far as to grab for the cab, hoping to jerk its occupant into an alleyway and fleece him. He missed his target, however, and fell flat in the garbage-filled gutter with a curse.

Through the ride, Sir Richard sat impassive, his regular features immovable as stone, his gray eyes cold. If his goal was amusement of the type his class usually sought in this neighborhood, he went about it with an odd implacability.

The hack pulled up before a broad, soot-stained building that turned a blank facade to the street. Its windows were obscured with bars outside and heavy draperies within. Wooden double doors, firmly closed, revealed only a carved peephole at eye level.

"You sure of that h'address, guv?" wondered the driver.

"Yes." Beckwith handed him a small coin, allowing him to see one of larger denomination in his hand. "Wait for me nearby. I'll call when I want you. There's a guinea for you if you come when I call."

The man stared at the money, greed warring with his desire to return to safer streets. "Right," he said finally.

Beckwith pulled up the hood of the domino and put on his mask, then knocked sharply on the wooden door with the head of his cane and waited.

The peephole opened, and a bloodshot blue eye surveyed him with suspicion. Abruptly, the hole closed, and the bolts were shot back, allowing the door to open a crack.

"I am here for the meeting," Sir Richard declared.

"Password," came a hiss from the dimness.

"Chaos," he answered, in a tone that suggested he found the word offensive.

The door swung open. Inside was a sharp contrast to the dirty street. A rich red Turkey carpet covered the floor, and the narrow hallway boasted French wallpaper and gilt sconces. Though the individual in charge of the door was distinctly rough-hewn, the footman who indicated that Sir Richard should follow him would not have looked out of place in Grosvenor Square.

He ushered Sir Richard into a large room at the back of the building. It was furnished with the armchairs and side tables of a gentlemen's club, but the inhabitants were not so familiar. Many wore domino and mask, like Sir Richard. Others had clearly cast off these disguises with their third or fourth brandies and were loud with the effects of drink. The buxom young women who served them endured their fondling and leers with good-humored impertinence, and a sharp eye for the banknotes that were continually being folded and thrust lingeringly into bodices.

The din was significant, and the air was heavy with the fumes of alcohol and candlewax and the clashing scents of pomades and cheap perfume.

Sir Richard found a vacant chair in a dim corner and sat down. When one of the serving girls came up to him, he ordered brandy, but he spoke to no one else. He had come with a purpose, his demeanor said, and he would allow nothing to distract him from it.

At last, there was a stir at the back of the room, and one of the other masked guests stepped from a chair to a tabletop there. "Gentlemen," he cried above the din. "Gentlemen!"

The volume of sound decreased somewhat.

"Gentlemen," said the man again. "We have a rare

treat for you this evening. Indeed, I think I may safely say we have a unique entertainment in store. Its like hasn't occurred in our time, at least. I couldn't vouch for our grandfathers."

This elicited a roar of laughter and vulgar sallies from the crowd, which was beginning to gather around the table. Beckwith joined them; he had recognized the voice of the speaker, and his lips were drawn tight in a thin line.

"May I present to you," continued the self-appointed master of ceremonies, "Bess Malone." He jumped lightly down from the table and offered a hand to someone. In the next instant, a slender girl had stepped from chair to table and stood facing the audience.

She wore nothing but a thin white cotton shift, as banks of candles behind her readily revealed. Her hair, jet black, tumbled over her shoulders in wild abandon. And when she raised wide eyes to the crowd briefly, they were shown to be vivid blue. Her skin was pale and dusted with freckles over the nose and cheekbones. She was exquisitely beautiful, and certainly not yet eighteen years old.

"Bess," declared the man, who had leaped upon another of the tables, "will go to the highest bidder tonight. And we expect the price to be high, don't we, Bess?"

The girl tossed back her hair, her breasts rising and falling with the movement and drawing ribald comments. She didn't look frightened, but neither was she at ease, particularly as the men began pushing forward and reaching up to caress her ankles and calves.

"Ah, ah, gentlemen," chided the master of ceremonies. "Bess comes untouched to her purchaser. Stand back and start the bidding."

"A hundred guineas," said a deep voice on the left.

"Two," responded a man in the front.

"Three," said Beckwith.

The master of ceremonies raised his head as if startled and turned to stare at Beckwith.

"Four hundred," said the first voice.

The bidding went on a full twenty minutes, one man after another dropping out reluctantly as the amount went above his touch. At last, only two were left—Sir Richard Beckwith and a nobleman of fifty or so in the front row, whose face was a map of debauchery and bitterness.

Silence spread through the room as the numbers mounted. When they reached fifteen hundred guineas, all conversation stopped. Only the quiet bids of the two stirred the smoky air, and the tension rose with each new offer.

At two thousand, the roué in front turned and stared pointedly at Sir Richard, gauging him. The older man's face looked devilish in the flickering candlelight. The room waited breathlessly to see what he would do, for most there knew him for a cruel and ruthless opponent. But after an interminable moment, he lowered pale lids, made a dismissive gesture, and walked away, signifying his withdrawal from the auction.

"Sold," said the master of ceremonies immediately, "to the gentleman in the rear, for two thousand guineas."

A sigh passed over the crowd as the tension released;

then someone called for brandy, and the group began to disperse. A footman appeared at Beckwith's elbow to escort him to a small study off the front hall. The masked master of ceremonies and Bess Malone joined him there. "Sir," said the former, "my sincere felicitations. You have acquired a diamond of the first water."

Bess took Sir Richard's arm and pressed herself up against him.

"I assume you have clothing," said Sir Richard. "Put it on." The girl drew back, piqued. The master of ceremonies laughed. "Protecting your property? Or merely eager to depart for some more private place? I can't blame you for that. Hurry and dress, Bess." The girl ran out. "And now, sir, there is the matter of two thousand guineas."

Beckwith pulled a fat roll of bills from an inner pocket. "Who gets the money?" he asked.

But the other's eyes were riveted on the banknotes. "You carry such a sum on your person? In this part of London?"

"It is not my habit. Who gets this money?" He began to count it out, and the other man watched, fascinated. "Who?" repeated Beckwith with some asperity.

"Eh? Oh, half to the club, half to the girl."

"I see."

His tone made the other defensive. "It was her idea, you know."

"What?"

"Indeed. She came to, er, a member and proposed the plan not two weeks ago. I... he was taken aback, I may tell you."

Sir Richard laid the bills on the desk. The man snatched them up and fingered them as if they had the texture of velvet. "Two thousand," he murmured.

"I'll wait for the girl at the front door," said Sir Richard.

"What? Oh, to be sure. I'll have her sent to you there," was the reply. But the man's eyes did not waver from the money.

Sir Richard made his way back to the entrance, conscious, now that the business was concluded, of spreading whispers behind him. He hoped that they concerned his identity, and that none here knew him well enough to recognize him behind a mask.

At last the girl he had purchased appeared at the back of the hall and moved slowly toward him. Bess now wore a shabby dress of white sprigged muslin and a threadbare blue cloak, both garments clearly the long-ago castoffs of some more prosperous lady. But her dark hair remained unbound, and her eyes flashed as she examined him. Looking at her face, one forgot the clothes.

"Come," said Beckwith. "I have a hack waiting."

Someone in the room behind snickered, but Bess merely walked forward and took Sir Richard's arm, molding herself to his side and gazing up at the mask he still wore. Side by side, they went through the door the footman was holding open for them.

Outside, the mist had thickened, and the chill was even greater. Beckwith disengaged his arm and looked for his cab, hoping the driver had not lost his nerve and deserted him.

The jingle of harness and the sound of hooves on

the cobblestones relieved him of this worry. The hack emerged from the mist and pulled up before the pair, the driver eyeing Bess Malone with amused appreciation. "A good night, then, guv?" he said.

Sir Richard merely stated his address in Mayfair and helped Bess into the carriage. In a moment, he had followed and shut the door, and the sound of hooves muffled by mist resumed.

Bess nestled close to her new protector, one small hand slipping over the buttons of his waistcoat. "Aren't you going to be rid of that mask, then?" she asked, in a lilt that called up visions of Ireland.

"We will talk when we reach my house," replied Sir Richard, removing her hand from his chest.

Bess straightened and eyed him. "Talk?" she echoed. "Aye, if you like. I'll be pleased to get acquainted before... what comes after talk. I've not done such a thing as this before, you see, and 'tis unnerving."

Beckwith merely grunted.

"Do you doubt me then?" flared Bess. "I swear I've never in my life..."

"No one has doubted you," interrupted Beckwith, and she subsided to watch his silhouette in the dim light filtering through the hack's window.

They made the journey in silence, broken only by Sir Richard's instructions to the cabbie when they reached the quietly elegant street where he dwelt. The driver steered into the mews at the back and deposited them before a narrow slatted gate next to the stables before departing with the promised guinea.

Bess pulled her cloak closed and gazed about with disfavor. "Why do we come here?" she asked.

"I should think that would be obvious," replied Beckwith, taking a key from his pocket and unlocking the gate. "Follow me."

The girl glared at his back, but did so.

He led her along a narrow walk to a cobbled yard, then through the back door into the kitchen. The servants had gone to bed, and the fire was banked for the night. Beckwith turned to face the girl, pulling off his mask and letting the domino fall onto a wooden chair.

"Ah," breathed Bess, "a fine handsome man you are, too."

"Come here," said Sir Richard.

Two

At the same hour that Sir Richard set out on his surprising quest that evening, a stream of carriages before the Earl of Leamington's Berkeley Square mansion paused to allow a very handsome family party to alight. The daughter first drew the eye, for she was a remarkably lovely girl of twenty with smooth black hair and large pale green eyes strikingly set off by sooty lashes. She was above medium height and slender, dressed in a white brocade gown that proclaimed its cost even as it avoided all extremes of fashion. Her parents were similarly clad—well but conservatively—and rather older than most progenitors of hopeful debutantes. Their faces were amiable, and they clearly derived much pleasure from their daughter's beauty and success.

They left their wraps and walked together up to the landing where the Countess of Leamington and her newly presented daughter waited to greet them. "Sir George and Lady Devere. Miss Julia Devere," intoned the butler.

"Julia!" cried the countess surging forward. "Allow

me to be the first to wish you happy. I'm sure I shan't be the last tonight. Such a fine match! When I saw the announcement in this morning's paper, I said at once to Alice, 'If only you do so well, my dear.' Did I not, Alice?"

"Yes, Mama," murmured Lady Alice.

"Sir George, Lady Devere, you must be delighted," the countess went on. "A positive paragon—wealthy, well born, without a hint of that distressing unsteadiness so common in the young men today. All London wondered where Sir Richard Beckwith would find a wife to match his high principles, I vow. Until Miss Julia appeared, of course. 'Tis like a fairy tale."

The older Deveres, embarrassed by this effusion, muttered incomprehensible replies.

"Such a handsome man, too," continued the countess. "A fair match for Julia there as well, eh?" She turned twinkling blue eyes on Julia.

Julia Devere showed no signs of discomfort. Her answering smile was lovely and unself-conscious. "Thank you for your good wishes, Lady Leamington," she replied. "We mustn't keep you from your other guests any longer." And gathering her parents with a glance, she walked on into the ballroom.

Behind her, the countess shook her head. "That girl deserves her success if anyone ever did; she has the sweetest temper on earth. Take a lesson, Alice."

"Yes, Mama," murmured her daughter again, and they turned to greet the next arrival.

Lady Devere, on the other hand, was deploring the manners of the aristocracy. "I shall never understand it," she complained to her daughter. "Sometimes it seems that the higher their rank, the greater their vulgarity. I shouldn't dream of speaking so to Lady Alice, should she announce her engagement."

"Their ideas are different from ours," agreed Julia absently. Her thoughts were focused on the party ahead. She would be the center of attention this evening, she knew. Any newly engaged girl was the object of congratulations, and envy, and she had the added luster of having won one of the most eligible bachelors of the *haut ton*. She looked forward to the furor with some trepidation, but her main emotion was happiness. She had liked Sir Richard Beckwith from their first meeting, and everything she had learned about him since then had strengthened her regard. She knew herself to be very fortunate—to be creditably settled in life with a man she could wholeheartedly admire.

The Deveres were indeed surrounded by well-wishers as soon as their arrival was noticed. In the flood of congratulations and questions about the wedding, Julia missed the first set, and she was led into the second only after her partner pointedly excused her from a pair of talkative dowagers.

"That was very rude, Mr. Whitney," Julia told him as the waltz began.

"Rude? You accuse me of petty sins when you have broken my heart?" he retorted.

Julia laughed. "You know I have done no such thing."

"I shall never recover," protested her partner. "Where is the infamous Sir Richard tonight, by the by? I should think he'd be much in evidence, flaunting his triumph in our faces."

"He had business to see to. He won't be here."

"The cad. Leaving you alone to face all these congratulations. Don't you wish to reconsider your acceptance of him under these conditions?"

"No, Mr. Whitney. But I am beginning to wish I had not accepted your invitation to dance. Do be serious."

"Ah, you and Richard, always so serious. I do wish one of you would fly up in the boughs just once. A wild adventure, a tempestuous scene. Don't you wish for it sometimes?"

Laughing again, Julia shook her head. Mr. Whitney heaved a dramatic sigh and turned the subject.

The ball continued much in this vein for Julia. During the supper interval, she was the center of a lively group of young people, and afterward she danced with a variety of partners. If she wished that one of these was Sir Richard, she did not let it show, and when one of her admirers went to fetch lemonade late in the evening, she awaited his return with a serene smile. She didn't even notice the arrival of two latecomers, one a young man whose handsome face was marred by chronic worry and the other the middle-aged roué who had bid against Beckwith an hour before. The two separated at the door, the latter stopping to scan the crowd, then moving with calculated nonchalance to a position just behind Julia, though partly screened from her by a curtained doorway.

"I must tell you the most extraordinary thing, Seldon," he said in a penetrating voice to an acquaintance he had taken in tow as he moved across the ballroom.

Julia's head turned slightly, and she started to move away as she recognized one of the most notorious libertines in London.

"What's that, Lord Fenton?" answered Seldon.

"Beckwith came to the Chaos Club tonight," was the reply. Julia froze.

"I don't believe it! Propriety Dick?"

"I tell you, he was recognized. And not only that, he laid down two thousand guineas to buy himself the loveliest little lightskirt I've seen in fifteen years."

"No!"

"I saw it myself."

"But he's never mounted a mistress. He's always deploring the morals of the *ton*."

Lord Fenton smiled slightly, his eyes on the rigid shoulders of Julia Devere a little distance away in the ballroom. "Perhaps his decision to become leg-shackled gave him pause," he said very clearly. "That certainly makes a man think of what he's missed."

Julia moved away, returning to her parents, numb with shock. She had not been able to resist listening once she heard her fiancé's name, but what she'd heard was so unbelievable that she couldn't even think just yet. She fled instinctively to the protectors of her youth and sat down beside her mother. Julia's hands were trembling, and her skin felt icy; a void seemed to have opened inside her.

"You are very pale, Julia," said Lady Anne. "Are you feeling ill?"

"Only very tired," she managed to reply.

"All these congratulations are fatiguing. Shall we go home?"

Julia nodded emphatically, and her mother turned to speak to Sir George. As the three of them rose and looked for their hostess to say good-bye, Lord Fenton watched from across the room. His lined face showed both malicious satisfaction and an almost diabolical glee. He gazed about the ballroom as if wondering what he could do next to sustain the entertainment.

On the carriage ride home, Julia was silent. Her parents, chatting desultorily about the evening, noticed nothing amiss. When they reached the house they had hired for the Season, Julia stepped down first and went directly to her room, submitting to the ministrations of her maid mechanically and allowing herself to be put to bed without speaking a word. The maid, who was new to her service, fell silent also after her first few remarks were ignored and simply did her work as quickly as possible.

When she was at last alone, Julia gazed up at the canopy above her bed and allowed an unaccustomed tide of emotion to surge through her. Its strength was such that she had to clench her hands and jaw to keep quiet.

Julia Devere had been reared with loving, but strict propriety by middle-aged parents. Her principles were high, her ideas somewhat rigid, and her life up to this point had offered no upheaval that put these views to the test. With her engagement to Sir Richard Beckwith, it had appeared that this serene state would continue, unruffled.

Now, her certainty had been swept away with a suddenness that left her breathless. Even more unsettling was her reaction. Instead of calmly reviewing the circumstances and judging them by the measures she'd been taught, Julia was swinging wildly from scandal-ized condemnation, to hot anger, to hopeful disbelief. She'd never felt such turmoil. It was as if her mind had filled with a chorus of alien voices, and she was shocked to find that she could surprise herself this way.

Julia had been carefully educated in many subjects, but not in the lore of feelings. These, to her parents at least, were things to be kept under sedate control. A civilized person did not indulge. A proper young lady did not even acknowledge their existence. For the first time since early childhood, Julia failed to rein in her emotions.

Silently, she struggled with herself.. Stories like Lord Fenton's malicious gossip circulated constantly among the *haut ton*, Julia knew. And though as an unmarried girl she was not told any of them directly, only the most unobservant or stupid deb failed to pick up scraps of information, and Julia was neither of these.

It was the connection of Richard with scandalous behavior that set her pulse pounding with a muddle of emotion—humiliation at the idea that Richard should find a mistress on the eve of their engagement and make her the butt of vulgar jokes, anger that he had deceived her about his character, amazement that she could have been so deceived, and overriding all else, an astonishing, fierce possessiveness that urged Julia to rise and fight for the man she intended to marry, and not to let some doxy steal him away.

The latter feeling surprised Julia most. If she had been asked earlier in the evening whether she loved Richard Beckwith, she would have replied, with a mildly reproving glance, that she admired and respected him, that she found in him her ideal of manhood, that she enjoyed his company and conversation. The hot emotion she felt now had no connection to any of those phrases. Julia wondered if she'd fallen prey to some kind of madness. There seemed no other logical explanation for the sudden, radical change in her character. Had some lunacy been growing in the hidden parts of her brain, she wondered, only to burst forth full blown now? But even as this fear surfaced, she dismissed it. She was furious, not insane.

She made a heroic effort to gain control of herself. She did not know that Lord Fenton's vicious story was true, a prim inner voice pointed out. Fenton was certainly not a trustworthy person. He had been pointed out to Julia at her first *ton* party as someone she should not know, and she had never even spoken to him in the course of the Season that was now waning. Was she, she asked herself, ready to take such a man's word about the conduct of Sir Richard Beckwith, whom she knew so well and trusted absolutely?

Of course not! She'd been distressingly unsteady, Julia realized, to allow this incident to overset her. It could not be true. And from what she had heard of Lord Fenton, it was likely to be a cruel jest. Julia flushed in the darkness of her bed, ashamed of herself for falling victim to such a hoax. Nothing had changed, she told herself; she would wake tomorrow to discover that Richard was the same as ever. And they would marry in six weeks as agreed and settle to a life much like her present one.

Thus reassured, Julia was finally able to close her eyes and fall asleep.

About the Author

Jane Ashford discovered Georgette Heyer in junior high school and was captivated by the glittering world and witty language of Regency England. That delight was part of what led her to study English literature and travel widely in Britain and Europe. Her books have been published all over Europe as well as the United States. Jane was nominated for a Career Achievement Award by *RT Book Reviews*. Born in Ohio, she is now somewhat nomadic. Find her on the web at janeashford.com and on Facebook, where you can sign up for her monthly newsletter.

Also by Jane Ashford

The Duke's Sons

Heir to the Duke
What the Duke Doesn't Know
Lord Sebastian's Secret
Nothing Like a Duke
The Duke Knows Best

The Way to a Lord's Heart

Brave New Earl
A Lord Apart

Once Again a Bride
Man of Honour
The Three Graces
The Marriage Wager
The Bride Insists
The Bargain
The Marchington Scandal
The Headstrong Ward
Married to a Perfect Stranger
Charmed and Dangerous
A Radical Arrangement
First Season / Bride to Be
Rivals of Fortune / The Impetuous Heiress
Last Gentleman Standing
Earl to the Rescue

agreement may have been initiated, but it was never completed. Not signed or paid. It seems they changed their minds. Can't we drop this dispute?"

"No!" Fairclough pounded weakly on the bed-clothes. "It's a matter of principle."

He looked worn out, Roger saw. He should leave him to rest.

The sly look returned to the old man's face. "You could still marry Fenella. That was our original solution. Put that bit of land into her inheritance. Tied up the loose ends all right and tight."

Roger couldn't believe her father would mention this idiotic plan. Hadn't it caused enough trouble? And then he was even more startled at how differently he felt about it today. The outraged rebellion of five years ago was gone.

"Now you're free again," Fairclough added.

As if Arabella had been nothing but an impediment. The phrase, and the old man's tone, cut too close to the bone. "My wife died," he said.

"Well, they do. Look at Foster over at Deeping. He's had three."

Roger stood.

"That was a jest, Chatton. No need to poker up about it."

"It's difficult to laugh at death."

"Well, I beg your pardon. You have my condolences, of course."

Roger bowed, and felt like a fraud. He'd felt relief, among other things, at the sad end of his marriage, he admitted silently. Guilt washed through him, with a twinge of pain in his stomach. He wished for the